D0341017

Amy & Lan

AMY

&

a novel

SADIE JONES

LAN

HARPER

An Imprint of HarperCollins*Publishers*

AMY & LAN. Copyright © 2022 by Sadie Jones. All rights reserved. Printed in the United States of America. No part of this book may be used or reproduced in any manner whatsoever without written permission except in the case of brief quotations embodied in critical articles and reviews. For information, address HarperCollins Publishers, 195 Broadway, New York, NY 10007.

HarperCollins books may be purchased for educational, business, or sales promotional use. For information, please email the Special Markets Department at SPsales@harpercollins.com.

Originally published in the United Kingdom in 2022 by Chatto & Windus, an imprint of Vintage.

FIRST U.S. EDITION

Library of Congress Cataloging-in-Publication Data has been applied for.

ISBN 978-0-06-324090-2

22 23 24 25 26   LSC   10 9 8 7 6 5 4 3 2 1

For Mark and Tarn, with love and thanks

Foys Wood

Four Acre

The Rough
and
Barrow

New Cottage
Em

Finbar's

Yard

Track

Wood Store

Baldy Wild

Tumbledown

Woods

The Hay

Cowhouse
Connells

Colin →

Farmhouse
Honeys

Workshop

Orchard

Chickens

Carthouse
Hodges

Frith

Dutch Barn

AUTUMN
2005

I

Halloween

LAN

Me and Amy are both seven now.

Down here at the stream the water is icy cold and makes our feet ache. I can't stand in it but Amy doesn't mind, so I stay on the bank or up in a tree and she walks through the water, chatting about things she hates or what isn't too bad.

The main thing is we want to light the bonfire ourselves and we're hungry.

Amy comes out the water and tries to get her wet feet back in her boots but they won't go. *Damn-bloody wellies*, she says, and we walk home with them half on, and the empty welly-feet sticking out so it looks like her legs are broken. She forgets about socks almost every time.

It's a long way up the hill. I go backwards so I'll be slow enough to stay with her. I can see the woods bobbing up and down behind her as we go. Birds fly up from them making empty sounds. We get to the top of the field, then onto the lane and over the bar gate, and cross the Yard with Amy still chatting and clumping along on her welly sides to the house.

It's a lot warmer inside and the smells are all pumpkin soup and sausages. She kicks off her stupid boots and we drop our stuff by the door. The kitchen table is covered in heaps of Walkers Ready Salted crisps and white buns, because of the party, and big pots of cold water with carrots in them. Jim is kneeling by the Rayburn, trying to get it going, and our mums are standing with their arms crossed staring at him. We ask if we can light the bonfire, and Jim says, *we'll see how we go,* but he's not paying attention, because when the Rayburn goes out the whole Farmhouse is more and more freezing cold every second. *Put some socks on, Amy,* says Harriet. Amy just says, *Mu-um,* because she hasn't got any socks and she's not going upstairs to get some. Harriet notices things like bare feet. *My* mum hasn't seen us I don't think. Jim says, *there you are, Lan, would you pass me the WD-40?* His voice is round, not boomy and shouty, like Amy's dad. He's definitely got the nicest grown-up voice, and he always likes me helping him. I pass him the WD-40 and the spanner, and he says *thanks,* like I'm a grown-up man too.

Harriet is swearing at the Rayburn, and my mum is on at Jim. He explains it was only the wick last time, not a repair *as such,* but Mum keeps on at him, because they're married. *This is boring,* says Amy, and I say, *let's go.* I grab some crisps off the table, and Amy takes a handful of carrots, and we go back out, the carrots all wet and dripping on the stone floor. Amy gets another pair of boots from the pile, too big, with embroidered flowers on and fleece inside. Someone must have left them after coming to play or something.

The whole Yard is just watery mud. We can see the sky in it like it's a lake. When it's a big giant puddle like this us kids can slide really fast on our bums, and make long waves all across it, but me and Amy are in a hurry because we want to build up the bonfire – it's massive and tall at the bottom of the Yard. It's got crates and brush, and some old black planks poking out, and the tarp over the top makes it the same shape as a volcano. *It definitely needs more wood,* says Amy, *come on.* We go off to the wood store where the logs are.

Logs aren't bonfire wood but we can sneak some if we want.

At one end of the store are the split logs and at the other end are the logs that aren't done yet, and in the middle there's the wheelbarrow, with axes and saws hanging from hooks. Climbing up the woodpile makes the logs move, and when they slide we shout *timber-rr* – scrabbling on dirt and beetles all the way down, and some of the logs are really sharp. Me and Amy have always got splinters, nearly every day. We can both sterilise a needle with a match. Then we hold it flat, like Jim showed us, and brush the splinter up. We don't dig the needle straight in and make a hole, because that *hurts like shit,* Amy says. We do the little kids' splinters too. They always cry.

We finish the crisps and carrots, and lick our salty fingers, then I climb on a bucket and get the axe down. It's just the small one the Mums use, but the handle is hard to grip because it's shiny, and the blade is heavy, so I need two hands or it lops down.

I hold tight and swing it about, all round my head, while Amy stands staring out at the bonfire across the Yard.

It's ages till tonight. We are *so bored*.

I swing the axe a few more times, trying to do a proper figure 8, not a kid's 8, which is just one zero on top of another. I swing it up, round my head, down to the ground, and up again. I want it to make a whooshing sound, like a rope can, but it won't go fast enough. My shoulder hurts, and the swinging only works one way, the other way it's fast but jerky, and I lose my balance, because of it being so heavy. The axe pulls me with it. I spin, and turn, and almost let it go, but I don't.

I'm so dizzy.

Then there's Amy, right in front of me. She's right there where I'm swinging and my body doesn't know what to do, so the axe blade flies down at the ground, really fast, straight onto her foot, right into her boot, and through it, with a cutting-slicing sound.

Amy kind of yelps, like our dog Christabel when she got hit by the Lada. She's staring down at the axe. I am too. The handle is in the air and the blade is stuck through her foot into the ground.

My legs disappear, and I'm sitting on my bum. Amy makes a sound like she's been winded, and vomits crisps and carrot all over the place and on her feet.

But she isn't screaming. And I can't see blood. I haven't chopped her. The blade hasn't even touched her toes, just cut the whole toe end off the boot – except for a stringy thready bit, where it's still attached.

Amy drops onto her knees and starts crying, with bits and crumbs all falling out of her mouth. The toe of the boot that I chopped off just lies there, looking at me. We're both still staring at the axe like it's going to jump at us. Then, with our fingers all watery, we take the handle, together, and pull it out. I feel like it's going to burn my hand off, and Amy makes that sound again, like she really has lost all her toes. I'm imagining blood. She is too, so we look again.

There is definitely no blood. Just Amy's white toes, like a foot coming out of a sandal.

We put the axe far enough away so even if it moves by itself, which it might do, we're safe, then we lie on our sides, out of breath like we've been running. Her eyes have gone big, and I can see window-shaped reflections in the blue. I feel like I want to go to sleep. My chest is wobbling inside, and Amy puts her thumb in her mouth, which she doesn't even do that often.

When we get up, we take the stolen boots, and the chopped-off bit, and run out of the wood store when no one is looking, and shove them into the bonfire, till they're hidden, and Amy washes the sick out of her mouth at the trough. Water-mud squelches through her blue-and-white toes as we walk back over the Yard.

The sky isn't reflecting any more, the puddle is just dark.

'Grown-ups always say things are dangerous,' she says, 'but they aren't.' It's true.

'Yeah,' I say.

'We're careful,' says Amy.

Grown-ups always say:

Mind your eyes
Careful, that's sharp
Don't break your neck!

You'll burn yourself

But we've stepped on rusty nails that stuck deep into our feet, and we didn't even get lockjaw. We've both touched the hotplate on the stove. We won't do it again, we're not stupid. Dangerous things are always fine if you're clever like we are, and cool like us.

AMY

There's nobody in my house because they're all in Lan's kitchen still, so we've got the whole place to ourselves, *and* there's hot water because my house is heated by the Aga, which has never even broken *once*. Me and Lan run the bath until it's as deep as it will go. It's hot, but sometimes cold water drips on us from the ceiling, because of condensation. Our skin goes bright pink. There's dirt in the soap ridges, and scum floats on top of the water like ice-islands, and we can tap them with our fingers. They don't break if we do it gently. We imagine tiny miniature polar bears on them.

There are loud grown-up voices downstairs, and doors opening and closing, and Martin Hodge comes back from work. We jump out and wrap ourselves in big crispy towels, and go out onto the Rope Bridge over the Big Room, not even feeling cold because of the hot bath. It's nearly the party time now. The grown-ups have put Fran Ferdinan on the CD player with the nail-varnish decorations on it that me and Lan did, and it's *really* loud. We drop our towels and jump up and down on the Bridge, yelling along –

Well do ya? Do ya do ya wanna? Well do ya, do ya do ya wanna? Wanna go . . . where I've never let you before . . .

The Rope Bridge swings and dust falls, and I remember the axe going into my boot and it feels like my toes aren't there again, but when I look down they are, and we start shouting as loud as we can –

We're not dead! We're not dead!

It's so funny.

Amy and Lan! We're not dead! Amy and Lan!

The little kids come running in from Lan's kitchen – Josh and Eden and Bryn, and Bill Hodge and Lulu Hodge – screaming up and down the Big Room like racing cars. I say, *quick!* – and we run to get dressed up for Halloween before they can follow us.

Lan puts on a black velvet shirt of his mum's and a hat, and I've got a big black cloak, and the cowboy hat. We go to my mum's room for make-up, because Gail doesn't have any make-up, because she says she's a *natural woman*. My mum is just as *natural* as Lan's mum. She keeps her make-up for special, which is almost never anyway. We draw black rings around our eyes, and make our lips black. And draw on different eyebrows, and I stuff Finbar's hat with some of Mum's knickers, to stop it falling down, and we both put beads on. We look amazing.

The Farmhouse kitchen is full. It's got my family, Lan's family and Hodges, plus Boring Colin, and Ruby Wright, because they've come early, like always. Lan's baby sister Niah is lying in the cot Jim made, by the Rayburn, which he's got working again, so now Gail's stopped being mean to him and she's all, *oh, Jim's such a handyman*, and squeezing his arms and swinging her hair about.

All the little kids go crazy when they see how good me and Lan look. They want to get dressed up too, but we haven't even finished getting ready, so we say – *NO!*

'Love each other,' says Mum. She's always saying that.

Help each other
Include the little ones
Be kind
Love

When she's forgotten about us we go in the larder and put cooking oil on our faces and dig our hands in the flour barrel and slap it on to look like ghosts. Then Bryn and Eden and Bill and Lulu and Josh come barging in and we do their faces too, and we *all* look like ghosts, and Dad shuts the door on us, and bangs on it, yelling like a Frankenstein to make us scream. Except then Josh and Bryn get real-scared, not pretend, and cry, so Dad lets us out, and says *sorry*. They aren't old enough to be scared for fun like me and Lan are.

We run round and get in the dog beds, and the flour falls off in lumps, and the dogs lap our faces and it's really funny until Mum screams –

'Just get out! Oh my God!' She's terrifying.

She makes us go upstairs to help the little kids, but they only really want to wear what we're wearing, so it's not going to work. Still, we do our best. Jim always says:

Do your best, it's all anyone can do.

He's definitely the best grown-up for saying things.

My dad's the best for being silly and playing.

The Hodges aren't best for anything. But they're sensible. Which is good, I suppose.

*

When it's finally time, and it's dark outside, all the grown-ups and all of us squelch down the Yard with the food and lanterns. Gail doesn't carry anything, or do any helping, because she always says having baby Niah is *so exhausting*. Me and Lan gallop ahead in the smells of woodsmoke and apples, with our black clothes flapping. Suddenly the big cold bonfire is above us – way more dark than the night-time sky. We see a torch flash, and Finbar comes out from behind it like a tall crazy scarecrow with his roll-up in the corner of his mouth.

'So, kids, give me a hand with this tarp,' he says.

Me and Lan help him, and pull at the pegs and knots, then the three Dads come and help, and us and Finbar throw the tarp up and off, and a rat runs out the bottom of the bonfire. It goes straight past Rani Hodge's foot, and she screams –

'*Martin!* A rat!'

Me and Lan copy her, going, *oh, Martin, a rat!* – and fall about laughing.

We're desperate to light the fire, but we have to check it for hedgehogs first. Bill Hodge says, *if we cook a hedge-hog, can we eat it?* and Lulu Hodge says *eat it!* right after, because she's only *three* years old and she copies every single thing her brother says. Me and Lan think cooked hedgehog would be gooey, and we could break the shell open like we did with the sea urchins that time on the beach, but Jim says hedgehogs taste more like rabbit, and –

We don't eat hedgehogs, because they're rare and precious.

We've only seen a few hedgehogs, but we see millions of rabbits, all gentle, with their tiny little jaws making circles when they chew. Lan and me think rabbits are precious too.

It starts being a real party when the Village Families show up, and Old Friends From Before we came to Frith. The grown-ups bring the outside sofa to sit on, and everybody is just lazing around talking and being boring. It's just like that time we went to see *Jack and the Beanstalk* in Swansea, and I got so bored waiting I rocked on my seat until I fell off and bashed my face on the back of the one in front and got a nosebleed. Mum wasn't even that nice about it because she was *so pissed off* with me by then. Waiting for the party to start is *even more* boring than that. I can't even stand it. So I chuck back my head and scream –

Oh my God when can we light this fucking fire?!

And my hat falls off and all Mum's knickers fall out on the ground. The grown-ups – especially the village ones – *gasp*, like I've done a poo or something. But the Village Kids laugh – and so does Lan. Obviously.

LAN

Jim lets me and Amy light the bonfire with the blowtorch. We hold it between us, with our arms straight. The blue pointy flame shoots out, and it hardly takes any time at all till great big orange flames storm up into the sky. It's hot immediately, and the flour on our faces dries and cracks. Everyone has soup, and baked potatoes full of butter, and shop-bought cheese, and orange-drink in massive bottles. Us Frith Kids and all the Village Kids run round and play in the mud, and this kid from school says I look like a girl in my beads and stuff and Amy says, *who cares?* I don't. And there are sausages, and there's ketchup, which we never have normally, because of sugar or money. Harriet's made her Pasta Thing, with mayonnaise and tuna and stuff. She and Rani Hodge hand it round, and Mum sits on the log, feeding Niah out of her boob, with her shiny hair hanging down in front. Niah sleeps nearly the whole time. She's like a small potato. Every single person who sees her is amazed, because she's new and so tiny. Mum sits on the log with her, and Jim keeps coming over and saying, *how are my girls? How's my baby?* and kissing her and things.

I don't mind he's so crazy about Niah. We all are. Even if she is just the same as a potato. Bryn and Eden are just my little sisters. I don't remember them being born, so I don't think about them being my half-sisters. Niah being new makes me remember I'm not Jim's real son. I mean, I don't *mind,* it's just Niah makes me think about it more. I go over and try to snuggle into Mum's shoulder but I don't think she notices me.

'Lan!' says Harriet, like it's really important. *'Lan!'* I sit up.

'Lan, can you and Amy be in charge of the ice cream?'

All the kids yell – *ice cream!*

'Can you get it before I count to twenty?' says Harriet. And I forget all about Niah and Mum and not being Jim's real son and me and Amy *run.*

When everyone's eaten and we've all played, and it's really late, most of the friends go home, and it's just us: Honeys, Connells and Hodges. And Finbar of course. And we sing live music. It's the best bit. The night is cold and dark. The fire is massive and hot and scorching and sometimes it pops, or even whistles when it's got green wood in. Finbar can play any instrument in the world. Me and Amy sit with our backs to the giant bonfire and Finbar says –

'So, kids, what'll it be?'

I love looking at everybody's faces in the firelight, all waiting. Finbar holds his guitar staring down at it. He always starts out shy, doing notes like he's thinking. He looks like a pirate, or a rock star, and sometimes like a vampire, but in a nice way. Amy's mum cuts his hair for him, like she cuts ours, because he doesn't like going into town, even though he's twenty-seven. Or twenty-three. First he plays the song about smugglers and brandy and ponies. It's our favourite. It makes our backs feel crawly with fear and we love it. Bill Hodge is smacking Finbar's tabla drums. Bill's only five, but he is really good at drumming. Everyone plays and we all join in singing the choruses, then Finbar plays another, and another, and we all get closer to the fire because it's icy cold. The stars are glittering. Mum's shirt has got wet and I'm freezing, so Jim gives me his big jacket. Amy is hunched in her cloak like a bat.

Jim and Finbar play the song about the man who's *seen fire and seen rain*. I can feel it in my chest, like nice-sadness. *Yeah*, says Amy, *me too*, and we rock ourselves, and stare into the fire. Rani and Martin Hodge get up from the sofa and waltz around over the splashy Yard. They look like ghosts or dolls. Then Finbar and Jim play 'Country Roads Take Me Home', which me and Amy love. We're singing, *take me home where I am born, take me home where I am born* – over and over and over, until we're dizzy and our cheeks feel fuzzy.

When the singing stops, Harriet and Adam do a Love Kiss, on the mouth, and we all pretend to throw up and Amy goes, *Mu-um! Da-ad!* My mum has her head on Jim's lap, and Niah's little white potato face is behind a blanket. Bryn and Eden are curled up with them, half asleep. My whole family looks like a heap of puppies. I'm glad there's not space for me, I'm not sleepy.

'Mum,' I say, 'will you tell the Story?'

'Oh, Lan,' says Mum, 'really?' But we know she wants to.

'Yes, Gail, tell it,' says Amy. So Mum does.

The Story always starts the same: Seven Years of Bad Luck.

'I was married to Lachlan's father for seven unlucky years,' says Mum. She's the only one who ever calls me Lachlan.

'Poor Gray Parks,' she says, 'I was a virtual child.'

They met at university. She was too young for marrying, which was why they had the Bad Seven Years.

'Seven miserable years. Then! At the exact same moment I found out I was pregnant, I realised I was in the Wrong Life.'

Amy leans and whispers in my ear, *it was not her right life.* That's how the story always goes.

'It was not my right life,' says Mum.

She didn't want to be living in boring London with boring Gray Parks, so, the very next day, she left, with *half her things in a bag* and me in her tummy.

Lucky you were in her tummy, whispers Amy, and I nod. We've talked about it before. We always think Mum might have left me behind in the wrong life with Gray Parks if I hadn't been in her tummy, but I was, so Mum (and me) went to stay with Harriet and Adam, in Bristol, because Harriet is Mum's best friend from school. Harriet was pregnant too. And she was really happy to see her, so was Adam, because *old friends are the best friends.*

'And my luck changed,' says Mum.

Forever! whispers Amy, and her hands appear out of her cloak, like a magician. We love that bit.

Harriet always joins in when it gets to Mum's luck changing. She pulls off her hair tie, and her hair springs out and fluffs up in the firelight, like a golden fleece stuck on her head.

'Adam had a lot of acting work that year,' she says, 'so it was just me and Gail in the flat, getting bigger and bigger.'

After Harriet stopped work because of being pregnant, they just lay around reading the papers. Everything they read was *depressing*, like about the greenhouse effect and battery chickens. And Palestine. And hurricanes.

'All around us, the world was so dark and frightening,' says Harriet. 'But we were just pregnant. And we blocked it out.'

'But then!' Adam says, sitting up tall and putting on his professional scary-story voice. 'Fate intervened!'

They weren't even looking, I say to Amy.

It was just by chance, says Amy.

'I just happened to see an advertisement in the local paper,' says Mum.

Farm For Sale in Two Lots

Traditional Livestock Farm For Sale. 4/5-bedroom Farmhouse, requiring modernisation. A range of modern and traditional outbuildings. Fantastic opportunity for development. Cow House. Bull House. Cart House. Barns. 78 Acres. In need of renovation. Available as a whole, or in two lots.

They immediately called Rani and Martin Hodge on the phone. Rani and Martin have always been our parents' second-best friends, and make the Home Team. They lived in Bristol, too, and *that very weekend* all five of them came to see the farm together. They walked round all the buildings and all the fields. It still had the old machines, but no animals, because of foot-and-mouth.

'It was very run-down, and sad,' says Harriet. 'But it was so beautiful, and it was Frith.'

Except it wasn't called Frith, because the people who lived here were called Lacey, so everyone called the farm Lacey's Farm, but it's *real* name was Frith.

'Frith means sanctuary in Old English,' says Mum.

'It's actually Norse,' says Rani, who knows most things in the world.

'Whatever,' says Mum. She hates being wrong.

So Harriet and Adam sold the flat, and Rani and Martin sold their house, and Mum got as much money as she could out of Gray Parks, and they went to the auction, and bought the farm.

All in about two days.

When they started renovating they lived all together in the Farmhouse, and in a caravan, and in a tent, and Mum and Harriet got more and more pregnant and it rained every day.

'Tell us about Jim!' says Amy.

'All right,' says Mum. 'So: that spring, 1998, I heaved myself off to do a carpentry workshop near Ledbury.'

'You didn't even want to go!' I remind her.

'I didn't even want to go,' says Mum, 'but it's lucky I did – because guess who was running the workshop?'

'JIM,' say me and Amy together.

Mum says if you ever come across something completely good, you should hold on to it. Jim is Mum's Completely Good Thing. He's mine as well.

'And I looked at Gail,' says Jim, and we all go quiet because his voice is soft and he sounds very serious. 'I looked at Gail and I knew. That woman is the love of my life.'

The newspaper ad for Frith is glued on the first page of the scrapbook. All the pages are black cardboard, with beautiful curly silver writing Rani did, saying what things are.

There's a photo of Jim and Adam when the septic tank came.

And the Big Room before it even had a floor.

The best one is Jim making the Rope Bridge, and the three Dads lifting it up with a pulley.

There are loads of pictures of me and Amy on grown-ups' backs while they mend walls or pick stones, and quite often me and Amy are just lying in the background on rugs or something, while they make Frith *fit to live in*.

'Me and Lan were here first, and we're the best because we're the oldest,' says Amy. 'Then, after me and Lan was Josh.' She counts on her fingers.

'Then Mum and Jim had *Eden*,' I say, 'and *Bryn*.'

'And Martin and I had *Bill*,' says Rani, 'and *Lulu*!'

Bill and Lulu are asleep, so they can't join in.

Finbar flicks a guitar string so it makes a deep sound that goes on and on, until he puts his hand flat on the strings.

'And Harriet brought me home, too.' He does his smile

that looks sad, as well as friendly. 'Along with Brown Dog, strays that we were.'

'We didn't forget *you*, Finbar,' says Amy.

We don't remember when Finbar came to Frith, we were too little. And we don't remember Brown Dog – he died.

They stuck the Farmhouse and the Cowhouse together with the Big Room, and fixed up the Carthouse for the Hodges. And got Poacher and Christabel and Ivan. And the chickens –

And the goats.

And more chickens.

And some more goats.

And made the Orchard into an orchard again.

I yawn. Amy catches it and she yawns, too.

'Don't forget the turkeys,' she says.

The Story always just goes off, into smaller and smaller memories. There isn't any ending because it's the story of how we came to Frith. And we're never, ever, ever leaving.

2

The Surprise

AMY

We're off school for the day to go and see about a flatbed trailer. We're in the back of the Lada. It's going really fast, and our bums are banging on the hard seats. I've got my head pressed against the glass to stop it wobbling, and the hedges whip the Lada like they're trying to make it gallop. The grass is yellow and sun shines in silver flashes in and out of rain clouds. Some of the hedges flying past are high and wild, with little spotted leaves dangling off, but some of them have torn white ends like giants have ripped them up with big teeth.

Jim's in the middle, between me and Lan, and Mum's driving and Dad's next to her going on about how much fuel and feed we need for the winter. They found the flatbed trailer in the local paper. We've never had a proper one before, which is why me and Lan got the day off, but Gail didn't come because of Niah.

The Flatbed-Trailer-Man's house is at the top of the hill,

and we stop in front and all pile out. When the man comes to meet us, two dogs like big fluffy brown bears come racing out with him and nearly knock us down. Me and Lan tuck in to Jim's sides, and Dad pretends to look for something in the car. Dad is scared of strange dogs. And being ill. And disappearing. He says, *oh God, Harriet! I'm disappearing*, and Mum has to say, *Adam, it's fine, you're fine*.

'Get away,' says the Trailer-Man to the dogs, yanking their collars. He's really tall like his house, with bony eyes that look like they've got stains round them.

'They're all right,' says Jim, who isn't scared at all. The dogs don't even leap at him. He's like a god in a cartoon, who can put out his hands and *calm the seas and the wild beasts*.

In the house, the Flatbed-Trailer-Man puts on the kettle, and says his kids are at school, and Dad says me and Lan are only off because it's an *insect day*, which is a lie, because we take loads of days off whenever. Dad's really good at lying because of being an actor. He can say *anything* and people believe him.

From the window ledge we can see brown-and-white cows' bums all squashed together in a barn. The grown-ups start drinking tea and finally, after about a million years talking about antibiotics, we all go outside. The mud in the farmyard is like poo soup, and it's so smelly it makes our eyes water. Jim is the quietest grown-up at home, but when we're out he does all the talking, basically, because he's the only one who grew up in the country, all the others feel like fakers. Except Dad, who thinks he fits in every-where, when in actual fact everyone notices him, because he's very good-looking and noisy. The flatbed trailer looks brand new and enormous. They check it isn't broken, and me and Lan climb up onto a rusty machine that's like a centipede, and hang off the prongs, upside down to watch. It's only exciting for about one minute, then they keep *on* talking about it, so we drop back down into the mud and go off exploring. The two big dogs slurp after us and I say, *don't look round, Lan. Act natural,* because dogs know when you're scared.

There's a wire fence in front of us, with some chickens on the other side. Ours are much nicer. These all look the same. Then I stop walking, because past the chickens there's a horse.

The horse is brown, with a fluffy black forelock and a furry tummy. *That colour is called bay,* I say to Lan. Lan wants a horse too, but not like me. Not with his whole body and heart. The horse is standing totally still, with its long black tail and black forelock blowing to the side and its big eyes watching every single thing we do. I run to the chicken fence and Lan and me climb over and the chickens scoot off, all wobbly on their legs. One of the dogs does a big round *WOOF* to stop us, but we don't listen. We can't go over the horse's fence because it's barbed wire. I stretch my hand towards the horse, and the horse stretches its nose over the fence to my hand. The points on the barbed wire disappear in the fur on its neck. Its breath is huffing on my cold palm. I look into its eyes and say, *Lan . . . it's so cute,* but that's not what I mean at *all*. Beautiful, is what I mean, or important, maybe, or mysterious. *If it's a boy, it's called a gelding,* I say. Me and Lan can tell if goats are boys or girls, but we're not used to horses. I think it's a boy, though.

If it's a girl, it's a mare, or when they're young they're called colts or fillies. Boys are colts and girls are fillies – I can't stop talking. But then we hear Mum calling for us.

'Ooooo-eeee . . .'

She always calls like that, like a train. And we always ignore the first one. I don't want to leave the horse. But Mum calls again –

'Oooo-eeee, La-an . . . Amy . . .'

We wait as long as we can, but then run back through the ugly chickens and climb the fence with the dogs frowning at us.

The flatbed trailer looks too big and posh for the Lada even if it isn't brand new. Jim gives money to the man from his pocket bundle. They shake hands, and I pull Mum down to me and whisper in her ear about the horse. She just gives me a look like she feels sorry for me. *Can we come back?* I say. *Shush,* says Mum. She's *so* annoying.

Dad says –

'OK, kids, time to go. Hop in.'

I sort of forget the horse for a *second*, because the whole reason we came was to ride home on our new flatbed trailer.

Can-we-go-on-the-trailer-can-we-can-we-can-we?

Mum says we'll bounce off and probably die, but Dad says –

'It's fine, if they fall off, they'll scream, won't you, kids?'

And Jim thinks it's OK, so Mum gives in.

'That's not a good idea,' says the bony-eyed Trailer-Man, but we're already on, so sucks to him.

Jim waves out the window as we go. He does this really cool grown-up wave, without actually waving. Me and Lan practise doing it but it's never as cool.

The Trailer-Man shouts, 'Careful!'

And Jim shouts, 'Yup,' and the Lada pulls us out of the gate.

The lane is pretty steep and Jim's pulling us *so* fast. Me and Lan are on all fours, dropping miles every time the trailer goes in a hole, bashing our knees and screaming. Mum leans out the window and her hair tie flies off and her hair pops out like a dandelion. She yells, *hold tight!* and me and Lan are laughing so much trying to stay on, we can't even speak. The sun comes out super-bright suddenly, like flashing silver, and the wind feels like spikes. At the bottom of the lane, Jim tries to make us get back in the Lada, but we are *not* budging, so the grown-ups think about it sensibly, and realise the main road isn't nearly as bumpy as the track, and it's probably actually even more safe, and let us stay on. Mum gives me her coat, but Lan is the lucky one, because he gets Jim's jacket.

At home they peel us off the trailer like peeling off a plaster, because we're frozen solid. We walk funny, playing Cracking the Ice, all the way to the house. Dad comes inside with us and me and Lan wrap our hands in hot tea towels from the Aga.

Mum's going off to do the goats. The goats are Mum's, like the chickens are Gail's, and Finbar has all the vegetables because he says he *can't be getting attached to things with faces.* Mum shouts, 'Fucking hell, Adam!' at Dad, because he's so lazy, but he pretends he can't hear and goes off upstairs.

'My mum should be married to Jim, instead of Dad,' I say.

'Yeah,' says Lan, because we both know my mum and Jim are the best two grown-ups and Gail and Dad aren't.

'Then we'd be brother and sister,' I say.

'Like twins.'

When we've warmed up we go out the back. Mum is shaking the bucket over the electric, calling, *ooo-eeee, goatie-goatie-girlies* – and the goats dash over with their ears flapping. Hazel's belly swings off her bony hips when she canters. She's having her baby soon. *She's a wise old darling*, Mum says. The teenage goats are clambering over each other's backs. Me and Lan can remember when they were *born*, it was *fantastic*. Except one died. Luckily we didn't see, because we were asleep by then. All Hazel's babies are basically Mum's favourites, even Satan, who's naughty. *There you are my gorgeous beauties*, she says.

When she climbs back over the electric with the empty bucket, her round face is pink from cold and bending down. She keeps her kinky curly hair tied back, but the crinkles still show. Her face is soft and round like an angel, but her nose is big and bony and sometimes a different colour. When she's happy she looks golden, but when she's angry or upset she goes red and terrifying, with her hair sticking out like the sun on Gail's star charts and her nose all pointy. The time we put goat shit in my little brother Josh's bed was the most angry we've ever seen her. Much more than she gets with Dad when he's being annoying because he's *like having another child*. It wasn't even the shit in the bed that got her, it was that we did it to *Josh*. My little brother, even when he was two years old, was gentle, and the sort of kid who can be bullied. If we'd put goat shit in Lan's sister Eden's bed, or even in one of the Hodge kids's beds, my mum wouldn't have been nearly so angry.

Me and Lan are on our tummies on the floor in the Big Room by the shelf near the TV, looking at the animal books. *We've got hundreds of fields*, I say, *we can put our horse in one of them.* There aren't very many books at Frith: *The Self-Sufficiency Bible*, which is the grown-ups' favourite. *Cooking with the Seasons.* And *Top Tips for Smallholders.* Lan is looking at the pictures in the *Seven Stages of Goat Pregnancy.*

It's always really noisy when everyone eats together in Lan's kitchen, with all the little kids running round. We're celebrating the new flatbed trailer, so the Hodges have come up from the Carthouse, and even Finbar is here. Sometimes Finbar feels suffocated, and can't stay for all of dinner, so he always sits nearest the back door.

And Em is here too, who we keep forgetting about. She's one of the grown-ups' Friends From Before. She's sitting next to me because she's staying with us. Em's very small for a grown-up, and she doesn't speak much, so quite often we forget she's even *there*, until she says something, or we bump into her Sleeping Sofa in the middle of the Big Room. And she's always wrapped in millions of cardigans because she's from London.

Mum's made shepherd's pie, and brought it through from our kitchen in the Cowhouse. Dad's a good cook, but he always makes a massive fuss. He acts *being Jamie Oliver* when he makes spaghetti, and flicks tea towels around, and sings in Italian. Mum always goes, *Christ, Adam*, but she loves it. Jim *only* makes his cheese on toast, but he does do lots of washing-up when the other grown-ups cook. Jim was in the army before he was a lawyer, which was before he was a cabinetmaker, and he says the army is why he's so good at tidying, and why he hates fighting *of any kind*. Jim will do *anything* not to get in a fight – usually walking around outside, but sometimes not answering, or laughing, which just makes Gail more annoyed.

Me and Lan are *roaming*, so we can talk to who we want then grab bites of food off our plates. We *can* sit at the table, we're better at it than most of the little kids. Bill Hodge is the *worst*. He's got a huge big voice, and now he's running round and round the table, *bellowing*. Rani doesn't even tell him off, *ever*, she just shuts her eyes and whispers, *Bill, Bill, Bill*, and Martin doesn't either, he just bends right down over his plate like a big cloud. Bill's sister Lulu is such an idiot she just laughs at everything Bill does, except when he hurts her, then she *screams*. He's such an irritating little kid. They both are.

Josh is next to Mum. He holds his fork in his fist the whole time he eats, and concentrates. *Shut up, Bill*, I say. Then Bill starts hitting everyone on the back with a long spoon. He hits Mum really hard – she says *ow!* – and then, out of nowhere, Josh just sticks his leg out and trips Bill up. He doesn't even put his fork down. Bill runs smack into his foot, and goes face first onto the stone kitchen floor with a smack. Everyone goes crazy but he hasn't lost any teeth or anything, he's fine, basically. He's screaming his head off, holding out his bright red hands. Me and Lan start laughing and I spit my potato out by mistake, and the grown-ups try to make us feel guilty but we *don't*. They all go off at Josh for tripping Bill, but I don't care, hitting people with spoons is just *wrong*. Rani should've stopped him, but she never does. She says *her* Indian Mummy smacked her legs with ladles, and Martin's dad was a White Drunk in Basingstoke who gave Martin *the strap*, so they never even tell Bill off. Or Lulu. Ever. He's still crying, and his snot is basically everywhere, and Josh is crying as well, because Mum plonked him on the bench away from her for tripping Bill.

I feel really bad for him, so I hug him and whisper in his ear, *I think you're a hero, Josh. Bill Hodge is a shit.* Josh has his thumb in, but he smiles over it at me.

'Maybe it's time for bed?' says Em-from-before-who's-staying. We'd forgotten she was there again.

'Definitely,' says Rani. 'Enough is enough now. Back to the Carthouse we go.'

The grown-ups grab the little kids for bedtime, and me and Lan don't argue, even if we are the oldest. I'm tired, and I hang on to Dad's hand going up our stairs, which are really steep, with walls on both sides and scratchy matting. He's got Josh on his back. My legs are aching and hurting from the flatbed trailer, but in a nice way. I look at each step going up, and think about the bay horse. I remember his face. His eyes looking right at me, and his breath on my hand.

'Dad . . .' I'm scared of asking. They *never* say *yes*. '. . . Dad?'

'What is it, sweetheart?'

'Can I have a horse?'

We're almost at the top of the stairs.

'*Can I?*'

'Sure,' says Dad. Just like – *sure.*

The stairs tilt under my feet. My legs sort of stop working, like they haven't got any bones in.

'Really?'

'One day,' says Dad.

I let my breath out. I thought he meant it for a second. I wonder if he knows how bad I feel. How excited I was. Just for that tiny second, when he said *sure.*

'I promise,' he says.

He bends to kiss my head, and nearly drops Josh the whole way back down the stairs.

He *promised.* I jump up the last step to the top. If he promised, then it's true. Even Dad wouldn't lie about a promise.

We hear a tractor engine. Headlights flash bright across the wall. A metal slam. Footsteps.

'Sounds like Boring Colin,' says Dad. 'What's he want at this time of night?'

It's always Boring Colin. I don't care what he wants. Dad goes back down, and forgets to say *teeth*, and I'm not going to bother. Me and Josh go off to our rooms. Colin says, *evening all*, downstairs, like he does. It's probably about asbestos. My duvet is blue and has stars and I love it, but I hate getting undressed. I flop onto it with my face on the soft cotton stars, floating in blue.

'Hey! Come down!' calls Mum's voice, pulling me awake. 'Kids!'

'Come down!' calls Jim, and his voice sounds *serious*.

I scramble up. We tumble down the slippy stairs again, me and Josh. *What? Why?* kids shout from all round the Farmhouse and the Cowhouse. *What is it?* The grown-ups are putting boots on at the open door. The other kids' footsteps race and patter from the Farmhouse. The cold air smells of mud and stones, and Colin's sheep, and tractor oil.

'What's going on?' says Dad.

They're all in a crowd. Me and Lan push through the legs. Boring Colin is standing by his trailer, with his hand on the ramp.

'Ready for a bit of a surprise?' Boring Colin's voice makes *surprise* sound like *oh dear*.

'What's going on, Colin?' says Mum. 'Not – sheep?'

Sheeps! says Josh. He's still little.

'Nope,' says Colin.

He yanks the ramp. The hinges squeak. It lands with a clatter and a bounce. We all lean forward. The trailer looks empty, just straw, then Colin steps sideways – and we see, at the back, there's a calf. It's blinking in the light. It's so *small.* Lying on its side, half hidden in straw. I've never *seen* a calf so small. It has a flat, wet nose, and sticking-out eyes, too big for its tiny sort of face.

'Must have toppled off her feet coming down the lane, I reckon,' says Colin.

'It's a calf,' says Gail. 'What's it doing here?'

Colin's sheepdog Betsy is leaning out of the window of his tractor with her tongue flapping. Our three dogs nearly push us over coming to look, and Poacher barks to say *hi* because him and Betsy are best friends. All the dogs are curiously sniffing the smell of baby calf coming from the trailer.

'Her twin and the mother died. Five days old,' says Colin. 'John and Mary thought this one would die an' all. Tried giving her to another cow. *That* didn't take. Always risky. I thought you might have her. Frith always *had* cows, before.'

Colin has an oblong head like a breeze block, and all his jumpers have holes and even his fleeces have holes. He doesn't usually talk nearly so much. Normally he only says *righto* and *all right?* He goes up the ramp into the trailer and scoops up the calf, with all her legs hanging down straight. *I can't believe this,* whispers one of the grown-ups, and Mum says *fuck.*

'She's orphaned,' says Colin, looking at us all. 'I'm not having her. I've already got eight hundred bloody sheep to worry about, excuse my French.'

The calf looks a lot bigger in the house. She's still smaller than Ivan, but he's a wolfhound.

'Don't crowd her,' says Jim.

She's not very steady. Us kids are creeping forwards, wanting to touch. Bryn and Eden keep whispering *baby cow!* Josh has his thumb in, just staring.

'I only went in the Spar for a box of matches,' says Colin.

He didn't get the calf in the Spar, it came from the flatbed-trailer farm, but Leslie Robinson who works in the Spar told him about it.

'Leslie said you lot could do with a calf,' says Colin. 'And I agree.'

Finbar opens the back door and peers in, squinting in the bright light. He sees the calf and stops, like he's been hit on the head. He puts his hand on his chest.

'Fuck sake.' He walks towards her in his paint-splashy T-shirt, his bare arms all white and stringy.

'Hello there, my little beauty. Hello, darlin'.'

Then he actually kneels down in front of her.

'Finbar!' I say. 'It's a calf!'

'I can see that, Amy,' he whispers.

He stares at the calf and the calf stares back. Her white-and-brown coat is curly, with a patch of longer curls on the top of her head that look like a wig. He strokes her face and we do too. She's warm and a bit damp, like she's dewy. The little kids are too young to be excited quietly. Lulu Hodge and Lan's sister Bryn keep boiling over. *Boiling over* is what Jim calls it. *Bill's boiled over*, or, *Eden's boiled over*. When one of us boils over near the calf the grown-ups take us out.

Colin brings in formula and a giant baby bottle, and the grown-ups put towels down, and he shows us how to measure it, mix it, and how to hold the bottle. The rubber teat pings out of her mouth a few times, but then she gets it, and drinks, slurping and swallowing, her big eyes going dark. *Look at her eyelashes,* whispers Lan. I look.

'But where will we *put* her?' says Rani, in a sensible Hodge way.

'She can't be out,' says Colin.

We take turns with the bottle while the grown-ups have a serious talk.

It's going to be minus one tonight. There's no shelter, apart from the goats'. If Satan doesn't kill her, she'll freeze to death . . .

The smooth plastic bottle of formula rests on my hand. We watch the gulps go down her throat. I hand it to Josh for his turn. While the calf drinks, we all stroke her neck, our hands crowding over each other.

'We'll just have to put her in the Snug,' says Mum.

My eyes meet Lan's, amazed. *The Snug?*

'The Snug is an inside *room*,' says Eden.

'Well,' says Martin, 'needs must.'

Martin Hodge is the most boring grown-up of all, so if he says it, it *must* be happening.

We cross the Big Room to the Snug like a royal procession, with me and Lan at the front. Colin carries the calf. Dad runs ahead and opens the door.

There's a calf inside our house, and she's going to live next to my kitchen. It feels like tiny fleas or bugs are jumping around in my head and in my legs and making my eyes go funny.

'Just think, when Frith was built, there would have been carts in the Carthouse, and cows in the Cowhouse,' says Mum. She's practically as excited as me.

We pull the rugs off the Snug floor, and chuck them out into the Big Room.

'It'll be nice to have a neighbour,' says Em. 'She can keep me warm.' We'd forgotten she was there again, and her sofa is quite near the Snug door.

We clear everything out. Chairs and pictures. When me

and Lan drag a box of hinges across the floor Martin says, *shh!* and takes them from us. Nobody wants to scare the calf.

The Snug is just a tiny room in the corner of the Big Room, but it's got a door. It's meant to be a study for Dad, for when he feels like writing, but it's too cold. Anyway, Dad only writes in bed, and hardly ever. Jim and Martin bring straw from the barn. *Two whole bales,* says Rani. *Luxury,* says Martin, and he hugs her.

Colin gently lays the calf down on the straw and she does a quiet *moo,* like a little horn.

'A cow in the Cowhouse,' says Mum again.

Everyone stares, and talks, and stares.

Me and Lan lean against things and hang on grown-ups' hands. We aren't tired, it's just everything is muddling. There are too many things to concentrate on. I think Rani's brought a cake over, but we're not hungry. We're not *tired,* we're just not hungry, and we can't think very well. Except about the calf. We want to look at her forever. I'm not sure where the little kids are. They might be in bed. I don't think I can stand up, or get comfortable sitting down, but we aren't going to bed. They can't make us. I look around for the most likely grown-up, and settle on Dad. I pull at his hand.

'Can we sleep in the Snug?'

'Can we?' says Lan.

All the grown-ups look down at us, and then at each other.

'I don't see why not,' says Jim.

Mum and Gail help us get our duvets off our beds, and they keep giggling. The baby calf watches us making our duvet nests in the straw, looking interested.

'In you go, quietly, lie down,' says Dad.

She's close enough for us to reach out and touch and she's made the air around her warm. My face hurts from smiling so much. They shut us in, and all their faces crowd into the top half of the door to look. *They're jealous,* I say. *Poor them,* says Lan, *they're too big to sleep in here.* Then the glass fogs up. And we forget they're even there.

We lie on our sides – just to look at the calf, not because we're sleepy. I'm not going to close my eyes. I'm going to keep them open. The straw is sharp, poking me. And itchy. And it rustles loudly when we move, not like bed. *Look, she's gone to sleep,* whispers Lan. Our calf's eyes are closed. She flicks her ears. Her breath gets louder – *she's snoring!* I whisper. Trying not to laugh out loud makes us keep quiet. Keeping quiet makes us yawn. I reach out to touch one of her warm hooves. I want to say, *hey, Lan, let's polish her hooves.* I'm going to say it. Hooves. Snoring. Straw. Nothing.

3

No More Beds

LAN

We've called the calf Gabriella Christmas, because it's
December. We want her to be in our school Nativity Play
but they won't let us. We hate leaving Gabriella to go to
school, but driving with Adam is fun because we get to go in
the Last Remnants. The Last Remnants is superhero-red,
and it's got a CD player. Adam doesn't play his CDs on the
lane or they'll *get mullered*, only when we get out onto the
proper road, and he sings along really loudly, because of his
trained voice. Nobody else is allowed to drive the Last
Remnants – even Harriet. Adam says the car is the *last remnants of his life*. He doesn't mean he's dead, he means their
Bristol life, when he had more acting jobs. He used to love
going to the pub, he says, with all their friends, and having
takeaway Thai dinners listening to Oasis songs. Harriet says
everyone knows it's stupid, not letting anyone else drive his
car, but we need to be understanding and kind, because
not getting acting jobs makes Adam *question everything*.

The Last Remnants is a Toyota Corolla. We love saying that – *Toyota Corolla!* We're bombing along the B-road, and Adam's playing *La Traviata* and us kids are singing and going *cheers! salut!* with pretend wine. Sometimes he plays 'Purple Rain', which is the *exact* same length as the journey to school. We put our arms out the window and Adam yells, *air guitar, kids!* and we sing – *don' wanna be yourr . . . week-end lover!* – as the Last Remnants rolls into town. People tying up their dogs outside the Spar and old ladies turn to stare. We are the coolest, and everything is brilliant, then the music stops, and we're just at boring school. *Did you have a good day?* Amy's dad always says, when we pile back in the Last Remnants. *We* don't know, we've forgotten. We just want to get home to Gabriella Christmas.

It's amazing how much poo she makes. It's really sloppy, not like a goat's. Goat poo is nice, you could nearly eat it. Unless the goat is ill, then it stinks. Gabriella drinks about ten pints of formula a day, and it all comes straight out of her big arsehole like a fountain of chocolate cream cheese. We can watch it for hours. The grown-ups have got obsessed with cleaning, and make us wash her bottles and the Snug floor every minute. Em-who's-*still*-staying says it's so clean she can't hardly even smell Gabriella from her sofa, but we can smell calf even over in the Farmhouse, so maybe Em can't smell very well, or is being polite.

Nobody knows when Em-who's-still-staying will leave. She's nice, but there's just not anywhere for her to be. Her sofa is right in the middle of the Big Room. It's like a big giant bedroom now. Because it's dark and rainy all the time, us kids have to play inside, and now we can't play in the Big Room, or even practise piano if Em's on her sofa, we have to play in the rest of the houses. It's the same playing we always do, but now the grown-ups call it *rampaging*. They talk about where Em-who's-still-staying can sleep instead of the Big Room so much that me and Amy have made up a song –

> *Honeys in the Farmhouse,*
> *Connells in the Cowhouse,*
> *Hodges in the Carthouse,*
> *Finbar, Finbar – no more beds!*

Early in the morning, when it's still dark, we *tiptoe* past Em's sofa and come back with the wheelbarrow and buckets and clean Gabriella's night-time poos, then get ready for school after. We're doing our teeth in the Cowhouse bathroom, because it's the biggest. Mum's not up yet, because she's in bed with Niah. We lean out to look at my sisters carrying their clothes across the Rope Bridge, to get dressed with us. Bryn trips over her tights and says *ow!* – and they both sit down on their bums.

Mum's voice comes from her room.

'*Shush!* Em is asleep!'

They're always shushing us because of Em. We look down at her, through the netting side of the Bridge. She's fine, wrapped up, asleep. Amy rolls her eyes at me. We go back in the bathroom and start to whisper-sing and toothbrush at the same time –

> *Honeys in the Farmhouse,*
> *Connells in the Cowhouse,*
> *Hodges in the Carthouse,*
> *Finbar, Finbar – no more beds!*

'*Stop it!*' shouts Mum from her room. '*Shush!*'

We were *trying* to whisper. I'm annoyed, and Amy says *what?* but my mouth is full of toothpaste so I can't answer. I spit and take a mouthful of water. The tooth mug is blue, with a yellow duck on it and rough bits where the handle was. I'm holding it when I go back out to check on Bryn and Eden. Amy comes too, still in her weird short pyjamas with the ponies. We look down off the Bridge. We can't see through the big glass doors to the Yard because it's dark still, but we can see Gabriella licking the glass inside the Snug door, which she likes doing. Her tongue is so long. And, almost right exactly underneath us, is Em's sofa, and Em, asleep.

'Shh!' says Amy, pretending to be an angry grown-up, and I nearly spit my water out.

Bryn and Eden are fiddling about with their tights. Josh is in Amy's kitchen with Harriet, and I can smell frying so Jim must be making our breakfast in the Farmhouse. We stare at Em's white pointy face in her squashy grey duvet. Small puffs of breath come out between her lips, like she's a shrivelled granny dragon. Amy rolls her eyes again.

My mouth is still full of spit, and toothpaste and water, and Amy gives me a look, like – *I've got an idea.* She keeps looking in my eyes while she takes the tooth mug off me, and gets a big mouthful of water, as big as mine. Then she almost chokes laughing, and has to shut her eyes. When she opens them we both look back down at Em, with our mouths full of water, big as balloons. Mine is shaking now, I've been holding it in so long. We know we mustn't do it. *Mustn't.* But she's sleeping like a target underneath us.

So we just *dip* our fingers in the water in the tooth mug

and shake them a bit. The drops fall on Em. She doesn't even move.

'*La-an*,' says Eden. Bryn is grumbling her T-shirt is too tight to get over her head.

'What are you *doing*?' says Eden.

Tiny drops of water fall out of our mouths.

'Stop it!' says Eden, who's bossy.

There are drops in Em's hair. We shake our wet fingers over her. I really want her to sneeze. A sneeze would be the best, like a cartoon.

'Amy?' calls Adam really loud, and that's it – we spit all the water, straight down, right onto her, then Amy kind of yells and chucks the rest out, and it lands full *splat* on Em's face, right in the middle. And we bolt, just as she starts screaming.

There's lots of Bad Feeling in the Last Remnants. Adam is playing a CD we don't like, and not singing. He drops us off without saying one single word, not even looking at us, and our stomachs feel sick.

Amy says they might have forgotten about it by after school, but we know they won't. This is worse than goat poo in Josh's bed. We're most scared thinking about what Harriet will say. But most ashamed thinking about Jim.

After school, Adam is waiting on the corner. He's already opened the Last Remnants' doors for us to get in, but he's looking the other way. The only thing he says is *shoes*, meaning *be careful of the seats*. He still isn't speaking to us when we get home, he just says *get out* in a mean voice, and takes my sisters and Josh inside. He's gone into the Farmhouse, so me and Amy go in the Cowhouse on our own. It feels empty and silent. We just stand there in her kitchen, feeling awful and small.

Amy says, 'Let's go say sorry.'

She doesn't mean to Em – she means to Jim.

'Yeah, OK, come on.'

We feel so bad we don't even open the back door as wide as normal, just a tiny bit, and slither out into the Yard.

Afternoons after school in winter are as dark as anything ever gets, and crossing the Yard on our own is terrifying. Finbar's cottage and the Carthouse with the Hodges in it feel like they're far away. We run towards the lights in Jim's workshop, and don't breathe till we get there. It's the only door we ever knock on. The bright light inside makes us squint, and it's warm.

Jim is working on a piece of wood. Pale curls roll up from his planer and fall on the floor. He stops when we come in, and rubs his face and hair. There's always sawdust in his hair, so it goes thick and sticky-uppy, like wood.

'This isn't Gail's dresser,' he says.

He's making a *Shaker-style* dresser for Mum, but he's always interrupted by *things*.

'It's just a gate for Finbar, to keep the goats out. The wood comes from that big old pine tree we took down last year, remember?'

We don't really answer, just shuffle about a bit and look at the floor.

'What's up?' he says. He knows what we did to Em. He's just being a grown-up.

'We're sorry,' mumbles Amy. '. . . Em.'

I can't even talk.

'Em?' says Jim. He's going to make us say it.

'We . . .' Amy starts, but stops again. Saying the actual words out loud will sound really bad. I wait for her to carry on, but she just doesn't.

I can't keep waiting so I say, 'We spat on Em's face while she was asleep.'

I can't believe it, Amy is about to laugh. I can feel her, next to me, I can tell. It's so . . . *wrong*. I'm going to laugh too. I break into a panicking sweat. Amy gives a bark like a dog, trying to keep it in, and then, suddenly, she starts crying. *Crying*. It is not like her at all. I check to see if she's faking. She's not. Her tears are pouring, and her crying makes me feel even worse. I chew my nails and stare at her, while she calms down.

'I'm sorry,' she whispers, with her face all wet and eyes that have gone bright blue. 'We both are. Sorry.'

'Sorry,' I repeat, 'it was mean.'

Jim switches off the light over the workbench, and unplugs the circular saw in case the little kids come in the middle of the night and chop their hands off.

'Do you know what a barometer is?' he says, and hands Amy a man-size tissue.

We shake our heads.

'It measures the moisture in the atmosphere, so it can tell you if it's going to rain, or if it will be sunny and dry.'

Neither of us have any idea what he's talking about. I mean, we understand what he's saying, but not what it has to do with spitting on Em.

'You two are like barometers for this place,' he says, 'for Frith. You did a fairly awful thing, because you sensed the atmosphere at the farm getting stormy. It wasn't kind, but

you know that already. Apologise to Em. And let's all forget about it.'

'Do we have to?' we say.

'You very much have to. Promise?'

'Promise.'

Amy and me look at each other. It's over.

We race back into the Farmhouse about nine times faster
than we ran down, and Jim comes up after, doing his slow
walk.

Adam is in the kitchen standing really close to my mum
and talking. When we crash through the door he jumps
away, and grabs Amy, and swings her around, laughing.
She asks if he's still cross, and he says, 'Who could stay
cross with you? Who? Nobody,' and tickles her. I guess he
must have just forgotten about it.

Mum's cooking at the Rayburn. She doesn't turn around,
just keeps stirring something wet with lots of vegetables. I
wait, looking at her back, and trying to work out if she
hates me now. Niah is lying in one of the dog beds so she
won't roll around the floor, and Christabel is in the other
one looking conceited, like Niah is *her* puppy.

'Do you know where Em is?' I say, because we promised Jim.

Mum turns and puts down her wooden spoon. I think
of Rani's mother hitting Rani's legs with ladles when she
was little. Mum has never hit me with anything. Harriet
smacks Amy sometimes, but hardly ever, and only when
she's insanely angry. Mum picks up Niah and sits on the
bench. She moves her long hair from one side to the other

in a slow swish. She looks really serious, like she's going to say something about what sort of a boy I am. Mum's got dark brown eyes the same colour as her hair, and she stares at me until I feel uncomfortable. Everyone says me and Mum have the same eyes, which is good. I wouldn't want Gray Parks's eyes when I don't even know him. Niah's looking at me too, but she has no idea what's going on, probably even less than Christabel, who's just farted. Mum shifts Niah up her leg and takes hold of my hand.

'Lan. Haven't you got hot little paws?' she says.

I feel awkward and stick my foot out and stare at it. I've got a hole in my sock and my toe coming out looks silly.

'I'll give you some Causticum,' says Mum. 'And some Aurum metallicum. They're both very good for guilt. Hold Niah.'

She gets up and leaves Niah on her back, so I have to move quick to keep her from rolling off the bench. Mum clinks about in her special cabinet, mixing me a potion. If she's giving me her potions then she doesn't hate me. I smile at Niah and she smiles back, but she's got spit bubbles so she looks kind of gross.

Mum turns around, holding up a tiny brown bottle, and when she sees me smiling says, 'See? My magic is working already.'

Jim comes in and says, 'Everything all right now?'

Adam's flopped down in the armchair with Amy on his lap, like she's too heavy to hold on to, and she's hugging him.

'Everything is all right,' says Mum, and Jim kisses her on the head. She loves when he does that. So do I, so he kisses me on my head, too.

'Good,' he says.

'Gail?' shouts Harriet from the Cowhouse kitchen. 'Time to go! Adam! Josh's homework?'

Adam gets up from the armchair and does a limping walk across the floor, dragging Amy along the ground like a sack, so she screams.

'YESH, MASTER!' he says. He's got one shoulder up, and his arm waving around, and one eye shut. 'COMING, MASTER!'

'Where are you going?' I ask.

'The village,' says Mum. 'With the vegetables.'

It's wet and dark out, but being in trouble makes me want to be around her.

'Can we come?'

Once we're out on the road, with all the vegetables in the boot in bags and boxes, Harriet makes the Lada go its fastest. Mum is tuning the radio. She finds a station but it's Welsh. The Lada radio gets Icelandic sometimes, and once we heard Russian. *Respect the Lada,* Adam always says, in his scary Russian accent, *for she is the last of her line.*

We're zooming along and Mum and Harriet are giggling and eating apples.

'So what are we going to do about bloody Em?' says Harriet, and me and Amy listen like bats.

'Poor woman,' says Mum.

'Poor, poor woman,' says Harriet.

She's not poor-poor-Em because of us spitting, just because of her *horrible break-up.*

'Can you imagine?' says Harriet. 'Nearly ten years of marriage. A "younger woman". I mean, Em *is* young.'

'I know!' says Mum. 'She's my age! Thirty-six!'

'Well,' says Harriet. '*Men.*'

'And she's *such* a lovely woman,' says Mum.

'She's *so* lovely.'

Grown-ups are always going on about how lovely other grown-ups are. Em's *OK*. She's not a calf. Amy looks at me and shrugs, *Em's just a boring grown-up.* I nod.

The road signs flash the headlights, green and white. We're nearly at the roundabout. Suddenly, Harriet swerves into the side, and slams on the brakes and turns off the engine. It's very quiet. We're the only car on the road, all lonely and dark. She twists round and looks straight at me and Amy.

'Be nicer to Em, OK? And you too, Lan,' she says in her fierce voice. '*Kindness. Love.* Yes?'

I feel like her hair is going to escape and jump out, but it stays pulled back.

'OK,' says Amy. 'Sorry, Mum.'

'Sorry, Harriet,' I say. 'We will.'

'OK, good,' says Harriet, and starts to drive again, talking to Mum about which house we're going to first, and me and Amy let out our breath.

Later on, at bedtime, when we're back from the village, and all the three families have all eaten in our own houses, I'm lying in my bed thinking over the day. For a second I can't remember if we said sorry to Em. I can picture spitting on her, and Jim being nice, and everything being OK again – but I don't know if we actually said *sorry*, like we promised. Then I remember – we did. We both said it before dinner. And Em got off the bench and gave us hugs. We're not used to Em hugging us, so it felt a bit weird, but we were relieved, so we didn't pull away. I'm just dropping asleep when Amy squawks like a parrot in her room, over in the Cowhouse. I squawk back, and we make some more zoo sounds, and then Adam shouts *shut up*, because Em is going to bed. *Sorry, Em*, we yell, *sorry* . . .

'That's OK,' calls Em, 'it's fine.'

It was nice of her not to be even a bit angry about being spat on. Maybe it was *lovely*, even.

I think of Mum's back, when she was standing at the Rayburn, not turning round for ages. She didn't even say anything cross to me at all, she didn't even tell us off. When Harriet pulled the Lada over and was fierce with us, telling us to be kind, it was like being roared at by a lion, but I checked Amy's face afterwards, and she looked fine. Just normal. I don't think she ever worries Harriet doesn't like her. She never thinks her mum might just go off one day.

4

Vita and Virginia

AMY

I'm lying on Gabriella's tummy listening to my dad trying to give Lan an acting lesson for being a Wise Man. Lan's reading is rubbish, because of daydreaming, says Miss Pillar, but it's really because Gail never makes him and he's way more shy than me. He can't get his lines right. Dad is booming. I don't think Gabriella likes it.

'Come on, Lan. Imagine the bright star, shining over the desert! Open your chest very wide. Big gesture, and . . . Follow the Star!'

Lan's whispering, not *projecting*, and Dad's trying not to get annoyed, I can tell. Dad's an actor but he's not very good at acting *not annoyed*. I'm hiding, so I don't make it worse. I should definitely be a King instead of only being Donkey Three. I'm way more king-like than Lan. Mum says it's *sexist* and it is. I haven't even got any solo lines. Lan has lots.

Follow the Star!
(All) *Follow!*
Not far now!
Come on, camels.
Behold, I bring Myrrh.

'*Come on, camels*' is meant to be '*Come! Camels!*', but it comes out '*Come on, camels*' every single time, like he's *bored* hanging around with camels and doesn't even want to bother seeing the Baby Jesus. In the end, Dad says,

'Just forget it, Lan, I'm sure you'll be fine on the night,' and goes off to do something else.

I come out of the Snug and say, 'Who cares about the stupid play?' but Lan's gone floppy. He goes to the piano and plays the same note fifty times. Gail never helps him with anything, I don't even know where she is, but then Mum comes in.

'Come on, kids!' she says, and drags us out, and *makes* us go with her to Pick Stones in Long Field. I can't even *believe* it.

'Mu-um . . . !'

Picking Stones with Mum in Long Field is cold and horrible, and it's *winter*, but she's in one of her moods, and we have to do it even if our fingers are numb and the mud is like glue.

'Come on!' she keeps saying. 'The faster we do it, the faster it's over!'

She's having a great time.

'Lucky her,' I mutter to Lan.

It's like she's *playing*. She keeps *shouting* Lan's Wise Man lines, over and over.

Follow the Star! (Looking for a stone)
Follow! (Picking up the stone)
Not far now! (Trudging back to the trailer)
Come! (Throwing it on the trailer) *Camels!*
Behold! (Throwing another) *I bring Myrrh!*

Me and Lan join in, in the end. And I guess it's not that bad. It's kind of fun, in fact.

Then Mum suddenly says, 'There you go, Lan, you know them perfectly!' with this look of triumph on her face.

I stand there, my hands spiky with cold, and look at Mum and the pile of rocks on the trailer, with her big shiny nose, and she's like this electric, bright woman. And I look at Lan, with his mouth hanging open, realising he's been saying *all* his lines right. And loudly. And I can't even believe it.

'Christ, Mum,' I say, in the same voice she says *Christ, Amy* when amazing things happen. And she smiles, and I feel like we're best friends.

When we're back in the house, warming up, Gail says, 'Thanks, Harriet, thanks, love.'

She thanks Mum for the Nativity costumes as well, which Mum, Martin and Rani did. The easy ones were Eden, Bryn and Lulu, because they're angels, and Bill and Josh are sheep, so they're easy, too. Lan's Wise Man costume is just shiny stuff from around the place, but I'm meant to have *brown* tights to be Donkey Three, and a *brown* T-shirt. We don't have a brown T-shirt, obviously, and Mum said, *who has a brown T-shirt? I'm fucked if I'm going to go all the way into town to find one.* So I'm going to wear grey tights and an orange T-shirt for Donkey Three.

Gail's doing her remedies at the Farmhouse kitchen table, putting them in bottles with the tiny glass funnel Jim got her for her birthday. She's going to ask Leslie Robinson to sell them at the Spar. She and Rani made beautiful labels and tags for them that say *Frith Farm*.

'Maybe Amy wouldn't mind so much that she's only a donkey if she had the right costume?' she says.

Mum is scrubbing her fingers with the washing-up brush to get Long Field off them, but she stops.

'You could always dye her a T-shirt,' says Gail. 'It's not complicated.'

Mum is staring at Gail, and I suddenly think she might do something, like smash all her little bottles on the floor, so I say, 'I don't care, I don't want to be a boring brown donkey.'

Gail carries on doing her funnelling, and Mum looks out of the window.

'I think I'm going to go and have a bath,' she says, slowly. When Mum has a bath we all have to leave her *completely alone*, or she screams at us.

She dries her hands and starts walking off.

'Oh,' says Gail, 'are you OK?'

'Fine,' says Mum, and keeps going.

Then Dad calls across from our house, 'I can smell that cow! Can you kids come and muck it out. Now, please!'

'Kids, if you're going that way, can you take your mum some Rescue Remedy?' says Gail. 'And look, give her some Impatiens as well.'

She holds out two of her bottles.

'Sure – thanks,' I say, and take them, but I don't give

them to Mum, I pour them down the sink instead. I don't think Mum wants to be *rescued*, not by *her*, anyway.

The Nativity is in the Village Hall, so it's not like boring school at all. Lan has a crown with wine-gum jewels we keep eating so the teachers have to stick more on. Everybody from Frith comes to watch us, even Finbar and Em. Lan's really good at his lines and doesn't forget any of them, and he's mostly loud enough to hear. We've got way more grown-ups in the audience than any of our friends, like a whole big team, and they're all smiling and clapping, and we wave like we're crazy and jump up and down. We're not meant to, because of *spoiling the illusion* and *being disruptive*, but they can't stop us and it's funny. And then there's mince pies. We drive home screaming with all our face paint still on. And there's no more school, because of the holidays. And *Christmas*.

The Winter Solstice is on 21 December. Gail's always telling us. And it's Lan's and my half-birthdays, which nobody cares about, and it's the day we dig up our Christmas tree. We leave the silver star on top of our tree all year, and me and Lan go and talk to it sometimes in summer. We ride down on the trailer to dig it up, with soup, and marshmallows, and goat's milk hot chocolate, and Rani's bread. Rani and Martin have their own fake tree in the Carthouse. They bought it together, years ago. It's blue tinsel, and the dangly bits fall off it, so it looks sort of bald, but they think it's romantic. Martin didn't celebrate Christmas until he met Rani, and neither of them believe in Jesus or anything, *obviously*, because Martin is like us and Rani is a Hindu. Her family had a blue tinsel Christmas tree when she was little, so it's her tradition and it makes her happy.

We make a bonfire, and toast marshmallows, then Finbar digs up the tree while Gail recites a pagan charm. She's not in a robe, just a woolly hat. Me and Lan make fart noises while she's chanting and try to do actual farts but they won't come out, and Dad is really angry and bellows at us. I don't know why he cares so much, he's not a pagan. He's really impressed by all of Gail's white witch stuff, much more than anyone else at Frith, even Jim. Finbar wraps the tree's roots in sacking, and we all carry the tree to the trailer, with everyone going *careful!*, and then climb up next to it, and take it back up the hill.

We've been looking after two turkeys since the summer. They're called Vita and Virginia. Virginia is Vita's mother, and she's going to die first. All our turkeys are called Vita and Virginia: we eat Virginia at Christmas, because of the Virgin Mary, and then Vita in the summer. We don't think Vita will miss Virginia when we've eaten her, because she's a grown-up turkey now, and she's forgotten Virginia is her mother. Next year we'll get two new turkeys and start all over again. Me and Lan have never seen them being killed. Jim does it. He kills all the birds, but the goats go to Allens butcher's and get killed there. Dad slaughtered a chicken *once*, and everyone hopes he won't slaughter another, because he went on for ages about Hemingway, and being *face-to-face with the truth*, and how he felt *like Lady Macbeth*, trying to wash the blood off his hands, until in the end Mum said if he didn't shut up she'd slaughter *him*, and not feel bad at all, and just wash off his blood in the bath.

We take the goats to Allens in Boring Colin's trailer. Mum drives. She always cries. Sometimes Gail comes along to make her feel better, and sometimes we buy chips after. Me and Lan wait out front in the shop, looking at all the pheasants and chickens hanging upside down, and legs of lamb, and dark red beef with thick white fat in it, while Mum goes on and on at Tommy Allen about *standards* and *kindness*. Anyway, Tommy Allen is always really nice. Once, Mum said to Gail, *there's nothing sexier than a kind young butcher*, and they laughed for ages. It wasn't that funny. Tommy makes Mum feel better about the goats, and then gives me and Lan each a Murray Mint, and one for Mum. The Murray part is fine, but the Mint is yuck, and they're much too hard.

Whenever the pair of goats get led away, me and Lan promise never, ever to eat them, but then we forget. By the time it's shepherd's pie or whatever, it just doesn't feel like whichever goat it was, and it's hard to imagine it running round the field. Except, one time, Dad did a prayer in his jokey Vicar voice, *thank you, Gordon, for giving of your flesh this day.* Gordon was a happy little dun-coloured goat with a black stripe on his back, and I suddenly remembered him jostling for his feed. I started crying, and so did Lan, and the other kids caught it, and then there was *mayhem*. Martin said we should only give names to the animals we aren't going to eat. *That's just barbaric*, Rani said.

Everybody's definition of barbarism is different, Jim always says. *Nobody thinks they're on the wrong side of the line.*

Jim has a special knife wrapped in suede on the top shelf of his workshop. It's out of reach so the little kids won't be able to reach it and stab each other and bleed to death. None of the grown-ups had ever killed anything before they came to Frith, just bought meat in supermarkets and *tried not to think about where it came from*. They experimented with different kinds of slaughter before they decided the super-sharp knife is the best one. They talk a lot about the times they got it wrong, and say things like *writhing* and *screaming*, and put their hands over their faces. *Apparently*, going after a chicken with an axe is a *bad idea*. Me and Lan have fun catching the chickens to give to Jim, but we never stay to watch, he doesn't let us. But this year we really, really, really want to see Virginia being killed, because it's *important*.

'It's Christmas,' I say. 'It's like a *special ritual*.'

'Like a sacrifice,' says Lan. He's thinking about being a pagan, like Gail. Him and Gail and my dad can be pagans together.

'*Ple-ease* can we?'

Gail always does a pagan prayer for the turkeys. She doesn't bother with chickens, maybe they're too small. She used to go out with Jim and chant things, but she can't be bothered now. She checks on Virginia almost every day and reports back on how big she is. I think killing the turkey will be like fetching up the Christmas tree, but more exciting. My mum doesn't want us to watch, but she's the one who always says, *if people can't be realistic about killing, they shouldn't eat meat*. And we're old enough. And we're going to. So sucks to her.

Mum goes to fetch Virginia, and me and Lan go with Jim through freezing drizzle to the workshop to fetch the knife. Our breath makes clouds as we talk about Christmas dinner, and all the things we like to eat. *What's that stuffing? The cripsy one?*

'Crispy, not *cripsy*,' says Jim. 'Lemon and thyme.'

And mini sausages! And bread sauce! Bread sauce is yuck. No, it's not . . .

Jim trudges to the workshop door.

'Wait there,' he says, and goes inside.

We try to be serious, because *killing should not be fun*, but we can't keep the bounce out. Far away in the Orchard, we hear the chickens scattering, then Virginia gobbling, sounding excited to be caught. We look at each other and giggle.

Jim gets the knife, and we dance about next to him, all along the back track, past the Hodges' windows, to the Dutch barn opposite the tumbled-down ruin where we saw that snake, near the field called the Hay. When we get there he unwraps the knife and stares at it, close up, and then sharpens it on the whetstone. We watch him in silence, loving the rasp and scrape. It's not a very big knife, we can't see any of the handle when he holds it. We hold our breath as he tests it with his thumb, and then he sharpens it again. Then he plucks a hair from his head. We stretch our necks out trying to see. *What are you doing?* we say. *Is it sharp enough yet?* But he doesn't even answer, he just nods. He puts the knife down and goes for a bale of straw. Me and Lan help. Jim breaks it open and we kick the straw about, and make a golden bed under the meathook.

Mum walks into the barn, holding Virginia, who looks happy. She's used to being handled.

'Hello, Harriet,' says Jim.

'Are you sure about this?' says Mum, meaning me and Lan watching, and Jim shrugs. They look at each other without saying anything, having a conversation without talking, just like me and Lan do.

'Well. OK, then,' says Mum.

She takes Virginia to the bed of straw, and Jim looks down at the knife, and Lan and me look at each other, and our hearts surprise us with suddenly pounding really hard.

Mum puts Virginia down and she gobbles and tries to get away, and suddenly the fun-feeling is gone, and we both step backwards. My stomach feels like sour milk. Virginia is almost as big as our dog Christabel. We wouldn't cut *Christabel's* throat. Virginia struggles again. Her head darts from side to side, like she's in a hurry.

'If you want to go, go,' says Jim, 'there's really no need for you to see this,' but neither of us move.

I feel like now I've made up my mind, and because of begging for weeks, and how much I wanted to see, I can't back out. But it's already not like I imagined.

'There you are, old girl,' murmurs Mum to Virginia.

She kneels on the straw with Virginia under one arm. We always want to stroke Virginia, and she won't let us. Her feathers are grey with darker edges, but her scaly legs and wattle are *disgusting*. Virginia stares about with beady eyes, and makes a chuckling sound, and the red-pink flobbidy bits of her wattle tremble as she looks about, and it just looks sad. I can't tell if she can see us. She's good at seeing what's a food pellet and what's a piece of grit, but when she looks into the distance she looks muddled. Now her muddled look and her wattle make me feel ashamed of myself.

'Can't we stop?' Lan says suddenly. 'Do we have to? We can eat all the other stuff.'

Both grown-ups look up really *dramatically*. Jim is holding the knife and Mum looks like a burglar in a stripy T-shirt getting caught red-handed.

'Go, if you want,' Mum says, still in the same calm voice she's using for Virginia.

If Lan goes, I'll go with him. But he's frozen still. Virginia stops staring, enjoying Mum's strokes.

'It's all right, girl. There, there,' says Mum, almost chanting, like Gail over the Christmas tree, except Virginia is listening. 'Her breed was created by humans, solely to be eaten,' she chants.

Virginia rests against her. It's hard to tell with birds, but she looks loving. I forget to breathe. Jim moves softly across the barn and gets one of the paper feed sacks. He hands it to Mum, and Mum presses it around Virginia's body, and lowers her head to the ground with long, long, long strokes down her neck, over and over.

'This is her purpose,' she sings, softly. 'It's why she came into this world. She wouldn't exist if it were not for this. She wouldn't have lived, and she wouldn't have had Vita.'

Virginia makes soft sounds, back at Mum, like they're chatting. Me and Lan feel hypnotised. The cold air goes still, and everything gets clear, like it's been cleaned. Jim comes up behind Mum and kneels down. There's a hard lump in my throat, like after I swallowed a whole Murray Mint by mistake and Mum had to emergency stop the Lada.

'She's had a lovely life,' says Mum, resting her body on top of the bird. 'Lovely grass, lovely food, love . . .'

She holds Virginia's slim neck close to the straw, but not touching.

Jim puts the knife into the gap under Virginia's neck, saying something under his breath. I don't see him cut, but when he takes the knife away I can *just* see the blood, running into the straw. Virginia doesn't even move, she doesn't even know he's done it. My legs feel watery. Mum is still stroking her head. Virginia's eyes look the same – then her neck goes loose – then they look dead.

I feel like there's a big sigh in the air all around us. Virginia's body twitches. Me and Lan have heard about death spasms. Lan's gone white, like he's going to puke. His hair looks weirdly dark. Jim is helping squash Virginia down. It looks quite difficult. Next to me, Lan makes a small sound. The death spasm stops. Jim's and Mum's hands relax. After a few more seconds, Mum says, *there, definitely,* and stands up, and takes the sack off the turkey's fat feathery body and folds it, like she's folding a pillowcase. She wipes her eyes with the backs of her hands. Jim stands up and hugs her tight.

'All right?'

Mum sniffs and nods her head.

'It's just as wrong to be sentimental as to enjoy it,' she says to me and Lan, suddenly a bit mad-looking.

'Nobody enjoyed it,' says Jim. 'Are you all right, kids?'

I don't know if I am or not.

I say, 'Yes.'

Jim picks up Virginia by the legs, and her long neck swings. 'Twine,' he says. Mum hands him some.

Lan turns and runs out of the barn. I'm too surprised to follow, and also I don't want to. Jim ties up the turkey's legs and hangs her from the hook. Virginia's enormous grey wings stick straight out, wider than my arms, and show all the white fluff underneath. I could stroke her now if I wanted, but I don't. My toes are numb. I shake my feet and wriggle about.

'You can give us a hand plucking,' says Mum. 'The sooner we do it, the easier it will be.'

I look at the big scaly claw-feet and shake my head. Jim clears away the straw. He kicks earth over some blood that seeped through. I help, feeling practical, like Mum and Jim. Strong.

'I'm so excited about Christmas!' says Mum.

They pull out feathers with a snapping sound, like tiny teeth coming out. They land in a fluff-pile on the straw. A quick wind blows the feathers, and for a few seconds the barn looks like a snow globe of two grown-ups standing next to a dead turkey.

The carcass swings from the hook. The head drips one thick black drop of blood, which stretches before it falls. *Virginia's head*, I think, *Virginia's blood*, but it just doesn't seem like her, now it's dead.

'Why don't you go find Lan?' says Jim. 'See if he's OK?'

Lan! Lan!

My wellies slap on the muddy track. I don't think he's gone back to the house.

LAN!

I check over the gate of the Hay, and see him standing in

– 60 –

the field, pretending to be interested in something in the hedge. I climb over the bar gate and run over.

Whatcha-doing?

Nothing.

Whatcha-looking at?

Nothing.

His face is tear-streaked. I join in with pretending the hedge is interesting, and looking around generally. The Hay *is* a nice field. We always feel safe in the Hay, even just walking next to it. It's got big hedges on three sides and a nice stone wall.

Our horse could go in this field, I say. *One day.*

I want my mum, says Lan.

He runs off, and I go after. I guess Gail will want to know killing Virginia went OK.

Gail is in her giant padded coat by the Orchard fence, looking miserable and pale, just like Lan. All her chickens and guinea fowl are pecking around nearby, with Vita in the middle of them, just eating away with her tiny friends. She doesn't realise she's nine times their size.

'Mum!'

Lan runs into Gail's arms so fast she *has* to hug him, or she'll fall over backwards.

'Have they done it?' she says.

Lan can't hardly speak for crying. He says he *hates Jim* and he *hates Mum*, and he'll never eat meat again. He doesn't really hate Mum. Or Jim. That's silly.

Gail starts to talk about how much she loved Virginia, and what a lovely turkey she was. I feel bad, because I'm not as upset as them. Jim says death is all around us. We've heard all about the *proper* farms, and the big abattoirs, we aren't like those bad people. Part of me wants to say, *it's just a turkey.* I feel as if I'm watching Lan make up the story of how upset we were when the turkey was killed for Christmas. It's a new thought and I don't like feeling different from him, and separated.

'Why didn't *you* do it?' I ask Gail. 'Why didn't *you* kill Virginia? She's your turkey.'

'I couldn't!' says Gail, looking shocked.

'You're going to *eat* her,' I say.

Gail shakes her head and hugs Lan again, but only so she won't have to answer me. I've annoyed her. I can tell. I look at the chickens all pecking about near her feet.

'All right, Lan, let me go now,' says Gail, and shakes him off like she can't breathe when he's hugging her. 'I'll get you some Rescue Remedy.'

She goes off, shouting, 'Adam! Adam! They've done it!'

I hear Dad answer, then both their voices chattering. Gail laughs, and Dad laughs, too. She can't be *that* upset, if she's laughing at Dad's jokes. I think she just doesn't want blood on her hands, like Dad. He doesn't like difficult things either. They're quite the same in lots of ways.

5

Christmas Day

LAN

When we wake up on Christmas Morning, it's frosty and sunny and different to all the other days. It feels it. Amy, me, Mum and Harriet do Early Goats and Early Chickens, shivering in pyjamas and smashing puddles into splinters. While we're outside, the church bells start! We can't see the church, it's in the village, but the sound of ringing is all over the valley. Anything could happen – animals talking, or anything. Amy says Perdy the cat was purring on her bed this morning, which is a *sign*, because she's not that sort of cat. Finbar says animals can talk on Christmas. Harriet read us that book about a magic broomstick. When the girl was holding it she could hear a black cat *talk*. One day I'm going to find real-life magic, definitely. I used to think Mum was magic, when I was little, but she isn't a real witch. I suppose it's good she isn't, she can't just fly off.

On Christmas Morning, me and my sisters do our stockings on Mum and Jim's beds. Niah's stocking has only got baby wipes in, and she doesn't even notice. Amy and Josh are with their mum and dad, and the Hodges are in the Carthouse with their blue tree. We don't all meet up *officially* until lunch, when it's dark outside, and candles and fairy lights are all around the houses. It looks like twice as many as there are, because of the reflections on the windowpanes. The grown-ups play Christmas carols and normal songs while everyone cooks. You can hear music everywhere, even outside, and Rani brings samosas over so we don't all starve to death. Her and Harriet and Adam are in charge of the cooking, and Em-who's-living-here-now is helping. This morning, Boring Colin came down his hill with a box of Quality Street when nobody was dressed and gave us presents. Mine's a toy car and Amy's is a pink comb, and they make us feel guilty, because we don't like them and his mum is dead and he's all alone. When he saw Gabriella dressed as the Angel Gabriel with her tinsel halo he said, *I don't know what to think. Whatever next?* The grown-ups invited him for Christmas and he said *yes*, if the sheep will let him. We think he's joking, but we aren't sure. Colin was our First Friend at Frith, and we feel bad for calling him Boring. When the grown-ups first got here they were all from cities and not used to how dark it is in the country, and Martin got lost after work and couldn't find his way home. He drove around the lanes for ages, and in the end he had to knock on Colin's door. Martin says, at first, when Colin led him into his creepy house where his mother died and offered him a cup of tea, he thought he was going to push him down the steps into the cellar and *string him up and butcher him*, but he didn't. Obviously. He showed Martin home, and then stayed for hours and hours and now he's our friend.

Lunch is at night-time on Christmas. The turkey is right in the middle of the table, biscuity-brown and shining and steaming. It looks so nice, but I know it's Virginia, and I've decided I'm not going to eat it. All the other things are covering the whole table – Rani's special bright orange honey-carrots, and Brussels sprouts, which most people hate but we don't, and ten tons of roast potatoes. And gravy. And bread sauce. And two different stuffings. Adam throws handfuls of parsley over everything, shouting *green confetti!* – which makes it look special, even if it doesn't taste of anything and sticks in our throats.

Martin carves and everyone watches. I lean so close to the turkey I nearly go cross-eyed, and Martin says, *mind your nose.* The breastbone is white where he's sliced off the meat. It's juicy, and it smells amazing. Everyone's praising Mum for providing *the most important part of Christmas lunch.* I pile my plate right up, so nobody can see I'm not having any, I don't want her to be cross.

The grown-ups eat slowly but we eat fast, and then roll about groaning and eating Quality Street and stinky cheese in the Big Room, all over the beanbags and on the floor. Amy and me drop grapes in our mouths like Roman emperors. *Look at me, oh yuss! Deeelicious,* and the other kids copy us. Jim's put a baby gate on the Snug for Gabriella, and she's leaning over it, trying to join in. Adam takes millions of pictures of her in her tinsel halo. The dogs have licked all the plates and lie on the floor thumping their tails, then Christabel, who's an old lady, is sick and Ivan the wolfhound eats it, and everyone who's watching is nearly sick straight after, and Jim calls it the *domino effect.*

Just when we're thinking Christmas isn't even all that great, and we don't know why we were so excited for it, Adam tiptoes out. Amy's dad is the only person in the world who can tiptoe out so everyone in the room notices.

'Cover your eyes!' he shouts, from the Cowhouse kitchen. 'Finbar! Martin!'

We try to go see what's happening but the other grown-ups throw us onto the beanbags and jump on top of us and cover our eyes. Mum is on me. I can't breathe at all. Bill's knee is on Eden's hair and she starts crying. My eyes hurt from Mum's hand squashing over them. *Don't worry about the turkey, Lan,* she whispers. *I understand.*

'DA-NAAA!' shouts Adam in his *La Traviata* voice.

They all get off us and we open our eyes, all stinging and hot. Right in the middle of the Big Room is an enormous wrinkly white sheet.

'It's a cinema screen!' shouts Adam.

In the middle of the sheet is a square of light so bright it makes our eyes ache. Adam runs up and down with his sleeves flapping, going *oh my God-oh my God.* He says when he was *rehearsing* he did something to get the projector to the right height, but he can't remember what it was. He shouts *fuck!* and we all laugh, and then wait. And wait. The sheet trembles like when wind blows on water. Finbar suddenly gets up and leaves – out the back door, not saying anything.

'Finbar's done really well,' says Harriet.

'Is he suffocated?' says Amy.

Adam produces two DVDs from nowhere. One is called *Chitty Chitty Bang Bang* and the other one is black and white with old people hugging by a Christmas tree, smiling and looking stupid. We haven't seen either of them, but it's easy to choose.

Me and Amy are on the lights, and we keep having to switch them on again because nobody's ready, or they're worried the dogs will get the chocolate, or they need more wine and beer. The projector is from Martin's office, and Jim made the screen, but it was all Adam's *idea*, and he was the one who went to town in the Last Remnants for the DVDs, so everyone claps him, and Harriet only just stops him from making a speech. She puts the DVD in the laptop, and we unplug the blow heater because the laptop speaker is quiet, and huddle under duvets on Em's sofa and on our beanbags, and the movie starts.

It's a long film, and even longer because the projector keeps overheating, or the laptop goes to sleep, or people need to go pee, but nobody has ever been so quiet as us kids. I'm squashed next to Amy with grown-up legs behind us. We have the best view. Because of it being a surprise – and maybe even because it keeps going wrong – we love *Chitty Chitty Bang Bang* even more than *Madagascar*, or any film we've ever seen. Even if the kids in it are weird and annoying. They've got the exact same colour hair as Niah, and the grown-ups think they're *so sweet*, but they make us puke. Gabriella keeps putting her head out and mooing. When she stretches her neck, she can get her face in front of the screen, and Chitty's stripy wings move on her pretty calf face.

When the movie ends, Lulu, Eden and Bryn are asleep. Bill is drooling onto Rani's legs, asleep with his eyes open, like a zombie.

'He does that so no one can send him to bed,' says Rani, as if Bill is being clever, not just weird.

The grown-ups start clattering about the kitchen, and Mum goes upstairs to check on Niah.

Everything feels gloomy and cold now the projector is turned off. My eyes are itching and I can't decide if I'm hungry or not. Me and Amy give some cold roast potatoes to the dogs. My head is full of the movie, and I'm thirsty. I dip a potato in cold gravy, catching the floating fat, and the gravy soaks into the fluffy inside but then I don't want to eat it, so I just drop it back in. Then I remember the Lego that's my *main* Christmas present. It's an X-wing fighter, and there's a sticker on the box that says *complete*. I wanted it for ages and ages, and Mum found it for me.

'I see you sneaking off, Lan,' says Harriet. 'Come and help dry up.'

'I'm just going to get something.'

I run upstairs in my socks.

It's freezing. Even the carpet is cold. At the top, I tiptoe as I pass Niah's room and glance in, out of habit, because she always needs checking on. I thought Mum was doing it, but she's not there, the cot is in the dark, so I just carry on to my room. Except, ahead of me are Mum and Adam. It's quite dark, and at first I think Mum is crying, because Adam's hugging her, but she isn't crying – they're kissing each other's mouths.

'What are you doing?' I say.

They stop, and Adam holds out his arm that isn't round my mum.

'We're saying Happy Christmas! Come and have a hug with us, Lan!'

He says it in a normal voice, but when I get there to be

hugged, Adam isn't there any more, and it's only Mum. I look up at her. I can't think of what to say.

'We've had such a lovely day, we were having a kiss,' says Mum. 'Like this . . .' She kisses me on the top of my head. 'Did you check on Niah?'

'She's fine,' I say. 'I was getting my Lego.'

'I'll come with you,' says Mum.

She feels a bit overexcited. She comes to my room with me, chatting about how great it is she found the X-wing fighter I wanted, and she had to look in three shops, and there's no point buying new Lego, and people are mad getting new stuff when you can get it less than half-price.

'Lucky the first person bought it new,' I say. 'So we can have it.'

She says how clever I am in a fake voice, and we go down into the kitchen, where the washing-up grown-ups have gone super-lively and noisy. They've put music onto Martin and Rani's brand-new iPhone speaker dock. They gave it to each other for Christmas, because they've both got proper jobs. All the grown-ups are jumping around while they clear up. The Kaiser Chief is predicting a riot.

All the lights are bright again. I stand there feeling like I'm not sure what I'm meant to be doing, holding on to my Lego. I see Adam putting leftovers in a box, and suddenly remember him hugging my mum. He said it was a *Happy Christmas kiss*. But that's not true. I know it was a lie, because the kiss wasn't a Christmas kiss, but I don't know what kind of kiss it was. It wasn't a Love Kiss because they aren't married, but I don't know why they *were* doing it. It doesn't matter, anyway. I suppose.

There isn't anywhere to put my Lego. If I do it on the floor, it will get kicked, and I don't want to go to the Big Room now because some of the little kids are boiling over in there. I think I'll do it later on.

The song finishes. The grown-ups go *phew!* because they're all sweaty. The new song is soppy. It's that man. Adam has been putting him on all the time in the Last Remnants recently. The grown-ups go *aahh!* with happiness, and Rani and Martin look at each other and sing *you're the one I love, you're the one I love,* while they wipe things and scrape plates.

Harriet is sweeping a big pile of food and dirt, and she does dancing-sweeping across the floor towards Adam, and sings, *you're the one I love, you're the one I love* to him. Amy's mum is the best singer out of all the grown-ups. She does it when she's teaching us piano, to show us the tune. Her hair is in a big bright gold fluff. Her voice is round and nice, not annoying, like those really high-up lady-voices. It sounds so nice, like Christmas, and love. She's right in front of Amy's dad, but he can't see her I don't think, which is weird because she is right there. Then he sort of does – and he grins at her, but just for one half of a second, and then spins away to sing at Amy instead – *you're the one I lo-ve!* – in his *La Traviata* voice. He's completely different to how he was upstairs, a minute ago, with Mum.

Amy is by the back door staring at some fairy lights.

'*Hellooo?*'

She's asleep, just like Bill Hodge, except she's standing up. Adam waves at her –

The back of her hair is matted, and looks funny. She opens her mouth to yawn. Just looking at her makes me feel tired, too. Then I notice a *smell*. It's so strong. It's horrible.

First, I think Amy's farted. Then that the smell must be coming from Virginia's carcass on the table. I start getting scared. It stinks so bad. It doesn't even smell like meat. It's like dead fox, or a pond that's gone dry and slimy, or smashed eggs in the henhouse. Everyone's noticing now, and all the grown-ups stop what they're doing and say, *oh my God*, and sniff the air. Harriet turns the music off.

'What *is* that?' says Amy, suddenly jerking her head, like the jack-in-a-box dolls in *Chitty*. '*YUCK*—'

'Mum!' screams Eden from the loo. 'My poo's come back up!'

Jim runs out of the kitchen.

'Shit, Adam, it's the fucking septic tank,' says Harriet. 'You didn't call the guy.'

Then Adam yells, 'Christ, not now! Fuck! *Fuck!* This fucking farm! This fucking, fucking place!'

He's screaming. It's horrible. Gabriella moos from the Snug like she's scared too – and Amy bursts into tears.

'Oh God, sorry, darling,' says Adam, and rushes to hug her.

All the rest of us just stand there. I look down. I'm still holding my Lego, but the lid's come off, and all the tiny little pieces slip down the cardboard and fall out and scatter over the floor. People are all rushing around, they'll tread on it, but I can't stop them. I'll lose all the bits, and I'll never get to make my X-wing fighter, and I start to cry, too.

'Oh! No! Kids!' says Adam.

He pulls Amy onto his lap and hugs her, and Josh comes running and he hugs him too.

'*Wait*,' says Jim in a big voice, and everybody stops. 'We need to collect Lan's Lego.'

He gets on his knees on the kitchen floor, and starts picking it up. I can't stop crying, because we'll never, ever find all the bits, they're too tiny. But Rani gets down to look, too, so then I start helping.

The smell is still so bad it's in our *mouths*. Martin opens the back door so freezing-cold air comes in.

I've found Chewbacca's head and hold it tight. There's a lightsaber in a crack in the floor, under Adam's chair, and I squeeze under and bump my head on his knee. *Sorry*, I say. Amy and Josh on his lap look snotty but happy, and Harriet is kissing his cheek.

'Oh, darling,' says Adam.

'It's not your fault,' says Harriet, and he snuggles his head against her front like Josh.

I don't know if we've got all the Lego. I think we have. We put the box on the piano to be safe – *out of harm's way*, says Em.

Adam says, 'I'm sorry I was angry, kids, it's not *Frith*, you know I love Frith more than anything in the world – it's just *money*.'

That makes us feel better, because money always makes grown-ups mean, everyone hates it.

'We'd better sort out this mess,' says Jim, and gets his boots on to take a look at the septic tank. Everyone goes too.

Me, Amy and the little kids follow the grown-ups out into the dark, past the Goats, to the yucky gross septic tank.

They're flashing torches at the ground and the fence posts, but they can't see where the pooey bit starts, and they keep saying *stay back! Stay back!* And *eugghh*. The Dads accuse the Mums and say, *you've flushed tampons-and-towels!*

And the Mums get unbelievably angry about *misogyny*. It's really funny. Martin throws up his hands and says *whatever*, and goes squelching back to the Carthouse to call an emergency plumber, and Bill starts dancing about going, *Dad's stepped in poo! Dad's stepped in poo!* and we all join in, then Finbar leans out of his house and yells:

'Kids! God almighty, will you give it a rest?'

When we get back inside, I've stopped being tired, and so has Amy. And we're *so* hungry. It feels like years since lunch. The grown-ups are scattered, doing this and that, and squabbling, but everything's fine again.

'Let's eat our dinners in the Snug with Gabriella,' says Amy.

And I say, 'Yeah.'

I think if we're really, really, really quiet, then our calf might say something. I know magic might not be real, I know that. Everyone says I'll grow out of believing in it. I don't want them to be right, but know they might be. And that I most likely won't always believe in it, like when I'm a grown-up. But I don't want to think about that now. Especially on Christmas. Especially now. I don't want to think about secret rare things breaking. I want to think all the Good will last forever. We'll be silent. I'll stay awake. She might say something. Just my name or something. She *might*. And tomorrow I'll make my X-wing fighter, and keep my fingers crossed nothing's missing.

SPRING
2006

6

Sticks and Stones

AMY

So, basically, New Cottage is nearly finished being fixed up and Em is going to live in it forever. It's taking ages because New Cottage wasn't new at *all*, it was an old ruin. It's a bit down the hill from Finbar's. It had no floor and only half a roof and it's taking *so much money* to do it that nobody knows *how we will survive*. The grown-ups always say that, but we always do survive. Just like they always fight, and then they love each other again. When New Cottage is finished, Finbar will be able to look out of his window at Em if he wants, and she'll probably be able to see him on the loo.

It's raining so hard we're stuck inside with the grown-ups. It feels like being in Noah's Ark in my kitchen, with the dogs clicking about on the stone floor, and Gabriella mooing from the Snug, and Perdy mewing. Perdy is only small and she looks cute, but her mew is loud and she's a killer. Mum says she should be on a Christmas card with the word *psycho* in red glitter above her head. She's killed so many mice and baby rabbits she's got fat.

Mum and Gail are looking things up in their self-sufficiency books and on the internet, which takes about ten thousand years because of dial-up. It's raining *so* hard the windows look like someone's outside squirting a hose on them. Sometimes it goes to hail, and then it's like someone's throwing stones. I keep picturing Finbar out there with the hose, and Finbar throwing the stones, because that's the sort of thing he'd do in one of his really-really happy moods, but it's not Finbar, it's just *weather*.

We've got Lan's family to lunch with us today, but not the Hodges. My kitchen isn't big enough for Bill and Lulu. Lan's is bigger but ours is better because it's got our shiny tablecloth and me and Josh's paintings stuck up. And the Aga, which is way better than the damn-fucking Rayburn, which is just rubbish. Dad is making spaghetti sauce, and the smell of frying garlic is everywhere.

Every two minutes Martin *throws* himself through the door in his mac with the hood up, looking like a sea monster, yelling questions like, how much chick crumb has Gail bought, because he found the words chick crumb *just scrawled on a scrap of paper!* on his spike. Then he's back two minutes later, to go on at Dad for putting petrol for the Last Remnants on the farm account, when *it's a personal expense, Adam*. Dad goes all dramatic about how he was *forced* to put goat carcasses in the Last Remnants' sacred boot. *Goat carcasses!* he yells back at Martin, but none of them are really cross, they're having fun. Me and Lan have got our faces on the table, chewing bread with our mouths open and staring at the food going round because we're just so *bored*.

Then Mum says, 'Gail, shall we get a cow-friend for Gabriella?'

'Sheeps!' says Josh. He wants sheep almost as much as I want a horse.

'If we get one, we may as well get two or three,' says Gail. *A herd of cows!*

'Do you think we could get enough milk without separating them from their calves?'

They start looking, and the dial-up makes birdie sounds.

'Nearly ready,' says Dad. 'Kids? Table?' He means, *put plates and forks on it.*

Martin comes back in, pouring rain off his hood in a puddle and waving a big red file. Everyone goes, *shut the door!* and he slams it.

'Martin,' says Mum, 'what do you think about Frith building up a small herd of cows?'

Martin makes a noise like someone has thrown a worm at him.

'He *never* wants more animals,' I say to Lan.

'Herefords,' says Dad. 'But native Hereford, not like Gabriella.'

What's wrong with Gabriella?

'Think of the red tape,' says Martin, and does a massive snotty sneeze. He wipes his nose with tissue from his pocket then counts on his fingers for us, like we're all tiny kids. 'Foot-and-mouth. BSE. Corona.'

All the other grown-ups go quiet, and Martin starts on about the petty cash. Me and Lan slither off the bench onto the floor because we're going to die.

'Yeah, *whatever*,' says Mum. 'I'm with Amy and Lan.'

Martin is *definitely* the most proper grown-up. He wears a suit and he's the only dad who has hair with a parting. It's on the side. Rani has a parting, too, right down the middle of her really black hair, which she gets cut *straight* along the bottom and tucks behind her ears. They're both so neat. Martin goes to work in the New Business Park, which sounds really cool, like silver spaceship rides, but it's not like that at *all*. Me and Lan made him take us there once and it was a massive disappointment, there wasn't even *food*.

All the grown-ups work on *some* non-Frith things. Rani *consults*, we don't know what it is. And Em-who's-living-here-now does something boring that's about Law but isn't being a Policeman. Jim is *always* making furniture, and Gail does her potions, I suppose, but I don't think that counts. (Lan thinks it does, but I don't.) My mum does her piano teaching, and my dad does acting sometimes, but hardly ever. We're not allowed to say that. When me and Lan were still six, Dad was Angry Restaurateur in *Casualty*. We were so excited we used to make him say 'Get out of my restaurant!' all the time, and he loved it, but then one day he shouted, 'Look, it was just one shitty little job! Can we please forget about it?' And nobody ever mentioned it again. Now he's writing a blog about all the farming jobs that the Frith grown-ups are learning to do, and funny stuff that happens, like falling in poo. People fall in poo a *lot* in Dad's blog.

Martin goes back out into the rain, and Mum says, 'Well, I still think we should get cows.'

Gail says, 'We'll work it out.'

Dad pours the boiling water out into the sieve thing and the spaghetti slips out in a big flop.

'Cows would be great for "Exit",' says Dad.

'Why is it called that?' I ask.

'It's short for "Exit, Pursued by a Goat",' says Dad, and laughs. 'It's a joke. It's funny. It's a take on Shakespeare.'

Me and Lan look at each other like *oh yes, hilarious.*

'It's a joke, about being chased offstage by a goat,' says Dad.

'What stage?' asks Lan.

'A figurative one,' says Dad.

'It would be funnier if it was called "Exit, Pursued by a Chicken",' I say.

'No, it wouldn't,' says Dad.

'Yes, it would,' says Mum.

'Dad,' I say, 'a *chicken chasing you* is way funnier. Goats chase people the whole time, but if a chicken did it would be a surprise and, also, really scary, because chickens are basically only just stupid birds.'

'It wouldn't be funnier, Amy,' says Dad, sounding irritated, 'and they're not *any old* chickens, they're not stupid birds, they're Gail's guinea fowl.'

Who owns the chickens isn't even the point, but he says *Gail's guinea fowl* sounding all puffed up and offended, like a hen.

'*Oo-oh! Gail's guinea fowl!*' I say, copying him, and me and Lan and Josh fall about laughing, and then Mum starts laughing too.

'Stop it!' says Dad.

'They aren't even *mammals*, Dad,' I say. 'You're in *love* with Gail's chickens.'

Adam's in love with Gail's chickens! say the other kids and we all laugh, but Mum and Gail have stopped laughing, and don't say *anything*, really suddenly, so me and Lan stop, too.

'Lunchtime,' says Dad, putting the spaghetti on the table with a bang.

And then everyone is *quiet*. Just staring at the spaghetti covered in bright red tomato sauce, steaming. The back door opens but it's not Martin again, it's Jim.

'Delicious!' he says.

Nobody else in the kitchen is talking. Jim sits down, looking round at everyone.

'OK?' he says.

Dad's putting spaghetti on plates with the big tongs. I feel like he's furious, and I think he's going to tell me off, but I didn't do *anything* wrong and Lan didn't either, so *I'm* not going to say sorry. Instead of thinking about how the air's gone angry, I think about the tablecloth, and trace my finger around the flowers.

'What's these again?' I ask.

'Peonies,' says Mum, quietly.

'What's these?' I ask her.

'Tulips,' she says. I glance up at her, she's looking down at her food.

The ones in between are daisies, everyone knows that. The tablecloth is my favourite thing in any of the houses.

We can hear everyone chewing, and spaghetti isn't even crunchy.

Immediately lunch is finished, Mum jumps up and chucks things in the sink and says it's stopped raining so she's going to do Hedging, and me and Lan can go with her if we want. There's *always* Hedging to do, same as there's always Picking Stones.

The Lada makes giant water sprays, zooming down the valley on the track to Barrow, and when we get there she *leaps* out and *slams* the door, and cuts the twine on a bundle of hazel stakes with a slash, so they explode and clatter to the ground. It's all wet and splashy. She's not talking to us. She hasn't hardly said anything. She paces out the distances for the stakes with her boots making smacking sounds, and me and Lan stand watching, saying *can we help?*

Years and years ago, when we were babies and Rani was pregnant with Bill, he wouldn't come out, so she was trying to make him get born, drinking raspberry leaf tea, which kept her awake all night, peeing, and then in the early morning she walked all the way down the valley to Barrow, thinking about what Bill would be like. (She probably thought he'd be a lot nicer than he is.) She was watching the sun come up when she heard this sound and turned, and saw a dappled baby deer hanging on the loose wire in the hedge. It was all cut and ripped open by barbed wire, and its front leg was hanging off, and even though it had almost no blood left, it was still trying to get off the wire. Rani tried to help but it died, right in front of her. She says she's *never seen anything so still* as the baby deer hanging dead off the wire. That's why we have to get *all* the barbed wire out of Frith. And also because of birds, because if there's no hedges where will they even *live*? Problem is, lots of our hedges aren't hedges, they're just wire fences with a few bushes along them. We need *proper* hedges and *proper* fields, to put all the animals we're getting one day. Mum has *big dreams* for Frith, she's always saying.

She takes an enormous breath, and lets it out slowly, with her mouth in an 'O'.

'It's stopped being so cold,' she says. 'The wind has changed.'

She climbs up on the Lada bumper.

'Mallet, please.'

The mallet-head is a black iron lump. I get it off the front seat, swinging it about.

'Gloves,' she says.

I grab her Armor gloves.

'Dad gave you these on your birthday,' I say.

Her hands look enormous in them, like an astronaut.

'I can manage,' says Mum. 'I'm fine. You play.'

The banging mallet makes a hard ringing sound while me and Lan dig about in the mud for stone markers for our spear-throwing contest, because we're Ancient Greek Olympians. Then we play Spearing Bears, taking turns being the bear until our hands are hot and we're getting blisters, so we stop, and look for rusty barbed wire so Ivan won't get ripped in pieces hunting rabbits.

Mum is so out of breath we can hear her throat, like sandpaper. It sounds really weird. We look up. The whole time we've been playing, she's only bashed in two stakes. The rest of the hedge stretches away, miles and miles and miles.

'Look!' says Lan, 'Adam.'

Dad is coming down the long track, swinging his arms. We wave and he starts to run. By the time he gets to us he's out of breath, too.

'Need a hand?' he says, and smiles.

He's definitely the most handsome man in the world. He looks like the Kind Woodcutter who doesn't cut Snow White's heart out, who she should marry instead of the boring Prince.

'I'm fine,' says Mum.

She points at the two measly stakes she's bashed in, and Dad says how good she is at it, then squashes her against his chest with both arms, so she can't escape.

'What an incredibly strong woman,' he says. 'Aren't you?'

'Yes, I am,' says Mum.

'And I'm a coward.'

'Oh, Adam.'

The way she says it makes me and Lan put up our heads, like dogs hearing a strange sound.

'The whole *thing* with . . .' he looks at us, then back at Mum, '*her* . . . you know, it was always silliness. It wasn't real.'

'I know.'

'And it's forgotten.'

Then they do more hugging. It feels like something heavy and bad that I didn't even know was there has gone away, and everything fits together again. Then it's just yucky, basically, because they do romantic Love Kissing, and me and Lan have to pull on them to make them stop.

We help with carrying, and Dad and Mum bash in more hazel stakes together, laughing and talking about Frith stuff. She holds the stakes and he bashes them in. If I was her I wouldn't stand so close to Dad if he had a big mallet, but Mum trusts him, and luckily he doesn't smash her skull in.

While they're working, Dad tells the story of finding the

Prossers in the Fox and Badger. The Fox and Badger is a pub. It's not in a proper village, and it doesn't have snacks, and it doesn't even have bottles hanging upside down, they're just on a shelf. But sometimes there's cheesecake. You put money in a box. Me and Lan do *not* like going there because everyone stops talking when we walk in. Dad loves it. He goes round shaking hands, and puts on a local accent by mistake. Me and Lan have to go outside because we're so embarrassed. Finbar never goes to the Fox and Badger, *obviously*. Dad thinks it's the most authentic pub in England and we should support it. Rani hates pubs and doesn't even care if they all close, and thinks England should just have cafés like France.

Anyway, basically, one day, Dad, Martin and Jim went to the Fox and Badger and came home with Frankie Prosser, and Nick Prosser, who was his nephew. *Meet the Champion Hedge-layers in Europe!* said Dad. Frankie Prosser looked like one of the Seven Dwarfs, and had clothes like moss, and Nick Prosser had an orange fleece and showed us pictures of Frankie holding a Hedging Prize Cup. Everyone watched them do our hedges with buzz saws and choppers, and we gave them cheese sandwiches and they gave the grown-ups lessons. *It's not as easy as it looks,* they said. We thought the whole of Frith would have perfect hedges, like in the olden days, but the grown-ups had to pay them money, so the Prossers only came back once.

'The Prossers would have done this whole boundary by now,' says Dad.

Him and Mum are sweaty.

'Jim says *slow but steady wins the race*,' says Lan.

'Oh, Wise and Perfect Jim,' says Dad.

Mum and Dad laugh, and Lan goes red, and looks angry, but Dad isn't being mean – all the grown-ups are best friends.

The sun is setting and has mist over it, and the air is turning pink. It's so *quiet*, now they've stopped hammering.

'It's not a bad place,' says Mum. 'We do OK.' She means, *it's beautiful here, I love it.*

I look at the pink air and the hills and fields and the sky. I look up. Up and out. I don't know if I've ever realised before that Frith belongs to *us*. Or even how big it is. All the farm. All the land.

'It's all ours,' I say. 'Forever and ever.'

'Dangerous,' says Mum, and her and Dad both laugh. 'We don't really own Frith, we're just looking after it.'

'No. It's ours,' I say, because that's just silly.

'The Laceys had it four generations,' says Mum. 'More than a hundred years. They just couldn't afford it, after BSE. And the old man died – remember the daughter crying, Adam?'

'I do,' says Dad.

'I don't care,' I say. 'Stupid Laceys. They've gone. Frith is *ours*.'

'If invaders come we'll kill them,' says Lan.

'Yeah.'

I imagine us both leading our armies on big brave horses. I want a suit of armour, and Lan wants a flaming sword, so we'd probably have to use magic. Lan says if we had magic we could zap the invaders and kill them dead.

'See?' says Dad. 'The Middle East. Chechnya. Right there.' I think he means fighting over land is bad, but those places are on the news. We've seen them, they're all brown and horrible.

'Who cares about the stupid Middle East?' I say. 'Frith is nicer.'

'Maybe the Middle East was nice before it got blown up,' says Lan.

We decide when we have our Battle for Frith we won't use any bombs or guns, only swords, because shooting is horrible and it's better to chop people up.

It's not nearly so quiet now; the birds are singing, like they do before bed.

'Time to go,' says Dad.

Me and Lan drive the Lada up the hill, Lan on gears and me steering, sitting on Mum's lap. We zoom round the corner of the house and nearly hit the Last Remnants. Mum has to *slam* her foot on the brake – but Dad isn't even angry, he laughs. We all do, and me and Lan climb out of the Lada on our own, because they're doing romantic kissing again.

7

Boiling Over

LAN

It's March so it's nearly the Easter holidays and – suddenly – there's bright green grass everywhere. And sun. Winter was like living in a puddle, and now it feels like it will never rain again. The birds are so noisy they wake us up when it's still dark. It's because animals have babies in the spring. And Perdy's got *kittens*! Turns out she wasn't fat, she had kittens inside her, and now she's had them. She's hidden them at the back of a tiny tunnel in the bottom of the hay-stack in the Barn. We haven't even seen what colour they are yet, or how many, but we can hear them mewing tiny squeaking mews. We are under strict instructions not to go near them *at all* because if humans touch them, Perdy might reject them. *We are getting desperate*, Amy says, and we are. We want to see them while they're still little. When the kittens are big enough, Perdy will feed them baby birds. I don't think she'll have to regurgitate them – she'll drag them home, like lions do. Also, if there's a black one we're going to call it Hexagon. Like a witch's cat.

Gabriella is getting smellier and smellier, and now the weather is warmer it's time to move her out of the Snug, and into the Goats, to live with them. Then we won't have to muck her out any more. We've taken her for walks every day, so she'll know what to do. When the day comes, everybody joins in, including Finbar and Em. We put on Gabriella's halter, which Em knitted, and open up the doors of the Big Room. We all lead her, and she tap-taps out, on her clog-hooves, into the fresh air of the Yard, blowing a big spray of calf-snot.

'Hazel's saying hello!' says Harriet, pulling out one of the fence poles to make a gap.

Gabriella is way taller than any of the goats, but she is still only a calf. Her knees are knobbly and her swirls and curls and wiggy bit are still fluffy.

'Go on then,' says Mum. 'Let her go.'

Me and Amy don't want her to leave home, and neither do any of the little kids. It's The End, and makes us feel sad. Together, we slip the halter off.

'Go on, Gabriella!' says Mum. 'Be free!' I wish she'd shut up.

Gabriella stays still for a minute. She tucks her head between me and Amy. The other kids gather round and we all stroke her neck and face. We can feel the bumps on her head that are going to be horns. Proper farms chop cows' horns off. We would never do that. She rubs her head on our tummies – then stops, with a jolt, like she's just noticed where she is. She turns to look at the goats – all together, staring at her.

'Like walking into the Fox and Badger,' says Rani.

Satan's in front, looking mental. He reminds me of Wilfy Edwards at school. Harriet didn't want to send Satan to Allens butcher's, so she squashed his balls with pliers and let him stay, but he's still naughty. He dances towards Gabriella and does a handstand, flicking his tail and glaring. Gabriella sort of backs off a bit, and walks towards Hazel, thinking she might be friends with her, but Hazel walks off, swinging her bony bum.

'Poor Gabriella, we really should get another cow for her,' says Mum.

Harriet says she'd like to make mozzarella. Gabriella has started to graze. We all stand watching for a bit, feeling flat.

'I would like a field of our own wheat,' says Rani, 'and one of corn. We could make our own flour.'

Me and Amy want a flour-grinding wheel with a donkey to pull it. The grown-ups want olive trees, hops for Frith Beer, trout in the stream, and more wildflowers, and everyone wants bees.

'Springtime talk,' says Jim.

'Let's plant a thousand trees this year,' says Harriet.

'That's not a bad idea,' says Martin. 'With a grant from the Forestry Commission.'

'I love it when you talk sensible,' says Rani. 'Say *spreadsheet* to me, Martin, say *APR*.'

'*Budget*,' says Martin, in a yucky voice, and kisses her. He looks so happy, and we can see his face go pink because it's not hairy.

I think Gabriella's forgotten us. She's just eating. Me and Amy stand staring at her.

'Can we go and see the kittens?' says Amy.

'No,' says Harriet. 'Under no circumstances.'

She's so mean. *When then?* we all say, boiling over. *When?*

'Not yet!' says Harriet. 'Give them a chance, they were only born yesterday!'

Even if it is springtime and everything's growing, there's nothing to eat. It's like a desert. There aren't hardly any vegetables, except in the freezers. *Frith has practically run out of food,* the grown-ups say, there's always boxes of dinner defrosting on the Rayburn, dripping water, full of things you can't tell what they are.

Me and Amy are walking round and round Finbar's garden rubbing our tummies because they hurt, moaning – *we're in a famine! Feed us!* We pretend we're Sherlock Holmes and look through our giant magnifying glasses for leftover vegetables. Amy rips some soggy cardboard to see what's in it, and suddenly Finbar's standing over us, like an angry giant. We leap away, like shocked goats.

'Stop that! I've got seeds germinating!'

Sometimes he just appears. I think it's because his garden is magic. There's jam jars and yoghurt pots with the writing washed off by rain which look like rubbish but are there on purpose, with seedlings and things. And there's cabbages growing underneath glass Finbar got from building sites. Sometimes it gets broken – not by us, by hailstones, or balls – and Finbar has to tape it up. The glass is to keep things warm, and for keeping rabbits off. *Those little bastards are not at all dim-witted*, Finbar says. He doesn't hate rabbits, but he *is* in a war with them. And he doesn't hate caterpillars, even if they eat everything. He watches them chewing on leaves, with his eyes glittering. *Look at that*, he says, *Who could begrudge that little fella, he's aspiring to be a butterfly*. Finbar says if we're very careful, we're allowed to stroke caterpillars. They feel like fat furry bumps, and their feet aren't yucky, like a centipede's are.

Right in the middle of the garden is scare-rabbit. It's like a scarecrow, except it's a giant toy rabbit stuck on a pole. Finbar found it by the road. *Could have sworn he was hitch-hiking.* It's got one eye hanging out on a wire, so it looks like it's staring at us, wherever we are. If me and Amy were rabbits we'd be terrified but the real ones aren't bothered at all. *Aw, they don't give a shit*, says Finbar. He's got a nice accent. He grew up in different places in Ireland and England, and once he was in hospital in St Lucia, because he had polio. But he's very healthy now.

'What's those?' asks Amy, looking at the tiny green threads growing in a row in Finbar's seedbed.

He points with his little finger, because his other fingers are rolling a cigarette.

'Carrots. Peas. Radishes. Onion sets.'

'Can we eat them? We're in the famine and dying.'

'They're not ready.'

There are lolly sticks with strips of foil, and cider traps, and criss-crossed string to stop the birds. Sometimes birds perch on them to eat. We love Finbar's garden, but we're *not* allowed inside his house, because it's his safe private house, and he doesn't like visitors, except Harriet. Amy's mum is his favourite person. They met in the Polio Hospital.

The very first thing I remember, in my whole life, is standing on the water butt in Finbar's garden, with my mum holding me, so I won't fall. She's singing – *I'm on the top of the world looking down on creation.* That's the first song she remembers, too, from when she was little. It must have been when Finbar first moved in, and Jim was fixing up his house because I remember the smell of the new wood in the hot sun. And something to do with Mum's silver necklace. Amy doesn't remember that. Her very first memory is Ivan knocking her over in a puddle. Or it might be eating a boiled egg and looking at the daisies on her kitchen tablecloth. She doesn't know which came first. She shoves me. She must have been talking to me.

'Lan!'

'What?'

'Finbar said we can go *inside.*'

'If you want tea,' says Finbar.

We don't care about tea but we do want to go in Finbar's house. Normally he says *do not set foot in my house*, and I don't think I ever have. We nudge each other and follow him. His front door faces Four Acre and the Goats, not the Yard. He steps over Jim's goat-gate, through the hanging ribbons, and we climb over after him.

Inside, the floor is wood, and the ceiling is wood, and it smells of oil paints and white spirit, like being in a nice wooden box.

'Where's your paintings?' says Amy. 'Can we see? Can we do painting?'

'Upstairs, and no,' says Finbar.

There's one table, one kitchen chair, and one armchair. The window over the sink looks down the hill, towards the New Cottage building site, where Jim and Adam are working, putting down the new wooden floor Jim's made, we can hear the knocking as they bang the boards into place.

'When Em moves into New Cottage you'll be able to see her,' says Amy.

'I realise,' says Finbar.

'And she'll be able to see you.'

'You're not wrong.'

'Where's the toilet?'

'You can't use the toilet.'

'But is there one?'

'Of course there's a toilet, I'm not an animal. Behind there.'

Me and Amy go look, while Finbar fills the kettle. There's a curtain across the gap under the stairs, with rows of tins stacked behind, and kindling below, and a bulb on a wire. Ahead of us is a shower curtain with ducks on it.

'That was in our house,' says Amy.

'Used to be,' says Finbar.

Behind the duck curtain is a toilet and a shower with a mouldy smell and bottles of cleaning stuff in a neat line.

'You can't use it!'

'We aren't!'

We come back out again. He's opened up the wood-burner, it smells of cold ashes.

'I won't light it until I've planted those potatoes.' Finbar makes lots of rules. And then sometimes really loves breaking them. 'Take a seat.'

Me and Amy share the kitchen chair. He makes the tea and cuts big slices off a Rani-loaf, and puts butter on, and gives them to us, then he stares out the window while we eat and drink our tea out of burning-hot enamel mugs. We have to sip from them on the table because they're too hot to pick up. I like lots of milk in mine and Amy likes three sugars.

Finbar is still looking out of the window. Probably thinking about Em being there soon, and hoping she won't wave at him.

'What's polio?' asks Amy.

'What's what?'

I've just realised the walls are all completely covered with books. It's like the walls are made of them. I look up to check the ceiling isn't covered in books too.

'Polio,' says Amy again. 'What is it?'

'It's a virus that attacks the body and makes people ill, or crippled, and sometimes they die.'

'Oh,' says Amy. 'How'd you get it?'

'I haven't the slightest idea. Dirty water, maybe. Why? Do you think you have it?'

'No.'

We lick our fingers and pick the breadcrumbs off the table because we don't want to leave a mess and make Finbar not ask us again.

'You were vaccinated,' he says, 'you've no need to worry. Polio is extinct in this country, like the dodos. In the past if you had it, they put metal braces on your legs.'

This is very interesting. We've never seen Finbar's legs. He always wears jeans, even when it's very hot. I look away from the books, and stare at his legs.

'Do you have metal braces?' I say.

'Me?'

'Did they put them on your legs in St Lucia?'

Finbar turns round.

'What now?'

'When you had polio,' I say. 'In St Lucia.'

'When I had *polio*?' Finbar stares at me.

'When Harriet found you,' I remind him. 'In the hospital.' I'm surprised he's forgotten.

Amy kicks me to shut up. It's not fair, she talks all the time and nobody thinks she's weird, when I say things, everyone stares at me.

'Finished your snacks?' says Finbar. He takes our plates and washes them. 'I should get back to it.'

'Thank you for letting us in your house, Finbar,' we say.

'It was my pleasure,' says Finbar, drying the plates. 'Let's not make a habit of it.'

As we step out over the barrier, through the fluttering ribbons we notice something is different. First I think it's just that Jim and Adam have stopped hammering, but the change in the air is more than that. It's wrong. We can hear grown-up feet running, which they don't usually do, and a lady-voice – Rani – shouting *oh my God!*

'What's up with them all now?' says Finbar.

Around the corner of his house we see the backs of Adam and Jim, running across the Yard. I notice Jim's dropped his mallet on the ground, he must have dropped it while he was running. Em and Harriet are rushing out of the back door of the Cowhouse, and Harriet sees us and Finbar.

'Fucking Bill!' she shouts. 'The kittens!'

Me and Amy start running too, faster than Finbar, I don't know if he's still behind us. We catch up to Harriet on the track and ask what's happened, but I don't know if Harriet's heard. The air is cold, because the sun's gone down, and it suddenly feels wintery, the sky is sicky-yellow behind the big black barn, above us. We can see the backs of Jim, Adam, Rani and Martin, and some of the kids, but everyone looks kind of frozen. Amy looks at me, scared, and I shrug – we neither of us know what's happened, but there's a lump in my chest.

'It's not his fault!' Rani is saying, angrily, to Mum.

Mum says *stupid cow*, really spitting furious, but not looking at anyone. I'm shocked. She can't mean Rani.

My legs feel watery. Bryn is crying. She sees me and runs and grabs my hand. I look around in panic and see Eden.

'Eden?' I say.

Her face is white. Her fists are clenched. 'Bill's killed the kittens,' she says.

I almost sort of laugh, but then feel really sick. I grip Bryn's hand harder and we go closer, brave as we can, to see what's happened. Amy's at my shoulder, but then she runs up to Adam.

And now we can see inside the barn. Martin is on his knees on the straw, just below the meathook, and Bill is standing in front of him with his jumper all lumpy at the front, and his face bright red, and his arms stuck out like a scarecrow. Lulu is sitting bawling on the ground. Lulu cries so loudly it's practically deafening, and now it's impossible to hear what's going on.

'Shut up, Lulu!' Mum snaps at her.

'Don't speak to my child like that,' says Rani, like a hawk about to peck Mum's eyes.

Next to me, Bryn's sort of snotty, wet-mouthed crying has words in it, trying to come out. I kneel next to her.

'What happened?'

'B-Bill wanted to see – we only – I wasn't – it wasn't me,' she blubbers.

I hug her a bit, because she's so upset, and I won't yell at her. She's crying too much to speak, and she's only four, she can't help it. I drag her with me, closer to the grown-ups, and to Eden. Amy comes back from Adam.

'He pulled them out,' she hisses in my ear. 'Look –' she points towards Perdy's tunnel. There's a broken bale, and a big gaping gap where the narrow entrance used to be.

'Where are the *kittens*?' I say. 'Where are they?'

It's too dark to see. Past Jim and Mum, Bill is still stand-ing there, there's nothing wrong with him, but Martin's lifting up his jumper like he's checking him for broken bones. A little round ball falls out of his jumper and onto the straw, tiny legs, wheeling.

'Another one!' says Mum, upset and shocked, like she's been crying too. She runs over. We go with her. I let go of Bryn. Everyone's crowding round now, we can all see. Harriet has a kitten in her hand – two – but they aren't moving. There are two more on the straw, a black one, tiny with its legs straight out, like twigs, not moving either. I hear Amy make a sound, or it might have been me.

'Don't let them see,' says Jim. 'Hey, kids, here.' But it's too late. We've seen. We *can* see.

'It was my fault,' says Martin. 'Don't blame him.'

'Don't be stupid!' spits Mum. 'It's not your fault at all!'

The grown-up angriness is much bigger than anything else, and getting in the way of understanding. I want to scream too, or cry and get their attention, they're being mad, instead of calm, and it's making everything too scary. I'm trying to ask if any of the kittens are OK, but nobody's paying attention.

'Here, now, here now,' says Jim. He's blocking us with his body, all of us kids, with his arms out, like he wants to herd us. His voice is calm.

'Let me see!' shouts Amy.

'No, darling, it's not for you to see,' he says. And all the grown-ups join in fighting. All except for Jim.

'Jim, for God's sake!' says Mum. 'Say something!' She wants Jim to shout at Rani and Martin.

'Shut up, Gail, now's not the time,' says Harriet.

'It was an accident!' says Rani, blazing hot.

'Don't speak to me, I can't look at you,' says Mum. 'Your fucking little boy's a menace, little bastard shit—'

'Stop that, be quiet,' says Harriet.

'Don't speak to her like that.' That was Martin, meaning Mum.

'Jim!' shouts Mum, furiously. 'Jim!'

Jim acts like he can't hear her. He's still trying to keep all five of us kids together and calm us down. He's soothing Bryn and grabbing Amy round the waist – but nicely. I can't even move. At least Lulu's stopped scream-crying. Rani's picked her up and is holding her like a baby, over her shoulder. Lulu looks dazed.

'How many kittens are there, Jim?' I ask.

He looks at me, steady in the eye. 'There were seven,' he says, 'now three.'

Then he hugs me, too. I'm not sure how I get into his hug, but I'm in it. I could look over his shoulder now, I'd have a clear view – Martin, and Harriet, and Bill's jumper and the little balls of furry kitten, scattered on the ground. The dead black one. But I don't look. I shut my eyes as if I am a baby, younger than Lulu, and don't want to open them at all.

'What happened?' whispers Amy.

'Bill went in after them,' says Jim. 'He put them in his jumper. When Martin pulled him out, they got crushed.'

I try to swallow but I can't. I think how small their bones must be. I wonder how much it hurt them. It must have been a lot.

Martin pulls down Bill's jumper and tidies him up.

'All right?' he says.

'It's not my fault,' says Bill.

'Whose, then?' says Harriet, closing in.

'He's just impulsive,' says Martin. 'These things happen.'

'Jesus Christ,' says Mum. 'Impulsive? He has a syndrome.'

'If I hadn't dragged him out –' Martin starts.

'If Harriet hadn't *made* you,' say Rani.

'Oh! That's not fair!' says Harriet.

'Wait, this one's breathing,' says Adam, and then there's suddenly silence.

I pull my face out of Jim's jacket front, and all us kids, and grown-ups, too, turn to look at Adam, plucking a tiny kitten, smaller than his hand, up from the ground, and pulling bits of straw off it. The paws dangle down.

'Can it move?' says Harriet.

'I think so,' says Adam.

'That's four, then. Let me see,' says Harriet, and goes over to him. 'Where are the other live ones?'

'Over here,' says Em. I hadn't noticed her. She's sitting on a corner bale with her arms in a circle over her legs.

I feel as if seeing her sitting quietly there, and the kitten being picked up by Adam, has made everyone ashamed. They all go quiet. And then they apologise to us. I hate it and just feel embarrassed.

'We shouldn't have lost our tempers,' says Rani. 'Everyone was upset.'

'We're sorry we scared you,' says Adam. 'We were scared ourselves.'

Me and Amy first, then the other kids following, start going over – on tiptoe, practically – to Em, who shields the kittens from the cold air, and smiles at us.

'Look,' she whispers. 'A ginger, a tabby-and-white – like Perdy – and two tabby-all-overs. See how sweet they are?'

For a single second I forget how scared and sad I feel. We all do. The kittens' eyes are so closed you can't even see where they are. Their tiny paws wave in the air, with claws like hairs. They squeak a bit.

'We shouldn't have behaved that way, fighting,' says Jim, behind us.

Then Mum speaks, and her voice is as nasty as before, not kinder, like the others, not even a bit.

'Give me a break, Jim, *you* didn't. Not one word. Not a word from you, ever, is there? Not even to take my side.'

I feel cold all down my back, like if I look at her I'll be turned to stone.

'Oh, Gail,' says Harriet, sadly.

'I'm taking my children home,' says Rani. 'When you're ready to apologise to me, you can come over to *my* house, and do it. Come on, Bill. Come, Lulu.'

Martin gets up, and picks up Bill, and all four Hodges leave the barn. Us kids stay in a huddle round the four live kittens, and Em. Em's shivering.

'We'll put them back,' she says. 'Then when Perdy's ready, she'll know where to find them.'

Me and Amy don't go back with the others. We're cold and shocked and we just need to be on our own for a bit, and wait for Perdy to come back.

'I hate Bill Hodge,' says Amy. 'I really, *really hate him.*'

'I hate him too.'

It's a hard, nasty feeling. We've said we hate Bill loads of times, but I've never felt like this. We sit on the gate to the Hay and plan how we'll kill him. Poison. Or smashing him to death with a spade, and watching him die in front of us while we tell him he deserves it because he killed poor innocent kittens. They couldn't stop him, they were only just born, they had nobody to protect them. Feeling sad takes over feeling angry and we stop talking or else we'll cry. But we'll *always* hate Bill Hodge.

It really is *winter*-cold now, like spring has been scared off. We sit there, on the top of the bar gate, and shuffle up, arm to arm. Usually I don't really think about me and Amy being friends. We're always together, and I don't even notice her that much. I'm glad she's here now.

'Remember that hen Mum had,' I say. 'The one that rejected her chicks?'

'She was evil,' says Amy.

She was. She threw them on their backs and pecked them till they bled.

'Do you think Perdy would do that?' I say. 'If she rejects the kittens?'

'I don't know.'

An owl hoots, up in the trees, but we can't see it.

'It's not creepy,' says Amy. She means being in the dark, and the owl.

She's right, the dark isn't scary, like it normally is. We've got the Hay behind us and the stars are coming out. All the bad feelings were in the barn.

We can hear the four alive kittens in the hay-bale tunnel, squeaking.

'Do you think Perdy can hear them?' says Amy.

We send messages with our minds – *Perrdyy . . . your kittens need you, come back . . .* We wait, and wait, and shiver, and wait. We hear Harriet call her train-whistle call from the house, and ignore her.

And then, at last, we see the ghost-grey shape of something trot towards the barn. And white paws. Perdy, coming back for her babies.

8

The House-Warming
Birthday Party

AMY

The baby goats are charging up and down the straw bales
in the sunshine and jumping on each other. They do it all
day. Me and Lan keep getting electrocuted because when
we're laughing we forget not to lean on the fence. Bill's
trying to make Josh pee on it, but Josh isn't stupid. Martin
says he'll *never forgive himself* for dragging Bill on his
belly with kittens up his jumper, Bill knows *really* that it
was totally his fault. We've stopped hating him. I mean we
hate him in the *usual* way, but not extra. The four alive
kittens are Gremlin, Squeaker, Olympic and Tips. Perdy
lies flat-out, purring, with kittens stuck on her tummy,
and we lie on the grass and put our ears against them so all
the purrs go deep into the middle of our heads. Perdy's is
rumbling and dozy, and the kittens' purrs are so small
they sound like tiny clicks. When they've finished eating
Perdy licks them so hard they roll over, then stalks off to

hunt, probably, and we lie back on the grass and put the kittens on our faces. We'll have to put them back in Finbar's shed soon – that's where she keeps them now – because today is the New Cottage House-Warming, and also sort of Mum's birthday party. She's thirty-seven, I think, or sixty-seven.

Boring Colin came over practically at *breakfast*, carrying Carlings, and two massive brown-and-orange dishes with something white and lumpy in. *It's not a local recipe, it was hers.* He means his dead mother. He always says, *Mum wasn't from here, she was from Snitter,* so the white goo must be from Snitter, but we don't know where Snitter is. He always tries to give us lamb for our freezers, but we've got a Frith rule *not* to eat animals who are killed when they're less than one year old. The grown-ups always say, *we'd love some hogget, Colin!* which is one-year-old lamb and tastes nicer, but Colin doesn't have any. He says there's *no market for it.* Josh thinks normal lambs being slaughtered practically the minute they're born means Frith *needs* happy sheep. He doesn't say *sheeps* any more, now he's six. Mum misses it, so now she says *sheeps*, and so does everyone else at Frith, except Josh.

The two goats for the New Cottage house-warming party came back from Allens butcher's yesterday, and we helped smash big stakes through their mouths and out of their bums the other end with the mallet. We rubbed tikka and beer into them. They're roasting over the pit in the Yard with Finbar basting them. Lan isn't as excited for them as me. He still talks about Virginia sometimes, because he was too young to see her be killed. I wasn't, I'm more grown up. Girls just are.

Ruby Wright comes out into the Yard and waves at us. She's in a pink dress. Her boobs look all squashed inside. I bumped into her boobs once with my face, and it was so embarrassing. Her party sandals make her feet look like meat tied up in string, but she looks nice. She's brought us three jars of her own honey in a basket with ribbons. All Lan's sisters want in the whole world is bees. We all do. We want to find a wild herd and make them swarm and come to live at Frith, where it's safe from pesticides. Ruby's honey has tiny hexagons of wax floating in it, and sometimes a bee's leg. While we're trying to open the jars, and Ruby's asking us not to, our godfathers Jack and Joffrey arrive. Jack is my godfather, and Joffrey is Lan's. Joffrey says he hates children but he doesn't, he always talks to us for ages and we love them both. We forget the honey and everyone crowds round as they walk out into the Yard, like two royal kings. Jack is carrying Truly, their Maltese terrier, because she's got a bad personality, and bites other dogs. They say they've brought a house-warming and birthday cake but we can't look yet.

'Of course I made it,' says Joffrey.

Joffrey's American. He has a cake shop, and he and Jack are Old Friends From Before, and live half the time in London, and the cake shop is *famous*. Jack has shining silver hair, and they don't want our Frith punch, only their special red wine, and Jack isn't happy about sharing.

Village friends are here as well, and the Robinsons, and the Barkleys. There's way more than twenty people. Then the Bony-Eyes-Flatbed-Trailer-Man comes in with a sad-looking lady behind him. We think she's his wife. I don't think everyone is going to fit into New Cottage for the Opening Ceremony.

Kyle and Lily Robinson's mum is Leslie Robinson who works in the Spar shop. The Robinsons are farmers. Proper farmers, not like us. Once, when we were little, we fed a newborn lamb with a bottle in the Robinsons' farmhouse kitchen, but they sold their house to the Barkleys, and now they live in the village, in a small new house. They still work on their farm, but they have to drive miles and miles to get to it. Everyone in our class remembers when the Barkleys bought the Robinson Farmhouse because Kyle and Lily kept crying in lessons, and Leslie had to come and get them. The Barkleys knocked down the farm buildings and changed the farmhouse name to *Tugbury Grange*, to sound posh, Gail says. Now the lambing shed is gone, and the Barkleys have got a *swimming pool.* And electric gates. We made Dad drive up to them in the Last Remnants so they started opening then just drove off, *three* times in a row. We laughed so much our faces hurt, and Dad had to pull over to wipe his eyes, and couldn't drive because his arms went weak. But then Mr Barkley rang up and said they'd watched us the whole time on their burglar camera, and could we *please not do it again?* And once, they caught Bryn licking their car outside the Spar. It was really embarrassing but Bryn was only little, and the Barkleys' car is so shiny it looks like nail varnish, I can see why she wanted to try it. There are three Barkley kids. Me and Lan don't really know them, they're older, and they don't go to our school. Mrs Barkley has wrinkly pink lips, and when she says Leslie she says *Lislie*, because she's from South Africa.

'Aw, Lislie,' says Mrs Barkley, to Leslie Robinson, 'great to see you guys!'

Leslie and Chris Robinson stand so close they look like

their arms have been glued. They've both got really big arms, Chris's are muscly and Leslie's are fat. She has to go sideways to get out from behind the counter in the Spar shop. She has a big round face and black hair, pulled back *tight*, and red splots that aren't a rash on her cheeks. She's scary but nice. She gives me and Lan packets of Wagon Wheels when they go out of date.

Chris Robinson always has the same checked shirts and he's the only person we've *ever* seen not in a book whose hair is proper *golden,* like wheat fields. Me and Lan like Kyle and Lily Robinson *best*, out of all the village kids.

Mr Barkley grabs Chris's shoulder and slaps it, and his big watch rattles.

'Great to see you, Chris! Leslie!'

'We're so enjoying your house,' says Mrs Barkley.

I think that's a horrible thing to say, but Chris Robinson smiles.

'It's not our house, it's yours,' he says.

Kyle and Lily are staring up and listening. Lily looks sad but Kyle looks angry. Kyle is a super-skinny kid, with black hair like his mum and as tanned-brown as his dad, but his fists are white and bony, because he's clenching them, and I'm worried he might explode.

'D'you want to come and see Josh's chicks?' I say. Lily nods, and grabs Kyle, and we find Josh and run upstairs.

Josh has got an incubator in his room. Gail gave it to him because the poultry farm was just *throwing it out.* When the chicks are about to hatch, you can hear them cheeping inside the eggs. It's amazing.

'*Here*,' whispers Josh, handing her one.

Lily Robinson's eyes look into the distance, listening.

'I can't hear anything,' says Kyle. I'm worried he'll break the tiny egg in his angry fists by mistake. Then suddenly he smiles, because he's heard the chick inside go *cheep-cheep*, through the shell. His face changes from dark to light, and his hand holding the egg looks soft and normal again.

After putting the eggs back we stand on the Rope Bridge, eating crisps and counting the people. '*Twenty-two* grown-ups and *sixteen* kids!' says Lily.

'Look at Finbar,' says Lan.

Finbar's whizzing around below us in a super-happy mood, talking to everyone and filling up drinks.

'All right, Finbar!'

'All right, Amy! Lan!' He raises his can of beer to us. He's talking to the Bony-Eyes-Flatbed-Trailers.

'Finbar made Bony-Trailer-Man *smile*,' I say. 'Look at his *teeth*.' They're long and dark yellow, and his mouth goes up at the corners like it's being pulled by strings.

Downstairs, Jim puts Colin's orange-and-brown dishes of goo on the table next to the giant pyramid of samosas, then Finbar organises everyone into a chain all the way out the door, and we all pass plates of melting-hot goat up to the house. We have to hurry because the rain starts, landing on our heads and the plate edges in big fat drops. Truly is yapping and barking all round the goat table, and Joffrey holds her above his head to keep her out the way, which makes her gag, so he has to put her down, then she chases all our dogs. Poacher's a big fat Lab, and Truly is tiny, but she makes his legs wobble with fear.

Everyone crowds inside the Big Room, and me and Lan get stuck next to Gail and my Godfather Jack, because it's where the tikka-baps are. Gail's going on about homeopathy, holding Niah, sucking a goat bone. Jack asks if she's read something about herbs that his *imprint published, many moons ago,* and Gail says she *loved it.* She's such a liar. She doesn't read anything. She gets all her homeopathy from a lady called Susan who lives in Wales and is trying to Preserve the Corgis. *If the ache radiates, you should try Caulophillum thalictroides,* she's saying, showing off her Latin names. Jack's really impressed. People only like homeopathy because they get to talk about their boring headaches, or how they're *feeling terribly anxious.*

Josh, Bryn and Lulu are crawling under the table, and the three shiny-blonde Barkley kids are opposite us. They've only got the crisps in front of them, and me and Lan and the Robinson kids have got the tikka *and* the samosas, so *sucks to them.*

'After all,' says Jack, 'modern medicine is derived from the herbalists of yore.'

I look at Lan. *Herbalists of yore.* We can use that. *The Pirates of Yore. The Goats of Yore.*

Wilfy Edwards from school screeches up to Joffrey and stares at him.

'Hello,' says Joffrey, staring back down at Wilfy, who's shorter than me.

'Where's the Cokes?' yells Wilfy.

'They don't have *any* sodas,' says Joffrey. 'Isn't it ghastly?'

Wilfy stares at Joffrey and says, 'Are you from *Africa*?' then just goes off again.

'Extraordinary,' says Joffrey, but his face doesn't look surprised, because he says people say stuff like that a lot round here, because he's black. Rani gets the same thing because she's brown. She says she's never surprised any more, but quite often depressed.

'Let's go, this is boring,' says Lan and we slither off.

Mum's making everyone try Colin's goo and it *is* nice, but I can't stop thinking about Colin's long grey hands making it, and his kitchen smelling like the insides of cupboards and the flypaper that looks like scabs. Ruby Wright is talking a-hundred-miles-an-hour to the Bony-Eyes-Flatbed-Trailers. In her own house, with Ragtime on the windowsill, Ruby's confident and normal, but now she's not, she's nervous.

'I'm just a know-nothing from Cardiff! Not a proper farmer like you! I've not so much got a smallholding as a *tiny*-holding!'

The Bony-Eyes-Trailers just stare at her and don't say *anything*. They should answer, it's only *polite*, and Ruby *isn't* a know-nothing.

'*Ruby's got her own bees!*' I shout up at the Bony-Eyes, but they don't hear.

'Oh my God, what *is* this?' calls Joffrey to the sky, like an opera singer, holding a plate of Boring Colin's goo. 'What *is* it?'

Colin stares at him, looking scared. 'Panhaggerty,' he says.

'Hands down the best comfort food I've ever had,' says Joffrey. '*Gorgeous.*'

'My mother's recipe. She was from Snitter.'

'Snitter?' says Joffrey. 'In Northumberland?'

Colin nods.

'Marvellous,' says Jack.

'YOU CAN'T BEAT PANHAGGERTY!' shouts Finbar, so suddenly that some people even scream, and he jumps into the air and lands on the piano stool on his bum, and starts to play the blues.

'YOU CAN'T BEAT PAN-PAN-PAN-PAN-PANHAGGERTY! IT'S FROM SNITTER!'

'What's up with *him*?' says Jenny Barkley, twisting her blonde plait around her finger. She's eleven. 'He's *weird*.'

'Finbar's not *weird*,' I say.

'Yeah,' says Jenny, and does a nose-laugh, 'you're *all* kind of weird though?'

I look at her family and my family. Jenny and her older brothers and her mum and dad have all got clothes that look like they *just* bought them, and there's no hay on them, or any odd socks, or dirt, *anywhere*. Plus, their hair is *neat*. We're not weird. They're weird. I chase the little kids over to Finbar, so I won't have to join in with Jenny. She's pretty, but her mum and dad took the Robinsons' farmhouse away, and she is *not* my friend. Plus, her older brothers have been on the stairs with their Game Boys since they walked in, and won't let any of us have a go even for *one minute*.

We make Finbar play more songs, and try to get Lily and Kyle to dance. They're really noisy when we're playing and it's just us, but they're shy about stuff like dancing, and talking to grown-ups. Finbar's crouching on the piano stool, playing with his heels and elbows. Mum *hates* us kicking the piano.

'Harriet! Come sing for us!' shouts Finbar.

Mum sits next to him, but she doesn't sing, she just joins in the piano-playing.

'That's it! That's it!' shouts Finbar.

'Let's take it down a little,' says Mum, in her gentle

turkey-killing voice, and starts to play 'You've Got a Friend'.

Rani and Martin are talking above my head. They're not fighting, because they never do, but Martin's boiling over a bit.

'Jesus, Rani,' says Martin. '"*Are you opening a curry house in the village?*" is *not OK!*'

'Shock horror, Martin,' says Rani. 'He's *called* Racist Rick.'

I trip over Jenny Barkley's brothers' feet and fall on top of Lulu, who screams. The Barkley boys go, *fuck sake,* without looking up.

'If they don't like it, they don't have to eat it,' says Rani, picking up Lulu and marching off with her.

Finbar is playing the piano louder and louder. There's a huge crack of thunder, right above the house, and the rain starts to pour outside.

'It's time for the cake!' shouts Dad, over all the people talking and the weather, and everybody hears him, because of his *trained voice.*

'Hold on!' shrieks Mrs Barkley.

'Wait!' shouts Joffrey.

They bump into each other in the front door, going out to their cars to get their cakes.

'Mum!' says Lily Robinson. She runs over to Leslie like they've got a secret. I think Leslie's got a cake for us too.

'Funny that,' says Dad, smiling at Mum, 'it looks like people know it was your birthday.' She looks embarrassed. She says she hates people looking at her or paying attention, but I think she likes it really.

There's car-door slamming outside, and laughing and a

– 114 –

load of *fussing* about Mrs Barkley's stiff yellow hair getting rained on, and Joffrey and her come back in. They're both holding enormous white cardboard cake boxes.

'Pivlova!' says Mrs Barkley, proudly, holding hers up.

'Lemon-and-Lime Pound Cake!' says Joffrey.

The meat and other stuff is pushed away to make space on the table. They both put down their giant boxes and lift up the lids at the same time. Everyone goes *OOOH!*

'Aw, just a little something!' says Mrs Barkley.

'Happy House-Warming, Em,' says Joffrey. Joffrey hardly even *knows* Em. I don't even know if she's *here*, we haven't noticed her.

'And Happy Birthday, Harriet,' says Joffrey, behind his hand to Mum.

Joffrey's cake is on a golden platter, like for a feast in a fairy tale, and it's round, with a hole in the middle, and covered in swirly white icing with loads and loads of flowers on top – sugar ones *and* real ones, purple and yellow – and in the icing around the cake Joffrey's put green sparkly sugar grass and tiny sheep and bunnies.

'It's all edible,' he says. '*All* of it.' Everybody *gasps*.

Mrs Barkley's cake is stripy layers of strawberries and meringue.

'Like the Austrian flag!' shouts Finbar, 'Heil!' and everyone looks at him for a second.

'Why is it called a Pivlova?' I ask Dad.

'It's a *Pav*lova,' says Dad, 'it's named after a famous ballerina.'

'A *ballerina*?'

Ballet is stupid, but the Pavlova would probably be the most amazing cake we've ever seen, except next to Joffrey's it's rubbish. It's like putting a donkey next to a unicorn. I love donkeys *a lot*, but I've never even seen a unicorn.

Everybody goes totally crazy over Joffrey's cake – even the grown-ups – and Mrs Barkley's bright pink lips get so thin you can't even see them and her eyes go squinty like a *murderer*.

'Well, that's gorgeous, isn't it?' she says.

I nudge Lily Robinson and say, '*Sucks to her.*'

Lily doesn't answer. She's looking at Leslie, by the door, shoving a Caterpillar Cake back into her big Spar shop bag that she always carries around, with 'There For You!' in big writing on the side.

Normally we only get Caterpillar Cake when there's birthdays at school.

'Mum!' I say. 'Look!' But Mum doesn't hear.

Everyone's crowding around, cutting the two shiny-white cakes. Flowers are falling off Joffrey's like a mini waterfall.

'Lily's mum brought a Caterpillar Cake,' I say to Gail. She hears me but doesn't say anything.

Mr Barkley's got a big slice of *both* cakes. His rings are tight on his fingers and he's shovelling them into his greedy mouth.

'Off so soon, Leslie?' he says, seeing her by the door with her Spar bag. 'You must bring the kids up to the pool one day. They're welcome any time, really, any time at all.'

'Right,' says Leslie. 'Thanks.'

'They aren't *going* home,' I tell him.

'Great!' says stupid Mr Barkley, munching like a hippo.

Leslie looks like she's stuck in mud, just standing there, looking grumpy. Chris comes up and puts his arm round her shoulder.

'All right, love?' he says.

'I was just saying,' says Mr Barkley, 'you should bring the kids up to our pool one day.' He's got cream on his face from the Pavlova. How can he not *notice* he's got cream on his face? He looks like a *baby*.

'Thanks,' smiles Chris Robinson, 'I might do that.' He's just being polite.

'Great,' says Mr Barkley again. 'Come and check out the old homestead, nice for the kids. They'll love the pool, we keep it nice and warm.'

Kyle pushes past me, his bony shoulder digging into my arm, and stares up at Mr Barkley like an angry wolf. His voice is practically as high as the smallest recorders at school.

'I don't want a go in your *swimming pool*,' he says.

Mr Barkley looks down on him, from his grown-up height.

'Nor me,' says Lily, really quietly. 'You couldn't drag me.'

'Oi,' says their dad, in the same friendly voice, 'less of that.'

Leslie looks even more stuck in mud. Or like a big tree.

'Be polite to your elders,' says Chris.

'Sod that,' says Kyle, and spits on the ground – only a bit, not so you can see. 'I bet your pool is *mingin'*.

'Well, we don't *want* you in our pool, so – *whatever*.' I turn around. It's Jenny Barkley. She's eating Pavlova with a fork, like she's not even a *kid*. Eleven isn't *that* old, she's not a grown-up.

Gail looks at Jenny like she's a really interesting bug. 'Why not?' she says.

Jenny sniffs and does her nose-laugh. 'They'd have to wash off the *farm manure* first,' she says.

I can't even believe it. Nobody can believe it. Me and Lan and Lily and Kyle and Gail and the Barkleys and Chris and Leslie all just stare at her.

'Now, now, young lady,' says Chris, calmly.

Jenny does another nose-laugh, right *at* him, like she's laughing at the way he talks. I can't breathe. She *is* laughing at the way he talks.

'I'm so *sorry*, Chris,' says Mrs Barkley, with her stiff yellow hair wobbling.

'Jenny, apologise,' says her dad.

But Kyle isn't waiting around for Jenny to say *sorry*. He kicks her in the shins. Jenny *screams*, and drops her plate and it *smashes* like a *bomb*. She hops about, grabbing her leg, and her face looks like a strawberry with tears squirting out.

'Oi!' says Leslie Robinson. 'Mind yourself!' She smacks the back of Kyle's head. I've seen her do that loads of times, I don't think it hurts.

Everyone in the whole party has come to see what the smashing sound was. There's creamy-cake splatted on the ground. The dogs push through to lick it up and everyone tries to pull them away because of splinters.

'Oh God, look, I'm so sorry,' says Gail, flapping her hands around. I don't know why she's sorry, she hasn't done *any*thing. She just wants attention I think.

'Come with me,' says Mr Barkley, trying to take Jenny away without grabbing her.

Jenny turns around, and holds her fingers up at Kyle and Lily in an 'L' over her shoulder.

'*Loser! Whatever!*' she sings. '*Your Mum Works in McDonald's! For the Minimum Wage!*' She does the letters with her fingers, along with the words. *Your Mum Works in McDonald's* . . .

'Jenny!' says her dad. 'Stop it!'

'Wow,' says Gail. '*Wow.*'

'I'm so sorry,' says Mrs Barkley, but she doesn't *sound* sorry, I think she's *pleased.*

'It's fine,' says Leslie like she's got something stuck in her throat. Her red mottles have gone darker.

I hate Mrs Barkley. I actually *hate* her.

'I'm not going to eat any of your stupid *ballet cake!*' I shout, then see my mum's face, and slap my hand over my mouth.

'Amy . . .' says Gail.

'Forgit it, Gail,' says Mrs Barkley. 'Thinks for a – lovely day. Lit's go, kids.'

Jenny's brothers have turned up out of nowhere, still on their Game Boys. When Kyle sees them he sticks his chest and his chin out at them.

'An' you two twats can fuck off, an' all,' he says.

Leslie smacks his head again, but he just laughs like a wolf, he's really cool.

The Barkley boys put away their Game Boys for one second, to look down at Kyle.

'What is he, like, *eight*?' says one of them, and they both laugh.

'I'm sorry, lads,' says Chris. 'Don't know what's got into him.'

Chris Robinson is about *nine feet tall* but the Barkley boys turn away from him like he isn't even a *person*, and say, 'Yeah, whatever.'

Mrs Barkley says 'Sorry' fifty more times, and they drive out in their shiny car.

'Good riddance,' says Gail.

'Gail, forget it, please,' says Leslie. 'We should get going, too.' She doesn't look upset. She looks like a mountain.

'Oh my,' says Joffrey.

Him and Jack, and Mum and Dad, and Racist and Mrs Rick, are all standing around the Robinsons trying to make them feel better. Gail and Dad are the loudest. It's kind of like they're *too* loud and *too* kind. I don't think Leslie likes it.

'I'm going to speak to that Amanda Barkley about Jenny's behaviour,' says Gail. 'Where's Jim?'

I can't see him.

'No need for speaking to anybody about anything,' says Chris.

Everyone's just standing about. There's a lot of very *tense feelings*.

Then Dad shouts –

'NEW COTTAGE HOUSE-WARMING CEREMONY!'

Lan looks at me, like *really?* – but Dad's just trying to cheer everyone up.

'To Em's New Cottage!' he yells, and throws open the glass doors.

Everybody charges down the Yard in the rain. I can't see Em anywhere.

'Mind my vegetable beds!' shouts Finbar. 'Leave my feckin' house alone!'

No one's even *going* in his house, but he sprints inside and pulls the curtains shut.

The rest of us march up New Cottage's path, and *then* I finally see Em – standing at the front door. Jim and Dad found the door on a skip – but they made it *beautiful*. Em's hands are all shaky. I notice she's got a bright red skirt on, with flowers. I didn't even know she was here, but she is and she's *dressed up*.

Dad pulls a long green ribbon from somewhere. Em, Racist Rick and Jim cut the ribbon. People keep saying how freezing it is, and how will we all fit inside. Everyone's feet are totally muddy from the Yard. I feel sorry for Em, she's been waxing Jim's new wood floor for days, and her new sofa came all the way from Ross. But then I see her face – she's smiling so much she's nearly *crying*. It's nice she dressed up for her party, even if nobody noticed, I'm glad she's happy.

The grown-ups were just lying around in the Farmhouse being lazy, so me and Lan went and got the Caterpillar Cake from where Leslie left it, and waited for Bill and Lulu to go home. We're sharing with Lan's sisters, and Josh, huddled round it on my kitchen floor like it's a campfire. Eden shoves me to get closer and I tell her to get off – we *cut* fair slices, she's so greedy. The dogs are all sniffing round, but they aren't allowed any.

There's a kind of *thump-thump-thump* in the front wall, coming from outside. I get up to have a look out the window at what's going on, and see Dad sitting in the Last Remnants with his eyes closed. The *thump-thump* is Oasis. 'Don't Look Back in Anger'. It's Dad's favourite out of all his CDs. He says it *takes him away*. Or takes him back. I can't remember. Anyway, he's got it loud enough to shake the wall. Me and Lan kneel on the window ledge, watching. Dad puts both his hands onto his face and covers it. I suddenly feel like I shouldn't be watching. Me and Lan half turn our heads to each other, like we're going to say something, but then I think we both feel embarrassed, so we don't. A big slice of light falls out onto the ground as someone opens the Farmhouse doors. Dad jumps, and uncovers his face, and sees us in the window. We both duck down out the way, and when we look back he's turned the light out in the car, and we can't see him any more. Dad stops the music and gets out the car. He's looking towards the light – where the front door is – but we can't tell who he's looking at, Mum or Gail, or one of the other grown-ups. He smiles, and looks sort of *public* again. Then the light disappears off the ground, as the door closes again, and it's all dark.

'Why doesn't he listen to it inside?' says Lan.

I shrug. I guess he just wanted some time by himself, to think or something.

9
Rescue

LAN

Every year, Jim writes the date when the first swallow of the summer comes, on his workshop wall with a pencil. He worries when the swallows come early, because of global warming. We like knowing the list will always be there. It's like history. It feels important.

26th March, 1998. Very long winter. 1st swallow today.
1999 – 18th April
2000 – 20th March
2001 – 1st April
2002 – 25th March
2003 – 4th March
2004 – 11th April
2005 – 26th March
2006 – 13th March

It's the Easter holidays and we're playing kick the can in the Yard when he calls us over, brushing the sawdust out of his hair.

'First swallow,' he says.

We all watch him sharpen his pencil with a Stanley knife. The pencil is tiny from all the sharpening – Jim always keeps them until they disappear. *Are swallows African or English?* asks Eden. *They're from the sky,* says Josh. We all crowd round as Jim writes the date.

2007 – 10th April

I look at what the first date is. 1998. All faded. Me and Amy weren't even born then. We're eight and a half now.

We weren't going to all go together to collect the rescue hens, but then at the last minute they made it sound so exciting, so now we are. *We're in a convoy,* I say, because we've got all three Frith cars. It's very cool. The Lada is leading, with Jim and my sisters and Josh in it, and the Hodges in the Mondeo are *bringing up the rear*. Me and Amy are in the Last Remnants with Mum and Adam. Adam is playing all Mum's favourite songs, without even asking us what ones *we* want to hear, and they're talking non-stop.

I bet Eden and Bryn are having more fun than us, I say to Amy. *Even the Hodges are,* she answers. And Niah's home with Em, like always. Amy's mum stayed behind too, with her goats or something. It felt like there was something secret going on with her and Finbar, but then the grown-ups said *we mustn't be late for Hen Rescue* and we forgot to ask.

Hen Rescue isn't like we imagined. There's no barbed wire or searchlights, it's just a normal farmhouse. We were excited to meet the Hen Coordinator, but she's not even in a uniform.

'I'm actually a magistrate,' she says. 'I just fell into hens.'

She *shushes* all us kids and takes us round the back to some stables where the rescue hens are, and tells us they'll be very weak and scared of noise, so we need to be slow and quiet near them. I think how we run screaming through Mum's chickens the whole time, and promise we won't from now on. We probably will though. Another lady comes out of a stable with some more Rescuers, carrying their crate of hens.

'Take care, Ann!' they whisper as they go past. 'Let us know when the next lot come in!'

'It's like being in the Resistance,' says Adam, and Mum laughs. It wasn't even a joke. Mum is so annoying when she's with Adam.

We crowd to look in our crate – but we can only see some bald, pale skin.

'Right then,' says Jim, 'let's get them home.'

'Is it *over* – already?' says Eden. It is kind of a let-down – we thought it would be more exciting. Why did they make us come?

Bryn, Eden and Josh want the hens to go in with them, but the Lada is too noisy. Adam doesn't want poultry in the Last Remnants but he gives in because Mum says, *oh, Adam! Please?* She loves hens so much. We put them on the seat, between me and Amy. We have to be quiet all the way back, not to scare them. Not even any music. *Silence in the car.* Me and Amy do sign language through the back window at Bill and Lulu, and play I spy. Adam and Mum don't speak at all, they just smile. The Rescues don't smell or anything, they just sit there.

*

When we get back to Frith, we fall out of the Last Remnants into the fresh air.

'Don't slam the door!' says Mum. 'Hens!'

Amy wants to tell her mum we're back.

'Don't disturb her,' say Adam.

'Why not?' We always disturb Harriet, it's fine.

'She's talking to Finbar,' says Adam. 'Give us a hand with the Rescues.'

All the little kids are jumping around, trying to hold the hen box.

'In a *minute*,' says Amy, 'I'm getting *Mum*!'

'Hey! Kids!' Adam shouts after us, but we race off down the Yard, fast as we can, and crash into Finbar's wall.

'Mum!' yells Amy. 'We've got the Rescue Hens!'

'WAIT!' says Harriet inside, in a really strict voice.

Amy rolls her eyes. '*OK!*'

We walk around and kick at the grass. After a bit, we go up to Finbar's front doorway. The hanging ribbons flutter. They're talking inside. Finbar is, anyway. His voice sounds funny. It sounds different. Me and Amy look at each other at exactly the same time, because there's *something going on*. We don't know what. The air feels jumpy.

Finbar is talking very fast. We can't hear all the words. *I'm telling you,* he says, *I've heard them talking to each other.* For some reason I think he's talking about Mum and Adam, I don't know why. We can't hear the next bit. Then something about how Harriet needs to *break down her mental barriers.*

'What's he on about?' whispers Amy. I shake my head. I don't know, but it sounds urgent.

'. . . they don't do it in *English*, obviously,' says Finbar.

'They don't use *any* human language. They're smart!' It's definitely not Mum and Adam, they always speak English.

'*Who?*' mouths Amy.

'These creatures are *highly* evolved . . .'

Creatures? We lean in, our hands on Finbar's wooden floor, just inside the doorway. Ribbons flutter and drift.

'They're coming here, *now*,' says Finbar. 'We've got to *do* something!'

'Can you see Mum?' whispers Amy.

I can't. I shake my head.

'. . . you have to see the *pattern*, Harriet,' says Finbar. He sounds more and more scared and I start feeling scared too. 'They're out there, and they're coming here. You're not *listening* —'

'I am,' says Harriet. I still can't see her, but it's a relief to hear her say something.

'You're not!'

'Wait a moment. Look at me, Finbar.' She's got her turkey-slaughtering voice on.

We hold our breath, waiting for him to answer, but then there's clumping footsteps, and all the other grown-ups turn up – Adam and the Hodges – and they grab our hands and pull us up on our feet, and yank us away from the doorway.

'Bloody hell, kids,' says Adam.

'Dad!' says Amy.

'This is *nothing* to do with you!' says Adam.

Amy goes bright red. He didn't need to yell at her. I don't know why he's lost his temper. They all get in front of us so we can't see, and Adam pushes the ribbons out of the way and barges in.

'You're not allowed!' I say, and start crying because I'm so angry.

He didn't even knock on the door frame. He was rude. I don't understand. Nobody's explaining anything. *It's OK, Lan*, says Amy.

'Adam,' says Harriet inside. 'This isn't helpful.'

All the other kids are running in from wherever, catching up and asking what's happening. Rani takes me and Amy's hands, firmly.

'Come along with me,' she says, like Mary Poppins, and walks off with us. Now we really can't hear anything they're saying inside, just arguing.

'Carthouse!' says Martin, all sensible, and rounds up the other kids.

'*Quiet!*' yells Finbar behind us, in his house, louder than all the other voices.

Rani stops, suddenly, and turns to look, and so do we – all of us.

'They're *listening*!' yells Finbar.

Who? I say. *Who? Who?* we all ask.

'Come along, children,' says Rani.

'There's nothing for you to worry about,' says Martin.

But who? They march us down to their house and make us sit *inside* it, with them, and the other kids. Martin goes back out, and we all watch from the window, but we can't see anything interesting.

'Would you like some ginger cake?' says Rani.

She gives us juice and the ginger cake is warm. With butter.

'Video or dancing about?' she says.

She's so calm. I want to tell her what Finbar said, about

the Creatures coming to get us – maybe from Space – but now we're in the Carthouse with ginger cake, the fear feels further way, like I dreamed it.

'Shall we tell her?' whispers Amy to me, her eyes wide and round.

I don't know. I'm too confused.

'Jim's there,' I say. 'He'll know if they have to call 999.'

Then we see Rani looking out of the window, and we look, too.

Finbar and Harriet are walking up towards the Farmhouse and the Dads are standing in a group, watching them go.

Amy jumps up and runs out the door before Rani can stop her. She tries to make me stay behind, but I run out too.

We run over the Yard then when we reach them put on the brakes and walk alongside, almost tiptoeing, trying not to make noise with our breathing. I don't even know if they've noticed we're there, except when Amy takes Harriet's hand, Harriet holds hers back. I look over my shoulder at Mum, watching with Adam and Martin.

'We'll tell Eileen all about it,' Harriet is saying. 'She's a good doctor, and she's known you a long time. We can definitely trust her.'

They're walking very slowly, hardly even going anywhere.

'I don't want to be ill again,' says Finbar, in a quiet voice.

Me and Amy look up, suddenly. Ill? Maybe it's his polio. I check his legs.

'I know,' says Harriet.

'Are you OK, Finbar?' says Amy. She's brave. Something makes me not want to talk to him.

Finbar and Harriet stop walking. I look round again. The Dads and Mum, and Rani, with all the other kids, are following us up the Yard, like a game of What's the time, Mr Wolf? I look at them, and everyone's worried expressions, then back at Finbar. He's bending down to stare into Amy's face like he's thinking very hard. His hair is even wilder and spikier than normal and his eyes are glittery like Mr Wolf. *Dinner time!* I think, but he's not being fierce, he's very quiet, it's just something about him that's not right.

'Sure, Amy, everything's fine,' he says.

Harriet nods at him with the same look she gives us kids when she's proud of us.

'See you later,' she says to us, and we know we mustn't follow any more.

We watch them walk up the hill. She's holding his hand. It's weird to see it. Like he's a kid or something, and he's way taller than her.

In the Carthouse, Martin cooks fish fingers for all of us. Me and Amy eat four each. And frozen peas – with butter, not water. And Rani gives us *ketchup*.

'I've got a secret store, don't tell anyone,' she says.

Lulu's marching about the room in some plastic high-heel princess shoes she got off a girl at school. They play a tune when she walks, so she eats her fish fingers walking up and down the whole time, and humming. Me and Amy don't even stop her, because the sound is so normal, it's nice to hear it. We just sit at Rani and Martin's table next to Bill and eat our fish fingers.

*

After supper, everyone except Harriet and Finbar checks on the Rescue Hens. Harriet and Finbar aren't back. Mum's been there watching ages, sitting on the grass with Niah.

Jim made a new run and henhouse, specially. He carried it up into the Orchard from his workshop, and put it exactly where Mum told him.

'Thank you, Jim,' said Mum politely.

'Now I'd better see to finishing off your dresser!' said Jim.

We all look at the new hens.

'One of them came straight out, and drank water – masses of it,' Mum says. 'But the other one is still just sitting.'

They look plucked, ready to go in the oven, and their combs are pale, like they've been dunked in bleach.

'They peck at each other,' says Mum. 'In battery farms. And moult. And they had mites, but not any more.'

One of them only has one eye. We never realised how pretty Mum's guinea fowl and bantams are, with all their different colours, and big fluffy tails like fancy hats.

We all sit, watching. It's getting cold, so Jim wraps Niah in his jacket. It's weird to think she's only a one-year-old and won't remember, and doesn't even know yet how special it is to get Jim's jacket. But she looks happy, so maybe she feels it. He puts her between his legs, and I lean on his shoulder.

'What shall we call them?' he says.

It takes ages, with voting, but in the end we call them Magic and Molly. Molly sticks her head out the opening for a second, looks around like she might come out, then just lies down, where she is. It's sort of funny the way she leans sideways, but it isn't.

Em is standing at the Orchard gate, but she won't come in because it makes her too sad.

'Too many lost souls today,' she says, and goes back to New Cottage.

'What's wrong with Finbar?' I say.

All the grown-ups wait to see if one of the others will answer. None of them want to.

'Tell us,' says Amy.

'He's not very well,' says Jim.

'Is he going to die?'

Jim looks surprised and upset.

'No. You mustn't worry.'

'Is it his polio?'

He looks even more surprised.

'His what?'

'From St Lucia,' says Amy, 'when Mum rescued him. His polio.'

'Oh. Well. No. Not exactly,' says Jim. 'You've got your wires crossed. Bipolar, not polio. It's a mental illness, not a physical one.'

We think about this for a second.

'Is it in his brain?' I say.

'In a way,' says Jim. 'In his *head*, maybe.'

I get the scared feeling again. I think of Finbar shouting, and how different he looked, when he was staring down at Amy. Jim looks at our faces, and how scared and upset we are.

'Finbar will be all right,' he says.

'Did he get it in St Lucia, though?' I want to get things straight.

'St *Luke's*,' says Jim. 'It's a charity. It helps homeless people—'

'Finbar was *homeless*?' me and Amy say together. We've seen homeless people in Ross. Mum said, *poor them*. I didn't like the way they stared at us. They weren't trying not to look sad, like most people do in front of strangers, and it made me scared, like they might jump at me.

'Finbar wasn't exactly homeless, he was just in a bit of trouble,' says Jim.

I'm staring at Molly and Magic. I feel guilty. It's not their fault they're ugly. Or the homeless people's fault. Or Finbar's. I feel ashamed of being scared. I love Finbar, he's our friend.

'Did my mum rescue him?' says Amy.

'At St Luke's? They made friends, anyway, and he came here to help out, which was very good of him. And here we are.'

'Look!' says Lulu. Magic has put her head out again. The little kids aren't even listening about Finbar. They're too young.

'OK?' says Jim to me and Amy.

'OK.'

He gets up from the grass, lifting up Niah and making an old-man noise – he's not getting old for ages, he's just pretending.

'I'll put this little one to bed, then,' he says.

Adam goes in, too, and the others. Mum lets us help with the hens. We put Magic and Molly inside for the night, and check their water, and close the run against foxes, which makes me feel a bit happier, but not much. The bantams and Vita are all going inside too, some of them queuing and bustling, and some running off into the hedge and the broad beans.

'I'll leave you two to get the stragglers,' calls Mum, and goes back inside.

Me and Amy herd them out of the hedge and over the grass, being cowboys. White blossom falling from the apple trees, like snow. We try to catch the petals but it's harder than it looks. We hear a car on the lane.

'Is that Mum?' says Amy.

But it's not.

'I hope Finbar comes back tonight, and doesn't have to be in hospital,' she says.

'Jim said the doctor will make him better with medicine.'

Down the hill, the lights are on in New Cottage, but Finbar's is dark.

I think of him alone in his house, every night. When I'm scared or worried I've got my sisters through the wall, and Mum and Jim in their room, and sometimes a kitten on my bed, or Christabel or Poacher. And there's always Amy, just across the Bridge. Finbar is on his own.

Amy is shoving me. '*Lan!*'

'*What?*'

'I said, *do you think Spirit the Mustang can fly?*' She says it cheerfully, like she's putting it on. Like Harriet, talking to Josh.

'I don't know,' I say. I don't care. Why does she want to talk about Spirit anyway?

'I think he probably can,' says Amy.

I don't encourage her at all, but she won't stop going

on about it. She talks about it all the way up to the house, making me answer her, so I can't even think about Finbar. Then we do hear an engine. The Lada, stopping out front.

Harriet yanks up the handbrake, then she and Finbar get out and slam the squeaky heavy doors. They come around the house, and pass us, and Harriet nods 'Hi' as they go off down the hill. They're talking as they walk, and the air around them doesn't seem nearly so jumpy any more.

'Let's go in,' I say. 'I'm hungry.' Then I look at Amy. 'What?'

'Dad didn't let Mum drive the Last Remnants.'

'He never does,' I say. 'Come on.'

And we go inside.

We hate the last day of the holidays, it's just grown-ups washing uniforms and going on about homework. I don't want to go back to school. Ever. Amy doesn't mind so much, but I hate it. We're making a list on the landing wall.

ANIMALS AT FRITH
1 cow (Gabriella)
17 chickens (all kinds)
2 Turkeys (Vita and Virginia)
2 x Rescue Chickens (Magic and Molly)
2 Cockrels (Robby and Goliath)
10 goats (Hazel, Satan, Conny, Erica)
3 dogs (Poacher, Cristabel, Ivan)
10 chicks (plus 2 eggs)
5 cats (Perdita, Tips, Gremlin, Olympic, Squeaker)

'OK, now let's put what we *want*,' says Amy.

WE WANT

ONE HORSE

SHEEPS

DONKEYS

DO YOU LOVE US???

'They'll see it every single day,' says Amy.

'Let's do a horizon.'

We draw the horizon, putting in all the landmarks – the barn roof, the highest hill, and the one shaped like a dolphin's nose. We stand back and look. The landing wall was just big and white before, now it's got all our writing, and the horizon. It might not be as good as we thought.

'It was better with just writing,' says Amy.

'Let's get colours, and paint the woods in. We can do all the grass, and a big sun – there.' I point.

'Yeah!' says Amy. 'Brilliant.'

I look outside. Down near his house Finbar is bent over the raised vegetable beds planting something. He stands up straight and looks down the valley and lights the rollie that's in his mouth already. We see the blue smoke drift. He's got proper oil paints. And acrylics. Ours are all dried out and the little kids never put them back. (We don't either.) We've got crayons, but they're broken and rubbish and I don't know where they are. We could ask Finbar to lend his. He won't say yes. But he won't mind us *asking*, he never does.

SUMMER
2008

10

Sunshine and Rain

AMY

June the 21st is the Summer Solstice and it's the longest day, and has *sixteen hours* of daylight. The sun hardly even bothers going down at all. It's not actually light when I wake up on me and Lan's tenth birthday because it's raining, but the birds are yelling their heads off so it must be morning. I run into Mum and Dad's bedroom and wedge myself against Mum. I don't shove her, I just press and wriggle. Dad doesn't move at all. As soon as her eyes are almost open she tells the Birthday Story. *On the day that you were born,* she begins.

Josh comes in wrapped in his duvet and lies at the end of the bed like a sausage roll. The rain is pouring down outside. It's cold today, but it was super-hot the day I was born.

'Boiling!' says Mum. 'I was so uncomfortable! Gail and Rani put drops of lavender oil into a cool bath. Adam was annoying the midwife . . .'

Dad gets up, says, 'Love you, darling, Happy Birthday,' and goes down to make tea. When he gets back into bed, the story is nearly finished.

I'm the only baby who was actually born at Frith. Even Lan wasn't, because after Gail saw me coming out she changed her mind and had him in hospital. Mum says, *fair enough, it's brutal,* but I think Gail's a coward. Josh was Third Baby. He got his shoulders stuck halfway out of Mum, so he was born in an ambulance.

Mum says, 'I looked at your tiny newborn face, and I knew you had courage. I could see it in you. It made me feel confident about your whole life.'

She says it every birthday, and on other days. Dad's hair is sticking up.

'Birthday-present time?' he says. 'You. Will. Freak. Out.'

I immediately think – *horse!* I know it's not, it never is, it's just a habit. You don't put a ribbon on a horse and surprise someone. You have to talk about money and look for exactly the right one. And anyway, I still can't ride, because Jenny Barkley keeps saying, *you must come up to the Grange and ride Rollo!* but she doesn't ever actually ask me, it's just like her dad always says *you must come up and use the pool!* Lily Robinson says the only good thing about Jenny having a pony is the Barkleys rent one of their fields off them. But Dad did *promise*. He wouldn't promise if he didn't mean it.

He's reaching under the bed for my present. I stop thinking about horses and concentrate on reality. I am a *practical person*, everyone says. And Lan isn't. Teachers say he's imaginative, and a dreamer. They pretend it's a compliment, but it's not. You'd think they'd stop saying he can't concentrate now he's reading so much, but they haven't. Anyway, they're wrong: he's not dreaming, he's thinking. He *can* concentrate, just not on *them*, that's what they don't like.

My present is enormous, wrapped in our balloon birthday paper, which has gone soft from all the times we've used it. There's a clear plastic panel, and on the cardboard bit there's yellow and blue writing that says – *80x Magnification!* – and a picture of a boy and his father looking through a telescope up at the stars. I was careful with the wrapping, but I *rip* the box to pieces. The telescope is blue. There's a tripod, and a shining glass lens, all sitting in white polystyrene, perfect and new.

'Don't say fuck,' says Dad. The school keep complaining.

'A TELESCOPE!'

'Fuck,' whispers Josh, with his thumb in.

'Like it?' says Dad.

'Yes! HAPPY BIRTHDAY, LAN!' I yell, at the top of my voice, and after a second Lan shouts back, from over in the Farmhouse –

'HAPPY BIRTHDAY, AMY!'

My actual birthday was two days ago, and Lan's isn't until the 24th, but this is the day we always celebrate, because it's the Summer Solstice.

Mum folds the paper back up, and gives it to Dad to put under the bed. Me and Josh start getting the pieces of the telescope off the cardboard. We have to untwist all the tiny wires. Mum and Dad are talking about their day: Mum's cleaning houses and teaching piano, and Dad's writing

'Exit', and helping Finbar pick broad beans. I'm not really listening, the telescope is fiddly. *They're not 'green gold'*, says Dad, behind me, *they're just vegetables that make a few measly quid.* He sounds grumpy. I ignore him. Me and Josh start screwing the legs together. They're in two parts, and need feet putting on. Mum and Dad aren't even watching, they're still just going on about money. Josh hands me the black rubber foot for the first leg. *Sixty pounds isn't exactly going to pay the gas bill,* says Dad.

'Dad,' I say. 'Can you help?'

The leg snaps closed and pinches my finger. It hurts so much my eyes sting. I yell, but he doesn't notice, because he's started on about having a B & B again. *A B & B would not be the end of the world, Harriet,* he says. I suck my finger and Josh gets the bag of screws to attach the telescope to the tripod.

'We don't *need* them yet, Josh,' I say.

Josh tears the bag open anyway, and the screws all scatter.

'JOSH!'

'Sorry . . .'

Mum is pulling on her socks. She jogs me with her elbow –

'Mum!'

'Amy, fuck sake,' she says, 'do that somewhere else.'

Why is she so cross? Everything feels wrong. Me and Josh pull all the telescope bits closer. I try to make the legs the same length. Mum jogs me again, getting off the bed. *Just don't say monetise,* she says to Dad, *you don't have the first clue.*

Josh can't find the special spanner thing.

I tell him to look under the box. He's looking under the bed. 'Dad?'

Dad's got his laptop out, and he's all tucked up with his tea, and starting to write. *Are you really doing 'Exit' now, Adam?* says Mum. *Really?* I don't want her to nag him. *In case you hadn't noticed, it's raining,* says Dad. I've got the second rubber foot on now but my finger's still really hurting. There's a flat piece with holes. It looks important. I don't know where it goes. *I'm not happy with you selling our private lives, Adam,* Mum says.

'Got them,' says Josh. He bangs his head coming out from under the bed. Mum rubs it and Josh shows me the screws he's found.

'Yes, well,' says Dad, 'I think you'll find *Gail* agrees with me.'

Me and Josh both look up because suddenly it feels like a ripple going through the air in the room. It's like on TV when there's a nuclear bomb, and you see the waves. I'm not sure what they were talking about. Not exactly. I was trying not to listen. Now I try to remember. Mum was halfway through tying up her hair, but she's let it go and it's sprung out, like the lizards with ruffs that stick up when they attack you. She's standing over the bed, staring down at Dad.

'If you and *Gail* think you can overrule the rest of us and turn this place into a fucking theme park, think again,' says Mum. It's not normal swearing, it's bad. I want to cry. It's my *birthday*.

'I'm going to work,' says Mum. 'You might try it.'

And she goes, without even saying Happy Birthday again, or goodbye, or sorry.

'What do you think I'm doing?!' Dad yells. His voice is scratchy.

Me and Josh are left sitting with all the bits of telescope. I'm not old enough to put it together on my own, it was a stupid idea. I look at all the separate pieces. Some of them are tiny, and I'm too clumsy.

'We can do it later,' I say to Josh.

'But I'm *helping*—'

'You're too young to help, *Josh*.' I sound nasty. I don't mean to. 'You're making it *worse*.'

My chest feels hot, and my tummy does too, like I've swallowed something giant and mean.

'Hey, hey,' says Dad. 'Come on now.'

He puts down his laptop, gets out of bed and kneels next to us, and finds the instructions, and the special lens-polishing cloth.

'Here we go, Ames,' he says. 'Let's sort this lot out. Eighty times Magnification! Wow.'

'Dad, your *breath*! Yuck!'

Dad puts his arm round my shoulder and kisses my head.

'Happy Birthday,' he says.

It's still raining and Mum's out cleaning houses when Dad makes goat's cheese and courgette frittatas for birthday brunch, and *still* raining when I go down to Jim's workshop, to watch him and Lan doing woodwork. Lan got a set of tools for his birthday. He wants to make something for Gail – *obviously*. He's just like Jim and Dad, always trying to please Gail.

'You should make a sled,' I say, 'your mum's already getting a whole dresser. One day.'

'Amy,' says Lan, in a voice like I'm *thick* and he's a carpentry *expert*, 'they aren't chisels, they're gouges.'

'So *gouge* a sled,' I say. Then Rani knocks on the door with a plate of chirotis for us. She always makes them for our birthdays. She dips them in sugar syrup and covers them in icing sugar. They're flaking everywhere. I sit in the corner, eating them, and watching Jim and Lan work. The whole workshop feels sparkly and full of birthdayishness.

Dad helps set up my telescope in the Big Room in the afternoon.

'I can't believe Galileo and, like, *Shakespeare* had telescopes,' I say. '*Eighty times* Magnification, Lan. How can a bit of glass even *do* that?'

'You should pay more attention to your physics lessons,' says Dad, who doesn't know either.

'I don't *do* physics, Dad, I'm in Year Five.'

He doesn't answer, he's going off with Gail to get something from the shop again.

If it wasn't raining we'd be able to see everything. We could examine the expressions on the faces of the Bony-Eyes' cows miles away. But there's only floating curtains of rain. We stare and stare at them, drifting across the valley. We can't even see his *cows* let alone their *faces*. I hope it stops raining for the Ancient Monument, Kyle and Lily are coming over.

We go to the Monument for our birthday every year. Finbar says superstition is *the first step on the road to delusion*, but if me and Lan don't go to the Ancient Monument on our birthday I know something terrible will happen.

*

It doesn't stop raining, it gets colder. When Leslie Robinson runs Kyle and Lily up the hill for the picnic, they're in layers, like it's winter. *No time to stop*, she says, and goes back down to the Spar. She's left a sign on the door saying 'Back in 5 minutes' and she doesn't like being too long in case she loses her job. She doesn't even *like* working in the Spar – but it's a bit like Mum and her cleaning, she doesn't mind doing it. *It's the price of this beautiful place*, she says. The Robinsons have a proper farm, but it's sort of the same thing.

We all trudge up the hill in a long line, like packhorses going up the Himalayas: us Frith people, Kyle and Lily, Jack and Joffrey, and Boring Colin. Joffrey's brought cupcakes for us, all the way from his famous London bakery, and Jack has a bottle of red wine for the grown-ups *and* a bottle of champagne *and* actual real glasses, which clink together as we walk. We've got elderflower champagne Rani made in the summer. They don't *think* it's alcoholic, but it could be.

Bryn and Eden are singing 'Ten Green Bottles, Hanging in the Wall', and making everyone join in. Bryn still says *bockles* for bottles and it's so cute it makes the song less annoying.

'It's pretty amazing your birthday's on the same day as Lan's,' says Kyle.

'It's *not*,' says Lily, 'they just *say* it is.'

'You can go to prison for that,' says Kyle, and I tell him to piss off.

At the very back of the line are Dad and Martin, pulling the huge wheelie bin from the Dutch barn. The bin is full of rats. Live ones. I mean, it's *full*. We can hear them scratching and squeaking. It's tied shut with a bungee, so they can't all scramble out. Nobody's happy with Martin and Dad about it, but it is sort of funny. They met a man in the Fox and Badger, and he told them the way to get rid of rats is to grease the sides of a bin, put in snacks for the rats, like bacon rind and grain, and then, when they go in, they can't get out again. *Et voilà!* said Dad. Problem is, once they're in there, you're meant to smash them to death with a bat, or put bricks on top, or leave them to starve. Dad and Martin had had lots of beer, and the man was what Dad calls *a real countryman*, so I guess they got into the whole Fox and Badger *thing*, and thought they'd be cool with it. Turns out, everyone who sees the rats just screams and runs away. We can't even get *close*. They are *disgusting*. They're all heaped up in the bin, nearly *halfway* up, and they're *writhing*. Kyle and Lily gave me and Lan a DVD of *Ratatouille* for our birthday and Rani can't even look at the picture on the front now, and they're only *cartoon* rats. Nobody wants to smash them to death, and leaving them to starve is cruel. So now we've brought them with us on the picnic, and we're going to release them, miles off Frith land. And Colin's land. On the other side of the B-road. I am *not* going to do it. They make me want to puke and it's my *birthday*.

We all march along to 'Ten Green Bockles' and the sound of everyone's squelching footsteps, and the rain, and the rats inside the bin, squeaking and scrabbling.

'I bet they're eating each other,' says Bill, 'or having sex.'

Finbar is in one of his good moods, carrying the little kids on his shoulder and reciting poems. We're nearly at the Monument and we still can't even see it. Black-grey clouds push at us over the hill, big and looming.

'There it is!' says Josh, pointing through the rain. 'Yay!'

*

Sometimes we play that the Ancient Monument is a time machine, or an *essential beacon* in a War, but in real life it's just a grey pointy thing on some grey steps. We get to it, all bent over with our hoods up and water pouring off everything. I had imagined our birthday – us lying on the warm grass eating crisps, and thinking of the sun skimming just beneath the horizon, and watching the stars come out, but instead it's pouring rain, and we've got a *giant binful of rats*. Dad and Martin have left them down the field, so we won't hear them scrabbling while we eat. It's too wet to sit down. Some of Colin's sheep come and stand around us and stare.

Jack puts a tablecloth on the steps on the Monument with a *flourish*. Looking at him, you'd think the sun is blazing hot. He opens the bottle of champagne.

'Marvellous,' he says, and his hat blows off. 'I think it's clearing up, don't you?'

It isn't.

The Mums have brought birthday candles for the cupcakes, but there's no point even trying to light them. Joffrey gives little bags of sweets to all of us, tied with blue and pink ribbons. *Party favours*, he calls them. Dad stands on the top step of the Ancient Monument and clears his throat a lot, to get our attention.

'We are gathered here today to commemorate the births of Amy Connell and Lachlan Honey ten years ago, and their first Summer Solstice Birthday the following year, on this *very spot*.'

My dad has turned our Monument into a stage. I love him. I look around to check everyone else is loving him too, and they are. He raises his glass to everyone, one by one.

'Harriet. Gail and Jim. Martin and Rani. And our *good* friend, Colin. It was the first time you joined us—'

'It was on my land, wasn't it?' says Colin. 'Only fair.'

The rain is cold and wet, pouring onto all our heads, and down my neck, and running in trickles down Dad's face.

'As you remember, the reason we don't celebrate on one of Frith's seventy-eight beautiful acres is that *that* year, 1999, *frankly*, we were desperate to get away. We thought we had made a terrible, terrible mistake. The six of us were sharing the Farmhouse. We'd spent *months* pulling down asbestos, ripping up lino, getting rid of lead pipes. Everything that could go wrong, had gone so, so wrong.'

'Jack and me thought you'd be back in town within the year,' says Joffrey.

The rain is a bit lighter now. But we're all still shivering.

'We were barely speaking to each other,' says Martin. 'Any of us.'

'And I didn't know if I could get pregnant,' says Rani. 'I was *miserable*.'

If she'd known she was going to have Bill, I whisper to Lan, *she would've been way more miserable.*

'We were flat broke,' says Dad. 'We couldn't afford to celebrate your birthdays in a pub, let alone a *restaurant*.'

'What's a restaurant?' says Rani, and everyone laughs.

'So we toiled up that hill—' says Martin, pointing down towards the rat bin.

'On Midsummer's Day. Carrying you babies,' says Dad, 'because it turned out, to our great surprise, pushchairs are useless in the countryside.'

'I remember very well,' says Bryn. We explain it was five years before she was even *born*. 'But I do,' she says.

'So do I,' says Lulu.

Dad carries on the story.

'The day was hot. But it was cloudy. It was sticky. There were so many *flies*. We *sat*,' says Dad, dramatically. 'And we *looked*.' He points towards Frith. 'And ... *as we watched* – remember, Harriet?'

I look at Mum.

'Yes, Adam,' says Mum, in her soft voice. 'I remember.' She smiles at him, one of her best, most golden smiles.

'Suddenly, the sun broke through the clouds!' says Dad. 'And shone down on our farm, like a *spotlight*!'

'It flashed on the new zinc roof!' says Martin.

'Like a sign from heaven!' says Rani.

'It *was*,' says Jim. 'It truly felt like it.'

They all start talking about what animals we had back then (hardly any), and which dog we got first (Christabel), and Gail's first chickens getting sick (sour crop and fly strike).

'Hey ...' says Dad. 'Hey! It's stopped raining!'

It's true. Dad's right. The rain has stopped. The air is warmer.

Everyone says *Cheers!* and *Happy Birthday*, and raises glasses, or pretend glasses. Me and Lan are ten. Double figures.

'Happy Birthday, Lan and Amy,' say Kyle and Lily.

'You know you're all totally mental up 'ere,' says Lily. 'You know that? You give us a right laugh.'

'They can't help it,' says Colin.

I like being teased by them. We probably are mental, we aren't like anyone else at school. I don't mind – I like it.

And Kyle and Lily like *us*, and they're our friends, and that makes me *happy*. I'm not sure Leslie likes us, I've only ever seen her being grumpy. I reach for another cupcake.

'Martin!' says Dad. 'You'll be with me on this.'

'Oh yes, what?'

'That little tumbledown stone barn . . .'

'By the Dutch barn? Near the Hay?'

'Yes.'

'What about it?'

'It would solve all our problems, wouldn't it, to make it a holiday let?' says Dad. 'Get this B & B idea finally off the ground.'

The little kids don't notice the change in everyone, but me and Lan do. We want them not to talk about it now.

'There's going to be a beautiful sunset,' says Em, and I'm really glad she's there.

'Yes! There will be!' I say, doing a cheerful voice, so Lan looks at me funny.

'Come on, Adam,' says Mum. 'Leave it alone.'

'Hey, hey,' says Joffrey. 'Come on, guys.'

'Adam is right,' says Gail, 'a *small-scale* holiday let. Sooner or later, we need to make a decision—'

'But not now!' says Mum, sounding upset, not even angry. 'Not tonight. Frith is a farm. A *real* farm.'

'When *is* the right time, Harriet?' says Dad. 'When we've had to sell Frith, because we can't pay the mortgage?'

I look at Kyle and Lily. They had to sell their house. Finbar starts to tap his foot, and his head twitches like it does sometimes, like he's trying to get a fly out of his ear.

'Can we move on?' he says.

'*Not* the time, my darlings, and not the place,' says Jack, in a very commanding sort of voice, like he's everybody's father.

He starts to put away his special wine and glasses. His lovely silver hair is wet, and I can see his pink scalp through it. I wonder how old he is, and feel frightened about things changing, and weakness. I don't feel safe.

Our parents go quiet. We do, too.

'I tell you what,' says Colin, wiping his mouth with some paper towel, then pushing it up his sleeve, 'let's deal with these rats.'

Everyone looks down the hill at the rat-bin. It's wobbling.

Then the sun really does come out. Summer evening sun, like thick gold lighting up the rat-bin.

'I vote we chuck 'em out a mile or two that way,' says Colin. 'I'll give you a hand.'

'Sure,' says Dad.

'Yep,' says Martin.

'You know they'll come back?' says Colin. 'Like pigeons, they'll be home to roost.'

'Never mind,' says Martin, 'let's get started.'

11

Scything

LAN

The weather is dry and hot. We have to help Finbar with
the vegetables – all us kids and everyone – to get them in
before they all go mushy. In the early morning when me
and Amy come out from the kitchen, everything is wet
with dew. We can see all the tracks from what the animals
were doing during the night, when nobody was watching –
the badgers, and the foxes, creeping around the henhouses.
The chickens all wait in line to come out every morning,
like kids in the lunch queue, and if Mum hasn't already, me
and Amy let them out. Or me and Eden, if Amy's asleep.
She's started sleeping later than me some days. We slide the
doors up and they come down their ramp, all busy and
fluffing themselves up, pecking about for grubs and chick
feed in the Orchard grass. Magic and Molly look completely different now. They were all baldy when they came,
and we were scared they'd die. Now they're enormous,
compared to Mum's little bantams, and their feathers are

red-brown and glossy. Harriet's goats are all together by
the electric in the morning sunshine, with Gabriella in the
middle, with her pretty white face.

Colin gave Josh a pair of lambs at Easter. He named
them Rose and Lily. He loves them so much, he's easy to
tease (especially since he named Lily for Lily Robinson,
because he *loves* her). The lambs have collars Em crocheted
for them, and they follow him everywhere. Even up to his
room. Now they're six months, they're getting big. Luckily their poo is more like a goat's than Gabriella's. The
grown-ups are always saying –

> *Joshua had two little lambs,*
> *Their fleeces white as snow,*
> *And everywhere that Joshua went,*
> *The lambs were sure to go*

– and Josh did take Rose and Lily to school, into assem-
bly and everything. The teachers said once was enough.

Apart from Rose and Lily, who are pets, Frith is more
and more like a proper farm. There's the hens to do, and
the goats, and pigs. It's our third year with weaners. We've
got four. They came in the Easter holidays from the pig-
farmer man. They were tiny, and black, with smiling
mouths. You can hardly see their eyes behind their
flopping-down ears. The smallholder book calls pigs
ploughs with legs. Harriet says our weaners are the happi-
est pigs in the world. The book says the pig used to be
called *the gentleman who pays the rent* in the olden days,
because you can sell the meat. Harriet and Rani want a

proper herd, so we can sell pork and people will stop buying factory-farmed, but my mum doesn't want so much farm work to do, and nor does Adam.

Having weaners is the same as Vita and Virginia, you get them when they're small, and eat them later in the year. It feels like cheating. Especially because they're so sweet when they come, and playful. All the animals at the farm have got characters, from the dogs to the bantams, but the pigs are smart, too. You can see it in their eyes. The grown-ups spent ages looking for the best and nicest abattoir. We said, *why do you care, if you're going to kill them?* And there was a fight.

They said, *we aren't killing them because we don't like them. Large Blacks are a rare breed – we're preserving them.* We said, *growing them to kill them is like murdering.* They said, *no, it's like farming.* We said, *then we don't want to be farmers.* They said, *we haven't noticed you complaining about the meat at school. Have you seen the places they raise pigs?* We said, *why can't we just have them as pets?* They said, *we can't afford pets. Do you want a world with no farm animals, or a world with happy animals and healthy soil?*

We said, STOP GOING ON ABOUT SOIL!

On school days, Jim does breakfast as quick as he can and we're out the door, but now it's the holidays we do the animals first, and have breakfast after, and sometimes outside. Jim and me made a table out of some bits of doors we brought home on the flatbed trailer, and we put it on trestle legs. Jim's teaching me. He says I'm talented. And we used the Foleys' dump truck to dump all the stones from the Stone Picking pile onto the Yard near the house, and a man came with a massive giant roller and squashed them down, so now it's a proper terrace. Sort of.

Something weird happened to me today. We were eating lunch at the big table outside: Honeys and Connells, and Hodges, Em and Finbar – all of us, not just some. And everyone was talking about the jobs they were doing around the place, and we had courgettes, and the courgette flowers fried in batter, with lemon squeezed on, and lots of salt. It was hot and sunny, and everyone's hands were reaching out for more, and getting bread, and cheese, and we were all drinking elderflower cordial. And I suddenly felt like I was looking down at us, from up on the roof. We looked so happy. I looked at Amy to see if she was feeling the same thing, but she was just chewing and saying something or other. It didn't matter. But it was weird. Being far above, or outside. Then the feeling went away. Like my brain clicked back to normal. It was like when your ears pop, and you haven't realised there's water in them, and everything goes clear again. I can't explain. I don't think I'll forget it though.

So I started making lists of things that make me happy about summer. Mostly in my head, but sometimes written down. It's just normal small things. Like the wild strawberries we found next to Finbar's proper fruit cages which nobody even knew were there. They're not planted on purpose, says Finbar, they're *rogue*. Whenever we think we've eaten all of them, there's always one more left.

Also – pinching the ends off honeysuckle flowers and pulling the stalks out backwards and sipping honey off the end. And the smell of those small white flowers that grow up the wall at the back of my house.

The smell of loads of things. Courgettes, when they're still growing. They're stripy and they smell warm.

And the way the chickens shake out their feathers when it's raining. Magic and Molly especially. The first time they did it they just looked so pleased about it.

And rain on lettuces, because it looks like glass.

Watching caterpillars chew.

There's a lot of things. Just tiny things like that.

It's almost time to cut the hay. The grown-ups have been waiting for just the right time. If the hay gets spoiled we'll have to buy in and *we may as well just throw our money down the toilet,* Martin says.

'I think the grass in the Hay is almost ready to cut,' says Rani.

We're down in the cellar with the Mums and Martin, while they move things around the two working freezers and Martin tries to fix the third one. It's been broken ages and it smells. The Hay is the best of our fields. We've been waiting for the baby birds to fly, so we can cut it without killing them. The Carthouse is closest, so Rani checks it every day and gives us updates.

'Are you sure it's ready?' says Harriet.

The cellars are cold and damp, which is nice when it's so hot outside. Me and Amy are on our bellies, reaching down into the biggest freezer to get broad beans out the bottom, and giving them to Niah, on the ground by Mum, playing with coal. Broad beans are chewy when they're frozen.

'The grass will go to seed if we leave it too long,' says Rani. 'We don't want meadow hay.' Meadow hay is rubbish, nobody wants it.

'Look, I don't know what the hell I'm doing,' says Martin's voice, from behind the broken freezer. 'I'm covered in spiders, and I'll probably gas us all.'

We'd forgotten he was there.

We need a new freezer, but there's no money.

Rani says, 'Forget it, Martin, I'll look up how to do it on the internet.'

'You can't learn how to be a refrigeration engineer online,' says Martin.

'I bet I could.'

Martin wriggles out, covered in muck off the cellar floor.

'Yes, being you, you probably could,' he says.

When Jim pulled over on the lane today so Colin's Land Rover could get past, we asked him about cutting the hay, and he said, *they say it'll rain Wednesday, but I doubt it.* Chris Robinson reckons it will be *dry enough* for a fortnight, but our grown-ups are getting nervous. Gabriella eats a whole bale every day on her own in winter, never mind the goats.

'All right,' says Jim, at dinner. 'Let's do it. Let's cut it Sunday.'

The grass in Long Field and Four Acre gets done with a tractor and cutter – Chris Robinson comes up – and Bony-Eyes gets silage off some of our other fields, and he actually pays us, but the grown-ups cut the Hay by hand, with scythes, because it's special. It's full of different grasses and clover. *The other fields all wish they could be the Hay,* says Amy. *Give them time,* says Jim, *they had a difficult twentieth century.*

The parents are all in love with scything. Mum's got a friend in Wales called Barri whose whole life is scything, and he taught them how to do it on a course.

All the weather forecasts were right. Sunday is just blue sky and sun. We all bring provisions and a paddling pool for Niah and set up camp in the corner of the Hay, and Harriet makes her pasta salad, which is mostly raw broad beans and courgettes.

Jim puts the whetstone on a tree stump, and they hammer and sharpen their blades before starting. It's called peening. They keep saying, *nicely peened!* and laughing. They've been practising on patches of grass and nettles for days, saying – *Barri says* this, and *remember, Barri always says* that. It looks so cool, we want to look closer, but they make us stand back.

We start early. There's still dew on the grass. Me, Amy and the other kids sit with Em and Finbar on the quilts in the corner and watch. It's shady and Niah is on Em's lap, in a white cotton sun hat. Usually, the Mums wear jeans, or sometimes shorts, but they've dressed up for scything the Hay. Mum's wearing a skirt tucked up in her pants, and Harriet's wearing a white dress with flowers. Adam's taking pictures for 'Exit', and Harriet keeps saying – *can you stop?*

The Hay is only small, and not a proper square, but the hedges are the best hedges at Frith. Before they start, we all run round and round saying –

Whoosh! Whoosh! – so any birds, or mice, or voles, or whoever else is left in it, like grass snakes, have a chance to escape. *There are more birds every year,* says Harriet. The three dogs lie in the shade, and Perdy is crouching in the hedge, thinking we can't see her, waiting to catch any stray little animals that run out.

Harriet and Jim go first. Everybody watches. They stand in opposite corners of the field, far apart. The Hay's long, dark grass sits there waiting.

'They're far away from each other because otherwise they'd be walking about on bleeding chopped-off ankles,' says Eden. 'And there'd be bloody feet all lying around, and you'd trip over them on your bloody stumps.'

'Ready?' Jim smiles at Harriet, and they start.

Their first few swings are bad, but they get better. The air is full of butterflies and crickets hopping. The dew dries, and the smell of cut grass mixes with the swishing, slicing sound of the scythes. Jim gives his to Mum. Mum and Harriet are barefoot, they say it's easier. Their feet are white on the dark green grass.

Every time they stop to talk about how it's going, all us kids beg to try. In the end, they let us, but only me and Amy.

'All right then, come on,' says Jim.

We jump up and run over the soft cut ends to them. Jim puts his arms on either side of me, and puts my hands on the handle of the scythe. I can hear Amy say to Adam, *will I chop off my foot?* I suddenly remember cutting the toe off Amy's boot when we were little kids, and how scared we were.

'Will we?' I ask Jim.

'No. That's why the handle is so long. Here, put your hands here, like this. Now, with me.'

His arms shine with sweat, and they're covered with seeds and grass. I won't ever have arms as big and strong as his. Mine look like worms or twigs or something. *Concentrate*, says Jim. *Left, right. Slowly. One, two. Good.* I grip the wooden handle of the scythe. I can't even see my hands with Jim's on top of them. My hands are so far apart my arms hurt. *Look at the grass, look where we're walking*, murmurs Jim. There is a semicircle where the scythe has cut. *Again. Keep low, low, that's right.* The blade is the shape of a sliver of a moon. As it touches the grass, the grass just – drops. Far in the distance I hear the other kids clamouring, and grown-ups laughing and talking, but I'm concentrating, and Jim is behind me, and all my effort and his effort are concentrated on making the scythe sweep one way, and back the other. One way, and back the other. *That's it. That's right.* My chest is burning. *Breathe*, says Jim, *breathe.*

When me and Amy give up, finally, it feels like our muscles are on fire. We flop down onto the quilt, and drink water and elderflower, and wipe our faces.

Amy lies there on her back, laughing. *Let's go down the stream later,* she says, and I say, *sure.*

'I got some great pictures of you, kids,' says Adam. 'This is going to be a fantastic post.'

Rani is scything now, she's not very good. She's laughing. *Oh, wait! I'm getting it! It's like dancing, I can do that* – and everyone encourages her. Martin has a go, says, *not for me*, then Adam tries. He poses with the scythe and Harriet takes a picture. *It's for the blog!* he says, when everyone laughs at him.

Finbar and Harriet finish up, sweeping their scythes

closer to the middle of the field, and each other, and finally, he stops, then she stops, and it's done. He salutes her. Then they hug.

Some of the stalks left behind look a bit chewed, but others are cut clean. The only long patch not cut is where we're all sitting. We get up off the rugs, and pick them up off the long, squashed grass.

'But you didn't do this bit,' says Bill.

'That's all right,' says Jim, 'we don't need to cut it all.'

We carry everything away, leaving the cut grass lying in the sun, already beginning to turn into hay.

I'm adding scything to my list. My list of things I love.

12

Baling

AMY

We're in the Spar with Mum. It's boring, we're only here for the Twisters, but Mum's run into Ruby Wright, and they won't stop talking. Kyle and Lily are hanging round the back, looking bored too. *All right?* we say. *All right?* they say back.

'I was *sure* it would rain, so I just cracked on and asked Chris,' says Ruby. 'He baled it up for me last week. Now my hay bales are all out there, but I haven't brought them in yet. Oh, it's looking *lovely*.'

She puts her basket on the counter and hands the things to Leslie. Ketchup. Jacob's Creek. Olive oil. Lan shows me his tongue, it's totally green. I show him mine.

'Look at your filthy feet, Amy and Lan,' says Ruby. 'Why don't you put shoes on?'

I wriggle my grimy toes. I hardly *remember* shoes.

'They're fine,' says Mum.

'And my Dunhill's, please, Leslie,' says Ruby. 'Thanks, my love.'

Leslie Robinson slaps two fat packs on the counter and pings Ruby's things through.

'Of course, they'll still need bringing in,' Ruby says, adding *all on my own*, silently, like she does to everything. 'I've got B & B guests for the next few days. They love collecting eggs, though, *bless them*.' She means, *bastards*.

'How are you, Leslie?' asks Mum.

'Thieves came into our yard last night,' says Leslie, not looking up. 'Stole nearly three hundred pound worth of diesel. Didn't see nothing.'

God, Leslie! say Mum and Ruby. They sound much more upset than Leslie, whose diesel was stolen. She just looks grumpy, but I look at Kyle and Lily, and realise I was wrong, they're not bored, they're miserable, because of the robbery.

'Went up this morning, found a hose just lying by the tank,' says Leslie. 'Great big long thing. Police came pretty quick, to be fair. But what are they going to do? Lost three hundred quid, haven't we?'

Mum and Ruby try to be comforting, but Leslie has shut her mouth up, tight. She looks like a big rock.

'Can Lily and Kyle come to ours?' I ask, and Mum says *sure, no trouble,* because it's not.

Jack and Joffrey come for dinner, too, and a lady we don't know, because there are too many courgettes and broad beans to eat. It's hot again, and we're all outside. Niah is naked in the trough. She's fishing, she says. There are just frogs in there, but nobody's telling her. The grown-ups still call her the baby, but she's nearly four. She's got dead-straight blonde hair. She doesn't really bother speaking, maybe because everyone else is better at it, or because Gail doesn't try to make her. Eden and Lulu are running round in their vests with bare arses.

'Do you never put clothes on any of your children?' asks Joffrey.

'What a wonderful place,' says the stranger. 'Blissful.'

She's got glasses with red frames, and a wrinkly neck. *Who's she again?* I whisper to Lan, and he shrugs.

Eden, Bryn and Lulu are playing Police Dogs. Eden's got dibs on Ivan because he's a hound. Lulu's got a tiara on Poacher, and Martin is trying to convince Jack to get piano lessons with Mum. *My instrument is the violin,* says Jack, *I'm marvellous at it.* Mum tells them about the Robinsons' diesel being stolen.

'That gorgeous farmer lady?' says Joffrey. 'How terrible!'

'Rural crime is rampant,' says Jack. 'Small farmers are practically destitute.'

'We're not!' Kyle shouts, suddenly, sending a guinea fowl clucking off in a panic.

'He didn't mean *you*,' I say, quickly.

'No, no, I didn't, I'm so sorry,' says Jack. 'I didn't realise—'

'We're all right,' says Kyle, pushing out his chest. 'We got insurance.'

'Very sensible,' says Jack. 'So that's fine.'

I start going on about scything the Hay, to fill the silence, and Mum helps. Jack and Joffrey don't believe we hand-scythed it ourselves, so we all go to look, along the back track. We all stand at the bar gate and look over into the Hay.

There's mist floating, knee-high, over the ground. It's only in this little field, not anywhere else.

'It's because the Hay is magic,' Bryn tells Jack.

'I believe you,' says Jack.

'My God,' says Joffrey, standing very still and almost whispering it.

'What?' says Mum.

'The life you live.'

'Thank you.' Mum stands next to him.

'Just wonderful,' says the stranger in the red glasses. 'Wonderful.'

We still don't know who she is.

'We're baling it soon. And we're doing that by hand, as well,' Dad says. 'Kyle and Lily's dad will do the other fields, in the conventional way, but we've developed a special method for this field, because it's so special.'

It's *Jim's* method, Dad's just boasting.

'Amazing,' says the stranger.

She and Dad start going on about 'Exit, Pursued By a Goat'. She's from a magazine called *Herefordshire Life*, and she wants Dad to write a column. It is exciting and Dad's really happy, but they just keep saying *amazing* and *wonderful!* – so we run off with Lily and Kyle, and leave them to it.

'You're so lucky,' says Lily. 'You get to live on your farm.'

I feel proud and guilty.

'It's not a proper farm,' I say, 'and yours is way bigger. Want to stay over?'

Their dad comes up early next morning, to do the baling in Long Field. He won't be able to fit the baler round the house, so we all run all the way down to the bottom of our valley, to the big gate where Bony-Eyes' land starts. We hear him ages before we see him, the massive tractor, with the baler banging along behind.

We open up the gate, and Kyle jumps up next to Chris on the high seat. Me, Lan and Lily chase along next to them, watching the loose hay going up the belt into the tunnel, and the bales, all perfect, bumping out the other end onto the stubble field. Kyle stands balancing like a monkey, with his hands on his dad's shoulders.

Afterwards, Chris comes up to the house and we see Jim give him a bundle of cash. They shake hands, and he stays for beers and goat ice cream, then Kyle and Lily get back on the tractor, and they all roar off. We run behind, with the diesel blowing in our faces, shouting, *thanks! See you!* And Kyle and Lily wave and say, *don't mention it,* just like Chris does.

At dinner, Eden asks, 'Now Dad's paid him, can the Robinsons buy back their house from Jenny Barkley?'

'Maybe. One day,' says Gail.

Gail's just being nice. I don't think the Robinsons will ever live in their farmhouse again. Bryn looks happy, but she's only six, she doesn't know anything. I think of Leslie's face when she was beeping Ruby's wine through the till and telling us about her stolen diesel, and I wonder if she hates working there, or if she's just tired, like Mum says. Mum likes cleaning houses, she gets to look at other people's stuff. Cleaning the Barkley house doesn't make her jealous. She says it's so naff it makes her laugh.

'John Gaunt owes us for silage,' says Martin. 'He would have done that baling for free, and Jim's just handing out cash like we're made of money.'

'I paid Chris Robinson a fair price for a good job,' says Jim.

'Maybe the Robinsons could build a farmhouse,' says Lan. 'They've got loads of land.'

We can't believe they haven't thought of it.

'Mum?' I say. 'They could build a house!'

'Nope,' says Martin, sounding like he doesn't even care, 'it's the wrong kind of land.'

'What d'you mean?' says Lan.

I don't want Martin to explain. He made it sound like a babyish idea.

I think of the land around the Barkley house, grazed by the Robinsons' sheep, and the Robinsons' fields of wheat and oilseed rape that Kyle and Lily have shown us from the car so many times, waving and pointing at the long rows, going, *'That's* our farm, and *that's* our farm, and *that's* our farm . . .' It's not the *wrong kind.*

'Most agricultural land is worthless,' says Martin.

I get up from the table and go outside.

The flowers Mum planted are giving off a scent that's so strong it's sickly. The night is very warm. The fields look a different size and shape than they did last week before they were cut. Nothing feels like it fits.

Down the Yard, Finbar comes out of his house, whistling, and goes off for a walk. I look up at the sky. It's a good night for the telescope, but I feel annoyed and slow and don't want to go get it.

Lan comes out. He puts his hands in his pockets while

he looks around, just like Jim does, and then comes over. *All right?* He sits nearby.

'I hate Martin,' I say. It isn't even what's bothering me, it's just easiest.

Lan doesn't answer about Martin, but he heard me. Behind us, the grown-ups are clattering about in the house, and *yapping* on.

Ruby's going to build a pool!

She's not? What with?

That lovely Polish guy, Mihai. He's helping.

Ben Barkley's definitely having an affair.

He and Amanda hate each other.

They love the money.

He's probably never been faithful.

Has she?

Neither of us want to hear them. We walk further down the Yard, where it's quieter. There's still a tiny bit of pale sky at the end of the valley. Above us the sky is inky blue.

'Let's make a really good camp, way out in the Baldy Wild,' says Lan.

'Or in the woods.'

'And sleep in it the whole week, and not tell them where it is.'

'Yeah.'

Doing my teeth for bed, I close my eyes. I'm brushing, leaning on the basin, and I think about Ben Barkley having an affair. I don't think our parents should talk about things like that. It's all right for Ruby to have a boyfriend, she's a single lady, but the Barkleys are a family. I don't like them knowing

Ben Barkley, and I'm glad he doesn't come round. I think it must be the most unfair, mean thing you could ever do to anybody, to be unfaithful. Apart from killing them.

I brush, and spit, and brush. I think of Jim paying cash to Chris, and Kyle waving from the tractor like a grown-up farmer. Me and Lily Robinson could get jobs and save up and get a pony. I could clean, or give piano lessons to babies. We could teach ourselves to ride. It would be fun to have a secret camp. We can keep the pony there, and Lily will be the only one who knows where it is.

I open my eyes, and rinse from the old blue tooth mug, and remember spitting on Em off the Bridge, when me and Lan were seven – and it makes me laugh all over again, and water goes everywhere.

When it's really hot like this, I sleep on top of my bed, and I can hear the mosquitoes. There are spiders the size of fried eggs scrambling around my bedroom walls. I didn't used to care about spiders, but now I hate them. I take my pillow and my patchwork quilt out onto the Bridge, and lie looking through the rope squares at the Big Room, and outside. There's a huge moon hanging in the sky and lighting up the fields, so bright I can't see any stars. Some of the grown-ups are sampling elderflower wine outside. As I go off into my sleep, I hear them laughing. I love going to sleep hearing people talking and laughing, not knowing what they're talking about, like when I was little.

Jim's special baling technique is very complicated. Even Dad doesn't understand it, when he wanted to put it in 'Exit' Jim had to explain nine times.

Jim makes the wheelie-bin bales in the Hay with all of us kids. None of the other grown-ups can be bothered, so we get him all to ourselves. We've been turning the rows of drying grass for *days*, and now it's ready. It looks gold and slightly green and smells of sun, but when we start to gather it, it's like every insect in the whole world has moved in. And dust. The sun is burning. Niah is walking round waving a bucket and talking to herself. Me, Eden, Lan, Bill and Josh are the most organised, and we've got underwear. Bryn and Lulu realise pretty quick it's not nice having itchy bits in your bum-crack. When it gets too bad we rinse off in the paddling pool, or one of us runs for snacks or water. The paddling-pool water goes white and mucky, then brown, then doesn't even rinse us off.

We run relays, dropping hay in the bin while Jim squashes it down, until it's full up. He sings and marches and makes happy roaring sounds, all day, picking us up and spinning us round, even me and Lan.

Our bales get so good. We're experts. They're not *machine* bales, they are way better.

The afternoon is boiling, scalding, burning hot. We're sweaty and thirsty and sneezing, with raised red rashes and long pink scratches, but we've made *forty-five* bales of hay. I nearly murdered Bill this morning because he jumped on one and broke it.

Jim hoses us off in the Yard, and then we're clean and cool and shivering. We all sing, *I'm on top of the world looking down on creation*, and Gail leans out the kitchen and goes *that's the first song I ever knew!* and we shout – *we know! You sang it to Lan!* It's probably the best day of my whole life so far.

13

Dreams

LAN

Amy's trying to learn the right-hand part of a piece called
'Dream', by Ernest Bloch, that Harriet is teaching us, but
we're just saying 'Ernest Bloch' in German accents and
laughing. *Ernest Bloch.* Josh is in the Cowhouse kitchen
being comforted. He wrote a story about a flying pizza
and Mr Tindle wouldn't mark it because Josh *wasn't sup-
posed to write genre* and now Josh is crying – not about Mr
Tindle, but because Harriet was so angry. He hates any-
body shouting. Mum, Jim, Adam and Rani are in there too.
Everyone is angry. All we hear is their voices, talking over
each other about five different things –
  It's all right, darling.
  So you go and look up the fucking regulations!
  We'll get more, not less, can't you see that?
  Nobody's shouting, sweetie, everything's fine.
It's not what Finbar calls *conducive.*

Then Harriet suddenly screams, 'All right! All right! You win – happy now?'

'*Happy?*' Adam yells, and his yell is so loud it's like it's coming through speakers from all over the house. 'SINCE WHEN DO YOU CARE?'

Then Harriet screams again and her footsteps run up the Cowhouse stairs, and her bedroom door bangs shut.

Everyone goes quiet, and Amy looks frozen. I've never heard Harriet scream like that. Or Adam yell so loudly. Jim would never, ever yell at Mum like that. I wonder what Mum would do. She might stop going on at him. Or she might just leave. Nobody says anything. I feel like the whole of the Big Room is shocked, not just us. The whole house. Then we hear Josh's voice, and Adam says, *Yes, up you go to Mummy*, and Josh's footsteps go up the stairs.

Me and Amy sit still, on the piano stool. There's total silence from the grown-ups in the Cowhouse kitchen. I picture my mum, Adam, Jim and Rani, all standing in the kitchen, not saying anything. The quiet goes on. I don't know what to do. Amy's just sitting still now, and looking at the floor. I feel like she might be going to cry. I lean close to her ear and wait for a second. And then I whisper –

'*Ernest Bloch.*'

Amy explodes laughing so suddenly she gets spit on the keys, and I do too. We laugh so much we fall on the floor. So much it hurts. And it's like we're going to cry. We can't breathe. And our stomachs are aching, and Amy's just gasping, not even laughing any more. Finally, we stop. It's all quiet everywhere. We lie there, getting our breath back in the quiet, trying not to think. We hold up our arms and look at them, at our hands, and then above, to the long, high gap, up to the beams in the ceiling. I'm more tanned than her, but her arms are longer. She's taller than me now by miles. But my hands are bigger. Hers are full of cat scratches. I've got a blood-nail, where I smashed it helping Jim with Mum's dresser.

Adam comes in, breaking up our peacefulness.

'Has *nobody* seen the Lada keys?' he says.

We watch him march past us, then furiously back.

'*Anyone?*' he shouts. 'Lada keys?'

Mum comes in, putting on her jacket.

I sit up.

'Where are you going?'

'Lan. You don't always have to ask where I'm going. I'm never gone long,' says Mum.

I've annoyed her. She and Adam start to leave. I get up off the floor, and see Jim, standing on his own.

'Don't worry, Lan,' he says, 'Ruby called. She's in a panic about getting her hay in. It's raining, and she hasn't got it under cover. Adam and Gail are taking the trailer down there now.'

'Can we come?'

We're bored with piano and fighting. Adam and Mum don't want us, but we make them take us along.

Adam floors the Lada going over Colin's hill. He and Mum laugh every time they hit a pothole. 'OW!' shouts Amy as her head hits the roof. We screech to a halt outside Ruby's smallholding, on the edge of the village.

'Here come the cavalry!' shouts Adam, leaping out, and we pile out after.

'Got your camera?' Mum asks him.

'Yup, this will be perfect.'

Leslie Robinson is shifting bales already, with Kyle and Lily and some guys from the village who Ruby says are Polish students, who are helping too, but we're the only ones with a trailer. Ruby's B & B guests are watching from the deck Racist Rick built outside her spare room.

'Leslie closed the Spar to come help me out,' says Ruby, 'how about that?' Her face is all pink and shiny.

Adam pulls into the field, and we all start heaving the bales over the squashy stubble. Kyle and Amy are both stronger than me, but I'm stronger than Lily. Our arms and faces are shiny-wet with rain. Ruby's fussing about, heaving bales, with her big boobs bouncing around in her T-shirt. *I knew I should have got them in last week!* she says. The three student guys talk Polish to each other and English to us. *My family are having the same problem each year,* says one. *The hay. The harvest.*

They're proper machine bales, and very heavy. Adam's given Mum his gloves, but mine and Amy's hands are getting striped bright red from the twine. Ruby's B & B guests are sitting on their deck with Ragtime, drinking lemonade. They smile and wave at us. It's raining properly now.

'Bastards,' says Ruby, but then she feels bad when they come down and help. *This is wonderful,* they keep saying, *everyone in the village pitching in, it's so gorgeous.* They're just like the magazine lady with the red glasses going on about the countryside being so *amazing.* Me and Amy roll our eyes. *Oh, how marvellous!* whispers Amy, in a posh voice.

We get the bales onto the trailer, and Ruby's mini

Dexters stare over the fence at us, looking worried about their winter-feed supply.

'Alek and Jakub and the other guy make your dad look puny,' I say to Amy.

'Puny Dad! Puny Dad!' she shouts at him.

Adam doesn't think it's funny, nor does Mum, but they let us drive the Lada to Ruby's hay store. Amy turns the key the wrong way and it makes an awful noise. *Nice driving,* I say, and she punches me.

The minute we get the last of the bales under cover, the rain stops and the sun comes out. Fat flies came out in clouds, and the Dexters' coats steam.

'I'll be off, then,' says Leslie, and goes back to the Spar with Lily and Kyle.

'Thanks a million, Leslie! You're a star!' Ruby calls after her.

Leslie doesn't bother answering.

'Say *hi* to Chris!'

We still have to get the bales off the trailer, but we take a break. Ruby wipes off the chairs, and brings out tea and lemon drizzle cake.

'Hey, you're the crazy big family with the Lada,' says one of the students, 'we've seen you around.'

'That's us,' says Adam. 'Do you mind if I take your picture?'

'Sure,' they say, and put their arms round each other's shoulders, and smile for him.

'It's for a regular piece I do,' says Adam, 'in *Herefordshire Life.*'

He tells them all about it, and his blog, and Frith.

'We've always dreamed of doing that,' says the B & B lady. 'Getting out of the city. Living in the countryside. Always.'

'Well, I've certainly no regrets,' says Ruby.

'Neither do we,' says Adam. 'And we're renovating a little barn up at our place. So it looks like you'll have competition, Ruby.'

'Who says?' says Amy.

Adam starts telling them about the tumbledown barn just near the Hay, and that it's going to be a holiday let.

'With the exposure we get from my blog and *Herefordshire Life*, we hope it's going to really take off. People like a *story*, my editor tells me.'

'And we've got plenty of those,' says Mum.

'How exciting,' says Ruby. 'I've always thought Frith has fantastic potential for development. How do you—'

'We're not developing Frith!' Amy interrupts.

Ruby, the B & B people and the Polish students all look at her. It's not normal for a kid to butt in – I wouldn't. Amy's not like me. But she is blushing.

'Frith isn't a B & B,' she says. 'It's a *farm*. It's a proper farm. Mum says it is.'

Ruby goes inside to say goodbye to her guests, and the rest of us get the bales off the trailer. It's a lot easier than getting them on.

We say goodbye to Ruby, and she makes us take a cake home with us to say thank you. We're quiet going up the hill, blowing on our hands and checking our blisters. Amy's still angry.

Mum twists round in her seat to look at her. She smiles at her and takes her hand.

'Amy,' she says, 'it's all right. Dreams change. Your mum understands.'

AUTUMN
2009

14

Tumbledown

AMY

Dad sticks the sign into the ground outside the new holi-day cottage. Gail got Jim to make it, and she painted flowers round the edges, and we helped burn the letters: TUMBLEDOWN. Bill hammers it in with the mallet. We all stand back. It looks *stupid*. It's a stupid-looking sign. Em gets geraniums from her garden and plants them around it. *So much better!* everyone says. They're pretending. They've always hated Em's geraniums. Mum says they look like they should have a donkey in a straw hat standing next to them. I asked, *why would a donkey wear a straw hat?* And she said, *if it was in Bad Spain*. I think she hates the colour. They're the same colour red as the Last Remnants.

Everyone's worried the Carthouse septic tank will over-flow even more now Tumbledown is a cottage. Doing all the plumbing was a *nightmare*, and Racist Rick's digger kept having to come and dig more holes. Tumbledown has got a Power Shower and macerating toilet. Me and Lan can't believe macerating means digesting. The grown-ups asked us to write a notice, to stop people blocking it up with nappies and sanitary towels. We wrote –

ATTENTION! I ONLY EAT WEE,
POO AND TOILETT ROLL!

– but Gail made us write a new one. And one about the internet, because there isn't any:

There is no internet access at Tumbledown Cottage,
but internet is available to Guests in the Farmhouse.

It *isn't*. Unless they want to spend all day listening to it going *beep-whirrr-beep-beep* and watching Dad trying to upload photographs and swearing. The toilet makes a *fascinating* sound when you flush it. Eden and Bryn took Niah over secretly, and they did all their poos in it for days, until the grown-ups found out and put a rope across the front door. Dad says *he* was the one who paid for nearly the whole of Tumbledown, including the macerating toilet, with 'Exit, Pursued By a Goat'. If Mum doesn't praise him enough he goes for long drives in the Last Remnants on his own. But him and Mum aren't fighting. They're definitely a lot quieter.

Lan's and my new favourite thing is lying on top of the Killing Barn. We never dared try to climb up before, but we're big enough now. The grown-ups are fine about axes – and rivers and campfires – but the Dutch-barn roof is *high*. It was very difficult and dangerous to start with because we had to get a rope up and tie it, but now it's easy. We use the long haystack ladder to get up, and the rope to come down again – we've put knots in it. When we land back on solid ground, we shake *so much* we go wobbly, and have to lie flat on the ground. We always put the ladder against the haystack where it lives after, so nobody will discover what we're doing.

Up on top the curve of the corrugated roof is like flying down the valley on the back of a dragon. The metal is hot. And flaky and rusty, and thin – you can punch right through it in some places. The valley and sky are so big up here, and Frith looks *tiny*, and right below us is the new slate roof of Tumbledown Holiday Cottage.

Through the telescope we can see all the way over the tops of our woods, and far, far away to the distant green mountains. Without the telescope we can't even *see* the cars on the B-road, just the sunlight flash. With it, we can even see what colour they are. I'm trying to focus it so I'll be able to read the number plates as they zip through the tree gap, but even 80x Magnification can't do that. I look at some birds and leaves, and then Lan has a go. Then we just lie there, baking in the sun. I tell Lan about this boy I heard about who had his head smashed off out of the window of a train, and we talk about vampire bats and if ghosts are real, and the ozone layer, and arsenic poisoning, and if we care about the eleven-plus and secondary – which we do *not*. We're actually both quite scared, but we don't say it. We can smell boiling sugar and fruit from the Carthouse kitchen, where Rani's been making jam.

'Remember when I found that caterpillar in the pickle?' It had gone white and I ate it.

We lift our legs off the metal to see how long we can keep them up. We wriggle up to the highest part of the roof. We can spy on everyone from here. Mum's put Colin's trailer in with the Goats, so they'll get used to it, and two of them are on the ramp, looking around. *Just like us,* says Lan. Finbar is hoeing the vegetable beds. *I can see his smoke!* Eden and Bryn are standing on boxes to groom Gabriella. Her calf is due in a few weeks, and she looks *fat.* Jim is sanding a door on a pair of sawhorses in the Yard, and Mum and Rani are leaning on it, drinking tea.

'Look at Bryn, dust-bathing with the chickens,' I say. Bryn *really* thinks that she'll grow wings if she tries hard enough.

Magic and Molly are still always together, but they've made friends with a silkie. Gail lets them keep their eggs – it's only fair, after being battery hens for so long and never being able to touch them with their beaks or even *see* them. I move the telescope slowly round the Orchard looking at chickens but the trees get in the way, green and blurry. Then I can see the chickens, very sharp and clear. I can see Batty, who limps from having bumblefoot. And Goliath – and then I see Gail and Dad are in the Orchard, too.

'I can see my dad and your mum,' I say. I laugh, because it's so *weird* seeing people up close when they don't know you're there.

'What are they doing?' says Lan, turning on his belly to look.

'She's got something in her hair,' I say.

Dad's and Gail's faces are so clear it's like watching TV.

Dad is smiling, and saying something. He gets some grass out of Gail hair, and she lies back on the grass. Then he lies back too, next to her, and puts his hands behind his head.

'They're just lying next to each other. It looks like they're going to sleep in *bed*.' I laugh. 'They're so *lazy*.'

'Mum isn't lazy,' says Lan.

'Yes, she *is*.'

She is. Lan never admits it.

'Well, your dad is lazy,' he says.

'Yeah, everyone knows *that*.'

Then Dad sits up and turns his back to me, blocking out Gail. He moves a bit, and he holds up both his hands like he does when he's saying something important. I take one hand off to focus, and the telescope wobbles and falls. It lands on the roof, but I grab it before it rolls.

'It's OK, it's not scratched,' I say. It's just got a few crumbs of chalky bird poo on it.

'Can I have a go?'

We hear a car on the lane. Not anyone we know – we can tell by the sound.

'Who's that?'

'Strangers.'

'No! It's the Tumbledown Guests!'

'Shit!' We'd forgotten, and we said we'd help, and we're exactly above the new cottage, and if they see us we'll be in so much trouble.

They're at the gate already. They're getting out of the car, and stretching, pulling out bags and suitcases.

We slither down fast – rushing, scared – over the bumpy iron, scraping our fronts and burning our hands on the rope, and tumble, out of breath, falling the last bit, onto the grass.

'Tumbledown!' announces Dad, coming round the corner with two Guests as we stand and make ourselves look casual, folding our arms and smiling, but my heart is beating so hard my T-shirt is shaking, and we're both bright red in the face.

Mum is there, too, and half the other kids – Bryn, Josh and Lulu – come to look. *All right?* we say, like nothing's up. The two grown-up strangers look tidy and surprised.

'Look at the state of you two,' says Dad. 'You're filthy.'

Lan's covered in rust. Grazes. And something black – oil? I am too, but I don't know why Dad's going on about it.

'What's that rope doing there?' says Mum.

'It's a swing.'

'We were swinging on it.'

Mum's suspicious, but Dad's not. Lucky she hasn't noticed the ladder still leaning up against the barn. We'll have to put it back later.

'So! Meet the Barrs!' he says in his Fox and Badger voice.

'Hiya!' says the female Guest. She looks different to our mothers, with shiny hair and lipstick.

'Lan and Amy,' says Dad, 'say hello!'

Then Bill comes up with the Guest Boy dragging behind.

'This is *Toby*!' says the Guest Mum, in a voice like she's announcing someone famous.

Toby looks up. He's small and pale, in a black T-shirt that says *Star Wars* in slanting yellow.

'Toby's obsessed with *Star Wars*,' she says, like nobody ever thought of liking *Star Wars* before.

'So are Lan and Bill!'

'Hey, Lan, Toby's got a clone trooper on a speed bike,' says Bill.

'Well, this is a great start!' says the Guest Woman, and starts going on about what Toby needs, and how he's *feeling*.

Me, Lan, Bryn, Josh, Lulu and Bill look at the Guest Kid, and he looks back. I think he's *feeling* Boring.

Tumbledown has a floor that looks like wood from B&Q. And it's got a sofa that turns into a bed, and a spiral staircase up to the proper bed, which are all made from kits. Martin and Dad screwed them together and we helped. Jim didn't join in because it wasn't like making *real* furniture. *Oh, it's gorgeous!* say the Guests. *Wow, this is amazing.*

'I'll leave you to it, I've got a lot to do,' says Mum, and goes. She's not being very friendly. I know she hates them being here, and I want to hate them too, but it's quite exciting, and I didn't know they'd be so impressed with Frith.

Dad and Gail show them everything, and we explain all about the toilet. The Guests talk about the *horrendous* motorway, and how awful London is because of the *financial crisis*, and Frith is *stunning* and the countryside is so quiet. *Listen!* they say, whenever there's a pause, *it's so quiet!* It's actually quite noisy, with all the birds and sheep and Colin's tractor going, up the hill, but – *whatever,* I say to Lan.

'What is that amazing smell?' says the woman Guest, when we're outside again.

'I'm making jam,' says Rani.

'Oh my God!'

They say *oh my God* about everything. I give Lan a look and toss my pretend long hair like a supermodel, like, *oh my Ga-ad!* and we explode laughing and have to walk off.

'So,' says the woman Guest, staring at everything. 'What shall we do?'

They're surprised we don't have *local info* in Tumbledown, and they keep going on about footpaths. The grown-ups point them down the hill, and say they can just basically go anywhere, and in the end they go off down the track, holding hands, with Toby between them, their heads jerking around like chickens as they stare at everything.

We've mostly forgotten about the Guest Family. They stay in the cottage a lot. When they come out they go on about how stressed they are, because it's *the end of the world as we know it*. Bryn got quite scared and asked Jim if it really was the end of the world, and he said, *no. A lot of people lost a lot of money very quickly, that's all. It's fine.* Me and Lan knew it was fine. It's only stupid money.

The Guest Parents say they never normally see each other because they work so hard. They heard an owl last night.

'They were so excited I thought they were going to *cry*,' I said to Mum, to make her laugh, but she just said –

'Yes, well, there you are. We're very lucky to live here.'

She was digging up ragwort in Barrow, so the pigs won't get poisoned.

'The Guest Family think we're brave,' I said. 'The dad told Jim we're courageous, because we've given up everything.'

'Oh, fuck sake,' said Mum.

She was in a horrible mood, so I left her on her own.

Toby the Guest Kid is fine, but he's bored. The Guest Parents have gone for another walk, after covering themselves in sunblock and Toby with a different sunblock, which is thick and doesn't rub in. Gail says all the reefs are dying because of people like them but Toby's letting us play with his Nintendo so we haven't told him. We're against the wall in the shadow of the Carthouse so we can see the screen. Toby's demonstrating the *Star Wars* game. His tiny white fingers are really fast.

'*The stylus is my lightsaber,*' he says in a growling movie-trailer voice.

Lan and Bill are rubbish at it, which is embarrassing, specially because it's meant for twelve-year-olds, and Toby's only seven.

'*For twelve years and over,*' he growls. '*Fantasy Violence.*'

He keeps asking things like what brand Lan's trainers are. When Lan said *Clarks,* Toby laughed for ages, and told us about his friend who still has Geoxes with Velcro. *He's pathetic,* he said.

Come and see the goats, we say, *come and see the chickens.* We've taken him everywhere, but he's not having any fun. Whatever we show him, he just says, *is it poisonous?*

No, we say, *it's a salt lick.*

No, it's an ant.

We told him about all the grass snakes and adders. He

quite liked the goats, until Hazel chewed his T-shirt and he screamed.

'She won't bite, loser,' said Bill.

Josh wanted him to see his sheep.

'Sheep make you go blind,' said Toby.

'No, they don't!' Josh was really upset.

'Can I wash my hands?' said Toby. 'Have you got any rabbits?'

We were getting *desperate*. So we went to find some Mums.

Gail and Rani were in the Carthouse kitchen with the jam, sitting down and eating it with teaspoons and listening to Snow Patrol. We leant on the table and groaned and interrupted their *grown-up conversation*.

'Where are his *parents*? We're *desperate*.'

Rani told us not to be mean. 'Poor kid. You have to include him.'

'He's overwhelmed,' Gail said.

'By what?' But they wouldn't even help, so we wandered off outside again.

We found Toby sitting on the trough all hunched up, with his DS and his shiny white nose. We asked him if he liked hide-and-seek, and he *finally* looked happy – until he found out we had to play outside. *Can't we play in the house?* he said. *Don't you have cupboards?* We told him the rules. You can hide anywhere, except:

The woods.

Inside human houses.

Out the front gate.

Past the end of the Hay.

Woods or stream.

Barrow, the Baldy Wild or Foy's Wood (Foy's isn't Frith).

Get it?

He didn't, and it took ages showing him.

Now we've finally started, and Lan's seeker. I know he doesn't bother counting properly any more, he just goes in the house and then leans out and yells *sixty-four!* or *eighty-three!* and then goes back in. I'm running around pretending to look for a good place, but really I'm checking on Niah and the Guest Kid to see if they're OK. Eden is holding Niah's hand. I watch them go down to New Cottage. Niah's so excited, she's giggling like crazy, and running so slowly Eden has to stare at the sky to stop herself shouting at her. They duck behind Em's garden bench. You could see them from anywhere, but it's nice of Eden to include her.

'Ninety-four!' yells Lan.

I can't see the Guest Kid, or anyone else, so I just run to the water butt by Finbar's, and pull a tarp over me. Something crawly drops down my neck and I have to jump out and shake it off, then pull the tarp back over. I'm terrified what else is under there, but I keep quiet, listening for Lan, who's stamping around, shouting –

'Coming! Ready or not!'

He takes ages pretending not to see Niah and Eden, then creeps up on them, and they're caught. Then he finds Bill under an empty dustbin, and Bill points down the hill, right at me, and yells, *there's Amy!* He makes me so mad I could kill him. He must have seen me hide. Recently, I've hated him nearly as much as we used to when we were little. It's since he said I had boobs, and he tries to elbow me in the chest. Nobody else ever says *anything*. They're really small. Mum says you can hardly even *see* them. I wish Bill was dead.

'YOU'RE SUCH A FUCKING SHITBAG, BILL HODGE!' I scream, right when the Guest Parents are coming back through the bar gate.

They look shocked, and ask what we're all doing. I say we're playing hide-and-seek and they're suddenly so happy it's *weird*.

'Oh my God, that's so lovely!'

They go back to Tumbledown talking about *real* childhood, and *fresh air*, like *poor Toby* lives underground, and never sees the daylight when he's in *awful* London in the *financial crisis*.

We're happy the Guest Parents are pleased we're including Toby, and we hope he's having a good time and everything, but the problem is, we can't find him. Nearly everyone else is found. In fact *everyone* is – except Lulu, who isn't playing, just dancing around by the water trough in her princess dress, like an arsehole, singing to herself.

Josh's hiding place was the best – stretched out in the pumpkins, with the long stalks lying all over his body. He was totally camouflaged, we walked past about nine times and he was nearly asleep by the time we saw him. But we still can't find Toby. We've been looking *ages*, trying not to shout too loudly, because he's a Guest and a Stranger. We don't want to draw attention. But it is getting sort of worrying. We've checked the Orchard, the hedges, the Killing Barn. Under the flatbed trailer, in the empty feed bins, in the log pile. We looked inside all the houses, too, and in the goat house, and the henhouse – which is where we found Bryn, being a hen.

'To-byy! We're coming for you!' we shout, kicking things to make a noise and scare him out, but there's just silence and emptiness, all round the farm.

We stop looking for a minute when Mum calls, *Jo-oshy,
ooo-eee* – and Josh goes in for his piano lesson. Josh is the
worst of all of us at piano, but the best at practising, so
Mum can't stop teaching him.

'Itsy Bitsy Spider' comes floating out of the open doors.
It's his favourite. He's been playing it for years. *Down
came the rain, and washed the spider out . . .*

We all start looking for Toby again. Lulu is dragging
after us in her Snow White dress and leggings, moaning.

'I don't know where he *is*. I'm not *playing*.'

'I don't *care*, Lulu, just help *find* him, OK?' I say.

We can smell dinner being cooked, and the day isn't so
warm as it was. It's been ages.

We really can't find Toby. We've even asked Finbar. We
yelled – *have you seen Toby the Guest Kid?* through the
ribbons on his door.

'I'm working. Go away,' he said.

Eden is dragging Ivan along, but *he* doesn't care where
Toby is.

'Check basically everywhere, Sergeant Ivan,' says Eden.
She's going to be a policewoman.

We check all the same hiding places again.

TO-BY . . .

Silence. The Lada is coming up Four Acre. Jim's driving.
We run over and wave him down.

'We've lost Toby!'

'Who?'

'The Guest Kid.'

'Better find him then,' says Jim.

To-by, To-by . . . we give u-u-p, come out . . .

'Maybe he's fallen in the water butt,' says Lulu.

'I would have seen,' I say.

'And it's full of water,' says Lan.

'Then he'll be drowned!' shrieks Lulu.

We check it, just in case, shushing each other because of Finbar. We climb up on the brick pile and look inside. No fair head, bobbing in the water. No floating Nintendo DS. Nothing. We've run out of places to look.

Me, Lan and the others go back to the Carthouse, dragging our feet. Gail and Rani are still at the table, drinking wine and listening to The Magic Numbers.

'We can't find Toby,' I say. 'Anywhere.'

'What do you mean you can't find him?' says Rani and turns off the music.

'He's gone.'

'Don't say that.'

'He has,' says Lan. 'He isn't anywhere. We've looked.'

Gail and Rani put down their wine glasses. They get serious, fast. They make us all go up to the Farmhouse with them, and call Mum and Dad into the Big Room. I'm starting to feel frightened. Lan looks at me, like, *this isn't good*, and I shake my head, *no, it isn't*.

Josh is sleeping on Em's old sofa, with his head on Christabel's belly.

'Don't wake him,' says Dad, 'he'll panic.'

What's most scary is how scared the grown-ups are.

'Are you *sure* you've looked everywhere?' says Rani. 'Even in the houses?'

Yes – we told you.

'Fuck,' says Mum, tying back her hair. 'Don't tell his parents. Where are they?'

'In Tumbledown, I think.'

We look all over Frith again, with the grown-ups, calling –
Toby . . . Toby . . .

We sound silly and small, looked down on by the empty
trees.

'Can't you find him?' says Lulu, swinging her princess
dress around. 'Ha, ha, ha.'

'Shut up, *Lulu,*' says Bill.

We look. We look. All the same places. Nothing.

'We have to tell his parents,' says Gail.

Nobody wants to but nobody argues. We all start off to the
cottage, but before we get there we meet Dad, coming the
other way, with Toby's parents. They're all laughing. The three
of them look so happy and normal. Then Dad sees our faces.

'What is it?'

When Mum tells them, the Guest Parents switch from
happy to *completely out of control.* They go mental.

'What do you mean? Where is he?'

'When did you last see him? Oh my God, oh my God,
Toby —'

The Guest Mum starts running around the Yard, search-
ing under wheelbarrows, behind walls, under the dustbin
where Bill was hiding.

We've tried there, we keep saying. *We've looked.*

'THEN WHERE IS HE?' she screams in our faces.
'WHERE IS MY SON?'

Toby's dad grabs Lan's shoulders, really hard.

'*What were you doing?*' he hisses. '*Where were you
when you lost sight of him?*'

Lan just looks shocked. The Guest Dad's fingers are
digging in his arms.

'Let him go,' says Jim, 'you're scaring him.'

'OH!' yells Toby's mum, like she's crazy. '*Now* you're protective! *Now* you give a shit!'

Lan's gone all white. I probably have too. Bryn starts crying.

'He would have come out by now if he could,' says the Guest Mum, and she starts to cry too. 'He hates being left alone.' She covers her face.

We're all back where we started, in the middle of the Yard. The Guest Parents are clinging to each other's hands, and whispering. Then they both stop, and stare, suddenly, at the same thing.

'Who's that?' says the Guest Dad.

Finbar has come out of his house. He's got torn jeans and no top, and paint on his tummy, because he uses it as a cloth. He's got a handful of brushes, and he wanders over to the giant scare-rabbit and wipes the brushes on its fur so it spins towards us. The Parents both stare at him.

'I said, who's he?' says Toby's mother, her voice as hard as stone. She marches over to Finbar. '*Excuse me*,' she says, 'who are you?'

'What?' says Finbar. He doesn't want to talk to anyone.

'Who are you?' says the Guest Dad.

'Finbar,' says Mum. 'That's Finbar, he lives with us.'

'In what capacity?' says the Guest Mum.

She sounds like the police or something.

'In the capacity of living here,' says Mum, looking quite scary.

'OK, all right,' says Finbar. He raises two hands in the air. 'I'll be inside.'

He turns back towards his house.

'Wait,' says the Guest Dad. 'Stop there.'

Finbar obeys. He stops in his tracks. I feel ashamed. Nobody should talk to anybody like that. *He hasn't done anything,* I say, but I must have said it very quietly, and nobody's listening.

'Come here,' orders the Guest Dad.

All our grown-ups have gone quiet. They aren't standing up for him. Finbar comes a little closer.

'What now?' he says.

'Have you seen my son?' says the Guest Dad. 'About this high. Seven years old. Blond hair.'

The Guest Mum makes a whimpering sound.

Finbar looks at Mum, and smiles a big, wide smile.

'*Hello?*' says the dad, like Finbar's thick. 'Hello?'

Finbar doesn't answer. He looks like he's just thought of something clever, and has a secret. I really want him to say something sensible. Just say he hasn't seen him. Like he did to us, before. But he doesn't.

'You're the people come to rent out what used to be a very pretty little tumbledown barn for a couple of days' rest-and-relaxation from your exceptionally busy but no doubt essentially pointless lives,' he says.

I feel my stomach go like cold water.

'Answer me,' says the dad, 'my son. *Toby.* Have you seen him?'

'Your son Toby with the little beeping hand-held games console and the nervous tic?' says Finbar.

'Oh God, what—' the Guest Mum begins.

'Holy Christ, will you take a look at yourselves?' says Finbar. He gestures at the farm with his paintbrushes. 'He'll be around somewhere!'

The Guest Mum points at his house.

'We need to look in there,' says the dad.

'Why?' says Finbar. 'There's nothing for you in there. Not your boy, anyway. Hey, kids, have you seen this woman's son?'

No, Finbar, we all say. *He's lost.*

The Guest Mum and Dad begin to walk across Finbar's garden together, holding hands, like they're on thin ice or in a minefield, staring at everything as they go past: the kids' windmills in the soil, scare-rabbit, broken glass and yoghurt pots.

'Mum,' I say, 'stop them.'

None of the grown-ups even look at me.

Lan goes up to Jim.

'Jim?' he says.

Jim looks down at him and says, 'Sorry.'

'Come on,' says Gail. 'Get it over with.'

'We'll just be a minute, Finbar . . .' says Dad.

They follow the Guest Parents.

'Stay out of there!' shouts Finbar, suddenly.

'Finbar . . .' says Mum. 'Can I talk to you for a second?'

The Guest Parents, Gail and Jim disappear around the back, and Dad lurks about outside. We see their shadowy shapes through the windows. Finbar shakes his head. He's not laughing any more, he's getting upset.

'That's not right,' he says. 'That's my private house.'

I want to say something, but I don't know what. I want to stop them. Or run away. I'm close to Lan and we lean arms against each other but don't meet eyes.

'Let's just walk down here a second,' says Mum. Finbar thinks for a second, deciding, then he goes with her, and they walk to the bar gate. I'm relieved he's gone with her, but it's still not fair.

'I don't get it,' said Bryn. 'What's Finbar done?'

'He hasn't done anything,' says Rani.

Me and Lan say things silently, like *I hate this*, and *me too*. After a few minutes, the Guest Parents and Jim come out again.

'No,' says the Guest Dad. His voice is shaking. I'm scared he's going to cry.

The Guest Parents both walk away from Finbar's house. The haven't found Toby *obviously* but they don't even say sorry. They look like stubborn kids.

Everyone stands around silently. I feel so weak and tired, I nearly sit down on the ground.

Mum and Finbar are still talking by the bar gate, looking down the track towards the end of the valley.

Then Rani says, 'Have you checked the stream? It's still running.'

The Guests' heads snap towards her like velociraptors. *What stream? Where?*

'We weren't *playing* down there,' says Eden, but none of the grown-ups are listening to anything we say any more. They run off down the hill – all of them sprinting.

'Stupid,' says Bill.

'There's no way he went all the way down there,' says Lan.

'I think he's been murdered,' says Eden, and starts crying, and it makes Bryn start up again.

'He hasn't been murdered,' says Lan. 'Don't be *stupid*.'

'Then where is he?' says Eden.

'We don't know *at the moment*,' I say. 'We need to find him.'

'What's happened?' says Josh, behind me. He's just woken up. Christabel is waddling behind him wagging her tail.

'Toby's lost,' I say, flatly. 'We can't find him.'

'No, he isn't,' says Josh. 'He went off to the barn. With Lulu.'

MUM! MUM! MUM!

Me and Lan are the only ones allowed to search the haystack. Eden is so jealous. They've always said, *don't ever go up on top of the haystack – if you slip between the bales you could DIE.* But they must know we *do*, because when Dad sends us up here to look he says, *You two go up, you're used to it.*

'Anything?' calls Jim.

We're at the top of the ladder. Grown-ups are holding it at the bottom and looking up full of hope and worry. Chris and Leslie Robinson are outside with their tractor in case there's bales to move. They came right up, the minute Rani rang them.

'Careful!' calls Dad.

I know the situation is *terrible* and *serious* but there's something very cool about it. It's not pretending – we're on a real mission. *Doing a job.* Anyway, it wasn't *us* who sent Toby up the haystack, it was stupid Lulu Hodge. Now she's down there acting sorry, but it's too late now.

The barn is completely full, because we haven't even used any hay yet. I climb off the ladder first, onto the slippery bales, right up in the rafters, where the cobwebs and pigeons and swallows' nests are. The bales go off into the dark, so we can't see into the corners or if there's a gap by the wall. that Toby could have fallen down. Down on the ground, they're all talking at once – *can you see him?*

'No!'

We hear murmuring below, and the Guest Dad's voice the loudest, then crying that's probably Toby's mum. Our eyes have adjusted. The top of the haystack is empty. Just us. Lulu said she brought Toby into the barn to hide, and *saw* him go up the ladder, but he's not up here, so that can't be true. Unless he's fallen down a hole.

'Kids?' calls Jim, again.

'Not here,' says Lan, like a forest ranger.

He turns to me and whispers, *do you think he climbed our rope? Outside?* He's panicking. I don't even bother answering, because – obviously – *no.* Toby's a pathetic little kid, not a *ninja.*

We can hear voices far below, and Lulu crying. The bales are tight and smooth, Chris Robinson bales, not wheelie-bin ones from the Hay. But if Lulu made Toby come up here, and he *didn't* fall off – then where is he? A rat patters along a metal beam above my head. It might be a homecoming rat, from our birthday.

'Why wouldn't we be able to hear him?' cries the Guest Mum.

She keeps asking that, and they keep *telling* her: if he's fallen down, his voice will be muffled by all the bales, can't she understand?

'Toby?' I call.

He's not up here, we may as well just go down again.

'All right, kids?' says Jim.

'All right,' Lan says.

A dusty beam of sunlight shines onto the frayed end of a piece of blue baling twine right in the middle of the stack. I nudge Lan. The twine on *Chris's* bales is *orange.*

'Look,' I whisper, '*blue*. It's from the Hay.'

We crawl towards it. We can even smell the difference – the hay from the Hay is sweeter. The corner of the bale is broken. There's another Hay bale, and that's broken too, and there's a gap. A Toby-sized gap. We slither over – but not too close – the edges crumble and we stare down the edge of a deep, narrow hole. I put my arm down it, into the black.

'I'm not going down there,' says Lan.

'Me neither.'

'There's a hole!' shouts Lan. 'He could have fallen down it.'

All the grown-ups talk at once, then shush each other like crazy. And then we hear a whimpering sound.

'Mummy?' He's down there, and he's alive.

GOT HIM! we shout. *Got him!* I lie flat on my front with my face on the scratchy hay and breathe out. I'm nothing but happy. I start smiling. I hear Lan laugh right next to me – a really small laugh, like just for himself. Toby was swallowed by the magical Hay hay, and we're saving him. I roll over on my side. We are victorious.

'999,' screams the Guest Mum. They're all going mental down there.

I've always wanted to call 999.

'Come on,' says Lan.

I start to wriggle back along the haystack, with Lan in front of me, shuffling along with his shoes in my face. *Clarks*, it says on the rubber bottoms.

Even the Fire Brigade came. We didn't need them. The ambulance has left now, and the Guests are in the hospital with Toby. Leslie and Chris and the Dads are restacking the bales. The ambulance men said Toby's got: a broken arm and collarbone, and probably a broken ankle, and maybe another thing, but they couldn't X-ray him here, so they aren't sure. We thought he was *dead* when Leslie moved the bales, and his dad pulled away the last one, and we saw him lying there, all white and crumpled up, like a dead spider.

He fell a really long way. Luckily it was narrow, the bales slowed him down, a bit. We've slid down the stack loads of times, but never gone down a *hole*. That was straight down. Fifteen bales. More. We don't even know how hay from the Hay *got* in the middle of the Robinson stack. They're always kept separate. It's a mystery. If it hadn't been for them, he would have just stayed up there, waiting and crying probably, and been fine. Lulu said he *wanted* to climb the ladder, but that's a big fat lie. He was a little scaredy-kid, she must have *made* him.

'I can't believe Lulu even got him *up* there,' I say.

Lan has gone totally silent. He hasn't said anything for ages.

'Lan!'

'What!'

'How did Lulu get him to go up there?'

'I dunno,' he says. 'Force? She's pretty strong. She could have just been really mean to him. Maybe she cried.'

'Yeah,' I say. Lulu will do anything when she wants something, like Bill. That's *Hodges* for you.

We walk past Tumbledown on the way back inside. The door is open. The Guest Stuff is still in there, and Toby's *Star Wars* duvet on the sofa bed.

'Cool duvet,' says Lan, then, after a moment, 'He was just a city kid. He didn't know any better.'

'He's not *dead*, Lan. Don't say *was*.' Lan can be so *gloomy*.

We don't *think* Toby will die. We're sure he won't. The only people who still think he might die are his parents. They're just being weird. He'll have a cast. Three casts, maybe. He can get them all signed. I've always wanted a cast.

The Guest Dad comes back to Frith to take their stuff away the next morning – just the dad, the mum's staying with Toby in the hospital. He's been there the whole night.

'But he's fine?' asks Gail.

'FINE?' says the Guest Dad and everyone takes a step away from him, like he's a bomb that's about to explode.

'*Fine?* No, he's not *fine*, Gail. He's had a *horrific* accident.'

'I didn't mean—'

But he doesn't speak again, he just marches in to get their stuff, and we hear him banging around, stamping his shoes on the B&Q floor.

Rani and Martin have gone to hide in the Carthouse with Bill and Lulu, so they aren't there when the Guest Dad packs up the car, just Lan's mum and dad, and my mum and dad, plus the rest of us kids, sitting in a row on the wall, watching from a safe distance in case there's more yelling.

The Guest Dad gets in his car and backs it up, and nearly hits the Last Remnants. Dad starts to say something, but

Mum shoves his arm. The Guest Dad starts driving out, but then, when he's at the gate, he stops and gets out again, leaving his door open. He storms up to Jim and Gail. His face is bright red. He's wearing a dark pink shirt and it nearly matches.

'Why didn't you tell us that barn was dangerous?' he shouts. '*Why isn't there a sign?*'

'We're so sorry,' says Gail about fifty times, but Jim doesn't say anything, not a single word.

The Guest carries on yelling – he's not insane-mad-crazy, more like he's in charge and *everyone* is a kid, or working for him, or a *really* scary teacher.

'This whole place is a *deathtrap*. You're lucky your *foul-mouthed, filthy* children haven't all been killed, or maimed. Not that you'd even *notice*.'

He meant *us*. All of us kids. We're foul-mouthed, filthy children. I stare at him. I think my mouth is open.

He spins round and goes back to his car, but then he thinks of something else.

'You should all be ashamed,' he says, much quieter, and it's even worse. '*What sort of a way to live is this?*'

He gestures at the houses. And us kids. Then he finally gets back in the car, and screeches out the gate, and away up Colin's hill.

We all just wait. Nobody says anything, not even our parents. We've never seen anybody yell like that Guest just yelled, or be so totally rude and insulting. The sheep are *baaing* away in Colin's fields, and the grown-ups are look-ing like they've been hit on the head. I don't know if it's funny or terrible. It's like being on weighing scales, waiting to see how to feel. That man screamed at *Jim*. Nobody screams at Jim except Gail. Jim takes a big breath and raises his shoulders and then relaxes again with a big *puff*.

'Well,' he says. 'The man makes a fair point. We do things our way.'

It's like popping a balloon. Mum bursts out laughing – and so do we. And I feel better. Dad sort of laughs, but a bit weirdly. He rubs his face with both hands and walks in a small circle.

'Charming,' he says.

But Gail walks away from Jim to the middle of the Yard. She puts her hands on her hips and looks at him. Jim looks back, peacefully. Her face looks like she's adding up numbers from very far away. Sort of cold. I've seen her look at Lan that way when we've been bad, and at Bill quite often. I'm glad my mum and dad don't ever look at me and Josh like that.

'My God,' she says, like Jim has let her down, like he's done something terrible. Then she goes into the Farmhouse.

After a second, Mum and Dad go into our house, and close the door, and Jim is left on his own.

When the Guest Dad shouted at him, he looked calm and like he was sort of *interested*, but not upset. Now he looks very sad. He notices us watching, all us kids, silent, in a row. He notices us, then looks quickly away, and then back. His face is normal and friendly.

'All right, kids?' he says. 'Not to worry.' Then he goes off, whistling.

Me, Lan, Josh, Bryn, Eden and Niah watch him go.

'We're sitting on the wall,' says Niah. 'Aren't we sitting on the wall?'

'*Ten green bockles! Sitting on the wall,*' sings Bryn. '*Ten green bockles! Sitting on the wall*—'

'*Six,*' says Eden. 'There's *six* of us.'

She takes Bryn's hand, and Josh's, and Josh takes mine. They sing and rock from side to side.

'*Six green bockles! Sitting on the wall,*' sings Bryn, and the others join in.

Niah's on the end on her own so Lan takes her hand, and then, giving me a *sorry about this* look, takes mine, so now we're all joined up. And we all sing.

Six green bottles! Sitting on the wall. And if one green bottle, should accidently fall . . .

15

Fannies, Arses, Poo and Blood

LAN

We're at secondary school in Ross now.

It's OK.

We nearly went to a brand-new school called a Steiner, but Mum and Adam think we need to be what they call *better equipped*. They keep saying we have to be *prepared for the future*. They make it sound like going to war. I'm trying to stop myself worrying so much, and I think I've worked out how: the future isn't real. The past is real, and now is real, but the future is just imaginary. I said it to Amy, and she agrees.

Secondary is like a big, old version of Martin's Business Park. There are a lot more kids, and we're a bit scared nearly all the time. And I hate getting lost so much. But Lily and Kyle are there, and none of the other kids beat us up, which was one of the things I was most worried about. After our first day, when we got home we went to play outside. We covered ourselves in mud, naked except for our pants and Amy's vest. The grown-ups kept saying, *how old are you?* because we were behaving like babies. We waited until the mud dried and cracked, then wet it with trough water and made slime, and hosed *that* off. And rolled in it. And afterwards, shivering in towels, we ate leftover pasta salad out of the dish.

The grown-ups are always asking us how school is going but there's nothing to say. We don't know. The minute we get home, I forget it. But I think I like home even more than I did. I really like being here. When I'm at school, when there's nothing to do, like in a lesson, I think about Frith. I imagine things like the dogs lying in their beds by the Rayburn. Or feeding the chickens. Or grooming Gabriella. She's going to have her calf any minute, and all she wants to do is be groomed, and lick the fence. She went off months ago with her passport to have sex with a bull called Rocky III. No one was there when they mated, but we saw Rocky III in the field before we left her there. He had tiny piggy eyes, and his chest and shoulders were so massive his legs looked tiny underneath. His coat was more red-brown than Gabriella's, and he had what Jim called *a lot of swagger about him.* Gabriella came back a couple of weeks later and we've been waiting ever since. If it's a boy, we'll have to castrate it, or eat it, so we all want it to be a heifer. Everyone's hoping she has it in half-term, and we've been counting the days. It feels like the longest autumn term we've ever had. Now half-term is finally here, and it's pouring with rain. Me and Amy are staring over the fence *checking for signs*, which is mostly trying to get a good look at her vulva. It used to be small and wrinkly but it's getting bigger every day, which means the calf is coming. We used to say *ewwww* – but we're over it now. I mean, I guess we got bored with *ew*. It's like what Harriet says: *life is full of fannies, arses, blood and poo.*

'Look,' says Amy.

There's a long shiny string of goo dangling from under Gabriella's tail, like clear snot, with pink blood in it. I lean in to check it, like a farmer.

'It's about the same as yesterday,' I say.

Gabriella lifts her tail again. We half expect to see the calf poking out, but she just does a huge fountain of poo.

'I think she should definitely come into the barn tonight,' I say. 'Let's ask.'

We've made some of Colin's sheep hurdles into a stall in the corner, and spread straw, so the calf won't smash its head when it comes out.

The rain is pattering and drumming on the ground and the roofs, and running down Gabriella's flanks, but she doesn't seem bothered by it. Then Adam yells from the back door –

'Kids! The Guests are here! Welcome hamper!'

'Shit!' says Amy. We'd forgotten Guests were coming.

The welcome hamper is our main job. We leave it on the IKEA table in Tumbledown, with flowers in a bottle. Mum's plan is that the Guests will love all our produce so much they'll buy more, and tell all their friends, and we'll be famous. Some of them do, but most of them don't buy anything. Sometimes they don't even go to the Spar, they just bring every single thing they're going to eat or drink with them in their cars. Ruby Wright said if we want more money, we should give the Guests breakfast, but Harriet said, *absolutely not, I am not cooking damn breakfast for them, cleaning the place is more than enough.*

We run up to the house and tell Adam about Gabriella's mucus, and grab the basket and splash over to Tumbledown.

'What's this?' says the female lady Guest, all smiley, when she opens the door to us.

The family are squashed inside, staring out at the rain. A giant dad and two boys, older than us. One looks like he's in Year Eleven, and the other is younger, huddled on the sofa under a blanket.

'Here's your welcome hamper,' says Amy. 'Bread, butter, jam, eggs, bacon, goat's cheese, milk and wine. And over *there* –' she does a big gesture, just like her dad, '– is a complimentary selection of Frith Farm Body Lotion, Shower Gel and Soap, made with essential oils. *Everything* is from Frith Farm. Except the milk and the butter – the wine. *That's* from the Spar. And Australia.'

The female lady Guest picks up the milk, and examines it like she's on an alien planet.

'Look, John, a glass bottle.'

'Our cow, Gabriella, is going to have her calf soon, and then we'll have milk of our own,' says Amy.

'Are there any more logs?' says the dad.

All the Tumbledown Guests are obsessed with the wood burner. They're cold all the time.

'Is this on?' says the lady Guest, touching the radiator.

We plug it in for her, and the younger boy jumps onto the back of the sofa and says –

'Cool.'

We take their log basket and splash off through puddles to the wood store, we climb up the woodpile and chuck logs at the basket from the top.

'If the grown-ups hadn't pulled down the Laceys' barns, Gabriella could have her calf in one of them, like on a proper farm,' says Amy.

'Or if *you* didn't live in the *Cow*house.'

'Or New Cottage, if Em wasn't there—'

'Or if Tumbledown wasn't a stupid *holiday let*—'

'*Oo-oh!*' shrieks Amy, in her posh-lady voice. '*Do come and stay on our organic smallholding!*'

We hadn't noticed the younger boy is there, standing just outside, watching.

'Need a hand?' he says.

He's got a jacket like the cool kids at school have, with the hood up. Me and Amy slide down off the log pile. I try and do it standing up like I'm on a skateboard but I fall and roll on my shoulder.

'It's kind of done,' I say, when I've got up.

Amy doesn't say anything.

'Luke's revising,' says the boy.

I wait for Amy to talk, like I always do, but she's just staring at the log basket, looking dumb.

'So have you got, like, loads of animals?' he says.

Amy still doesn't say anything, so after too long thinking about it, because I'm bad at talking to people, I say –

'Yeah. Wanna see?'

Out in the Yard, there's a huge, bright double rainbow, right above our heads.

'Wow,' says the boy. 'Look at that.'

Amy's acting like she's not with us. I've forgotten his name. I show him Gabriella, and Rose and Lily.

'Why have the sheep got *collars*?' he says.

'They're Amy's brother's.'

He laughs. 'OK.'

'He's learning to shear them.'

He nods.

'Cool. Is that the cow that's going to have a baby? She's fat.'

Normally, Amy doesn't shut up about Gabriella, but she just stares off down the valley.

After a while he says, *see ya*, and goes off back to Tumbledown.

What? I ask Amy.

What? she says. *Shut up.*

It's finally time. All us kids lead Gabriella in from the field, fighting over who gets to hold the rope, and Josh brings in Rose and Lily so she'll have company and not pine for the others. Gabriella has a dopey, calm look, and her tummy sways from side to side. The Guest Family stand outside Tumbledown, watching.

'Come and see!' says Mum. 'Gabriella doesn't mind, she loves people.'

She's always trying to include the Tumbledowners in things around Frith. She wants to inspire them to lead more fulfilling lives.

We spread out more straw and fill a water bucket, and break open a bale of Hay hay. Gabriella is swishing her tail and licking Eden's arm like it's a salt lick, over and over again.

'Wow, that is *gross*!' says the older boy, Luke, pointing.

Everyone stares at Gabriella's swollen vulva, and the stuff hanging out of it. I want to put a blanket over her so he can't see. She's not gross, she's a cow.

'It's *natural*, Luke, not gross,' says their mum, but she sounds really fake.

It's really easy to see when sheep are happy, and Rose and Lily are really happy to be in the barn with Gabriella because they love being around Josh. He's keeping watch, but it's been a whole day and a night and no calf yet. She's eating a lot, but she looks less fat. Harriet says it's because the calf has moved into position, nearly ready to come out.

'Do you think she's nervous?' I ask, leaning on the sheep pen, watching. My mum was nervous to have me, that's why she went to hospital.

'She doesn't look it,' says Amy.

On our way back to the house we hear the Guest Boys behind us.

'Hey, where can we get a signal?'

We stop and turn around. It's the younger one who asked. The other, Luke, is holding a phone and checking it.

'*Michael*,' he says, 'shut *up*.'

He's holding up his phone, and squinting. Guests always do that. They can't believe they can't make calls.

'Is that an iPhone?' I say, which is just a normal thing to ask.

'3GS,' says Michael.

Our mums just have Nokias, and Adam and Martin have Motorolas. There are some kids at our new school with iPhones. I'd like to see it.

'They've put a mast up now,' I say, 'but the hill blocks it.'

'You can come in the house,' mutters Amy. 'If you want, like, Wi-Fi.'

Luke laughs, for some reason.

'No thanks. We're fine.'

He laughs again. Probably at Amy, because she's being so weird. She doesn't normally talk like that, all quiet and grumpy-sounding. The two boys walk on, away from us, still staring at the phone. Amy blurts –

'Up the hill it's better!'

'Yeah?' says Luke. 'Where?'

Amy looks at the ground again. She's beginning to annoy me.

'Top of Colin's hill,' I say. 'This way.'

We walk out the front gate and up the lane. Amy's trailing along behind the three of us. She's walking funny – looking girlie, like Lulu Hodge or something – and I don't want them to think I'm with her.

'What's that stink?' says Luke.

'It's just, like, a general country shit smell,' says Michael. They laugh. I do too, but I can't smell anything.

'Yeah?' asks Michael, meaning, *is there a signal now?*

'Nah,' says Luke.

'Up there,' I say. 'Top of the hill.'

'*Roight, ta-ap of the hill, roight thurr, thankin' you koindly,*' says Luke.

He falls about laughing. I'm not sure if he's laughing at me. I don't talk like that – I don't think. I laugh along a bit, just to show them it's fine and I don't care. At school, I don't let people know anything I'm thinking, hardly ever. I've got pretty good at it.

'Hey, wanna see something?' says Michael.

'Sure,' I say.

'What?' says Amy.

'Oh, *man*,' says Luke, 'come *on*.'

The brothers go into a huddle and argue about it. Luke turns round, finally, and looks at us.

'Yeah, OK. *You* can see. But not her, she has to go back.'

The three of us boys look at Amy. I feel like one of them. She's waiting for me to stand up for her, but I don't. I pretend to be looking at something interesting in the other direction.

'I want to see,' she says.

'You don't even know what we're talking about,' says Luke.

'Nor does Lan,' says Amy.

'Yeah, but, y'know,' says Michael, and shrugs. Why doesn't she take the hint?

'God, this is so lame,' says Luke, and walks off, staring at the phone. He must think we're so young.

'People get email just there . . .' says Amy, pointing to Colin's metal gate. I nearly tell him that we think the metal helps the signal, like an aerial, but I don't want to risk being laughed at again.

Luke stands on the bottom rung, and holds the phone up, turning slowly. Some sheep look up from eating and stare at him.

'*Got* it – 3G.'

Michael squashes in next to him to look. We can only see their backs. They look like they've got a secret, like there's something really important, but I can't think what it could be. It's just a phone, and there's nobody around. It reminds me of the time me and Amy found that shotgun in the mud, by Bony-Eyes's fence. It was rusty and rotted and about fifty years old or something, so it wasn't dangerous, but we were just little kids so we were terrified going near it, and ran home to tell Jim. That's how the two brothers look, kind of scared and excited, like they've found a gun – or a bomb. Amy is trying to get my attention but I pretend she isn't there.

'Wait, wait . . .' says Luke. 'Wait . . . Oh, *fuck*.'

'No *way*!' says Michael, as he sees something.

'I told you, man.'

'Hey, Lan,' says Michael.

I'm surprised he's including me, and feel really proud suddenly, and I run up. Amy crowds in behind me, trying to get in on it.

'Shit,' says Luke.

They're laughing. I can only see Luke's hand and the edge of the iPhone. I glimpse the screen, but hardly. Michael laughs again. They both do.

'Dirty bitch,' says Luke.

'Here . . .' says Michael, and makes space for me.

It's video. The daylight is too bright to see very clearly. Then I do. Legs, and then what looks like an armpit. It's not an armpit. It's a woman's vulva – or a girl, I don't know, it hasn't got any hair on it. A hand with red-painted nails is rubbing it.

'Let me *see*,' says Amy, shoving.

The image freezes, but they let her look. I feel her jump when she sees it.

'Shit,' says Luke. 'Fuck this shit.'

We're all pushing each other. I'm trying to keep Amy out, but she won't go. I shove her – hard – and she shoves me back even harder. I won't look at her. The picture stays frozen. We all wait. Then there's a different hand, a man's hand, hitting a lady's breasts. A weird laugh comes out of me. They laugh as well. It's not funny.

'*Dirty fucking bitch*,' says Luke.

A woman's voice says – *no, no, no!* I feel a kick of guilt, and just – shock. Then Luke shoves Michael sideways into me, and I lose my balance, and stagger into Amy.

'See – told you,' says Luke. Suddenly he's sticking the phone back in his pocket, and walking off. 'Told you.'

Michael goes after him, and the brothers fall over together, and wrestle on the road. Luke has Michael in a headlock, shouting, *that's your lot, you dirty boy.* Me and Amy are just standing there. Luke rolls off suddenly, and leaps up.

'Oh my God! Gross, *gross*,' he says. He's got sheep poo on his sleeve. '*Fuck, it stinks.* This whole place stinks. It's everywhere, man, it's *rank.*'

The brothers run back down the lane. Now it's just us two again. Me and Amy. We don't say anything for a second. I feel so embarrassed I don't even know what to do. What's she doing here? Why won't she go? But she doesn't, it's like she just wants to stand around and talk about it. I hate it.

'Did you see?' she says. At least she's looking at the ground, not at me.

I don't know what to say to her, so I don't say anything. I just start walking back.

'We should tell,' she says.

'No!'

She follows me.

'*You better not*,' I say, and go faster to get away from her.

'Lan?' she says, as we walk. 'Lan?' but I ignore her, until finally she gets it, and stops talking.

That was yesterday. Today, everything's exactly the same. I mean it's still raining, and Gabriella still hasn't had her calf. Except it's not all exactly the same, because now I've seen that stuff on Luke's phone, and me and Amy aren't talking. I mean we aren't saying *anything*. It's weird, because we haven't had a fight. We hang out with the other kids, or else I'm by myself. And the grown-ups, whenever they see me on my own, are like, *where's Amy?* They always do that, whenever we're apart, even for a *second*, they go, *where's Amy?* I hate it. It's weird enough already, without the grown-ups making a big thing out of it.

The only nice thing is that the Guest Family will be leaving soon, because it's nearly the end of half-term. We had really wanted Gabriella to have her calf before we went back to school though. *None of us are going to school till the calf is born*, Eden tells Mum. *If you force us, it's against Child Protection.*

Amy, Josh, me and my sisters are on the floor of the Big Room watching *102 Dalmatians*, surrounded by dogs and drying racks of school clothes. We've got goat's curd in a bowl, and Rani's sourdough crusts. Bryn drops off asleep, her head hits the floor, and she wakes up and says *ow!* – deciding whether to cry. It's a really quiet moment in the movie and suddenly Finbar bangs on the glass, and makes us all yell. His haunted-looking face is peering in between his hands.

'*GABRIELLA*,' he mouths.

It's time.

'*Oh my God oh my God oh my God*,' says Eden.

We're all creeping up to the barn – all the adults and all the kids, with torches and lanterns, and Colin runs to meet us in a head torch. We called him the minute it started.

I notice Amy walking next to me.

'I don't want to wake *them*!' she says, nodding towards Tumbledown. It's the first thing she's said to me all day. I want to say *me neither* – but I don't say it immediately, so then I can't, and we're back to not talking.

Gabriella looks happy to see us, and the sheep do, too. We run up and give them strokes and pats. Gabriella's little curly wig-hair is fluffy from all the brushing she's been getting. I suddenly think about her going off to meet Rocky III and have sex with him. She seemed fine after she came home, but maybe it hadn't been any fun. Maybe it upset her. Then I think of all the chickens and goats, all the animals mating or trying to mate, all the time. They aren't mean about it, they don't seem upset. Maybe it's just humans who hurt each other when they do it. But it can't be, our parents did it. Which I don't want to think about either. I push it out of my mind. I decide I didn't see anything on that boy's phone, and I can't remember. It's fine. It just means home is a bit more like school now, with things to ignore and pretend about.

Everyone fetches bales to sit on, and brings blankets from the house, and they've got all the farming books, and pages off the internet.

'Get comfortable,' says Harriet. 'She might take a while.'

Gabriella is walking about, snatching at hay. Sometimes she looks at us, or does a small moo. Her flanks are heaving. Everyone's gathered round in a semi-circle with the sheep. We just need Mary and Joseph to walk in with the Inn Keeper. I nearly tell Amy.

'The calf is in the birth canal,' says Harriet.

The word canal makes me picture the calf sitting on a barge.

'Like on a barge,' says Amy.

'That's what I was going to say!' I say. 'It's like a Nativity Play.'

'Yeah,' she says, 'where's Virgin Mary?'

And things are fine again. Like it never happened. With me and her, anyway. I stand there smiling for no reason, not even at Amy, just because I'm so relieved.

'Does she mind being watched by us?' asks Eden.

'No,' says Mum, 'we're like doulas.'

'What's doulas?'

'Like midwives.'

'Stupid,' says Bill.

'It's not stupid,' says Mum, 'it's from Hindi.'

'Nope,' says Harriet. 'Rani?'

'It is. It's a Hindi word,' says Mum.

'Christ, Gail, it's not Hindi – the Americans came up with it in the *fucking eighties*.'

'It's not Hindi, Gail,' says Rani.

'*See?*'

'*SHH!*' says Eden. 'Stop squabbling when Gabriella's giving birth!'

We've waited so long for the calf, but we still aren't ready when we see a semi-transparent white bulge coming out of Gabriella. It's small at first, but then it swells. Inside it we can see a hoof.

'Oh,' says Amy.

Gabriella's munching her Hay hay like she hasn't noticed. She doesn't look like a calf at all any more, she's a proper grown-up cow. I don't know when she changed, we didn't really notice.

'How can she eat?' said Amy. 'With a hoof coming out her arse?'

'Vagina,' say Harriet and Mum.

'You said it was a vulva,' says Bill.

'Come on, children,' says Harriet, 'you know this stuff.'

'You said it was her birth canal,' says Bryn.

'It's coming down her birth canal, through her vagina, and appearing at her vulva,' says Harriet.

'Appearing?' says Eden.

'Arriving.'

'What about her labia?' says Bryn.

'Bloody hell,' says Harriet. 'Fine. *Arse.* It's coming out of her arse. Happy now?'

'Well, they're certainly getting an education,' says the Guest Mum.

We all turn round. Luke and Michael are with her.

'My boys have never seen anything like this,' she says.

'Come watch,' says Mum.

Me and Amy climb over the hurdles to the other side of Gabriella, to be closest to her and furthest from them.

The three of them sit on a bale, and everyone else shifts about and makes space. Gabriella moos three times, loudly, like she want us all to settle down.

'SHH!' says Eden.

Gabriella's stopped eating. The gleaming bulge grows, then stays the same size for hours. Gabriella walks around, and occasionally turns to look at her tummy. Someone hands us a thermos of tea. Niah wakes up and says, *is it out yet?* and falls back asleep. Gabriella does mountains and fountains of poo, and we clear it away, and put down fresh straw. I hear one of the boys whisper – *that's disgusting.*

Mum climbs into the sheep pen with us, and sprays Gabriella's vulva with something she's made – chamomile or tea tree or something – and lays on her hands, and hums to her. The sticking-out bit gets bigger, and bigger. *This is good*, says Colin. *This is moving along fine.*

'I can't stand it,' says Finbar, and leaves.

Gabriella's front legs wobble, and with a groan she lowers herself onto the straw. She looks at us. *Clever girl*, we say. *What a beauty.* The fresh smell of Finbar's Woodbine comes floating in from outside in the darkness where he's waiting. Niah's woken up again, mumbling. Jim says, *not yet, darling.* I stare into Gabriella's eyes. She gives me a long wet lick on the back of my hand. The white, thick bag bulges and then, like an overfull balloon, pops, and a torrent of water gushes onto the straw.

'*Gross*,' says Michael, loudly.

'You just shut up!' snaps Amy, glaring. 'QUIET.'

We see two hooves through the thick white bag, then it tears. *Good*, says Colin. *That's good.* We've never liked his boringness so much. The tiny hooves are cream-coloured, and the hair above them is slick, and white. My heart is thumping hard. Gabriella's white tummy is heaving, her vulva in a tube, snug around the pair of hooves. Amazingly, she eats some hay. The two sheep are nose to tail, staring and chewing in their matching collars. I don't think they're interested.

'I'm knackered,' says Luke. 'I'm going in.'

'Oh, Luke, stay . . .' says his mum.

Me and Amy exchange looks. We don't care. He doesn't even matter. Gabriella lays her head flat on the ground, and rolls her eyes, and moos again. She sighs. She heaves.

Harriet climbs into the pen, kneeling next to Mum.

'Look, milk,' says Josh.

Gabriella's udders are dripping.

'Ouch,' say Harriet and Mum together, and they both laugh.

'There, girl . . . there, girl,' says Mum.

Each heaving push lifts Gabriella's back end up from the straw. Her back legs jerk, the tiny hooves ease further out. Fetlocks. Brown knees. She grips and squeezes, relaxes, and heaves.

'A nose!' says Eden. 'A head!'

The head is between the hooves. Gabriella lifts her head and rolls her eyes, so for a second she looks like she's having a fit, or is dead.

Nothing's happening. I'm scared. I can hear the grown-ups whispering. Mum and Harriet look at each other.

Gabriella gazes far away into the night, then, slowly, up at us.

'Can you stop taking pictures, Adam?' says Harriet in a super-calm voice. 'I'm going to kill you.'

'It's a record,' says Adam. 'It matters.'

We stroke Gabriella's face, and pull her ears. Most of her calf is still inside her.

'She OK?' says Finbar, coming back, then he goes again.

Gabriella is pushing. Her tail flops, uselessly. Low voices. Pages turning. Minutes. *Twenty minutes.* Ages.

'Vet?' says Adam.

Gabriella's breathing fast. *It's all right, Gabriella,* I whisper in her ear. She heaves, she pushes.

'Ears out,' says Amy.

The circle of people closes in.

'Finbar! You're missing it!' screams Eden.

'Quiet!' says Harriet.

'Is it dead?' says Josh. He's a worrier, like I am.

Gabriella's breath puffs against my hand.

I stand to get a better look. It's half out now, wet and smooth, not like a calf, more a snail, a slug. *Colin?* says Harriet. *Leave her be,* says Colin.

Gabriella groans. She sounds so tired. Then she seems to wake up. I hear a slither, and then a rustling, landing sound. There's a smell, the wettest smell I've ever known, wetter than blood, not like water.

'Its ears went flap!' says Josh.

Look!

Oh my God.

There, it's out!

Is it a girl?

A heifer?

Is it breathing?

'Is she going to eat it?' says Bryn. 'Like Pickles?' Pickles was a hen we found smothered in the bloody yolks of her own eggs, she was a psycho.

The two sheep have come to look, staring through the

gaps in the hurdles like they're watching TV. The calf lies slack and still, just skin on bones, half in, half out of the membrane bag, and that smell, rising in a mist. Gabriella is lying down flat. Harriet quickly rubs its side and wipes its muzzle. Gabriella lifts her head and moos. The calf sucks in air and moos back, a tiny sound. Amy is trembling next to me, her shoulder squashing mine.

'Back,' says Harriet. We take a step, and bump against the sheep hurdle.

Gabriella shakes her head, and pulls herself together. She gets her front legs up, and stands. A bit dizzy, she shuffles round.

'She can't see it,' says Josh. '*Mum?*'

'She's fine, she'll smell it. It's a little heifer.'

A heifer. We can keep her *forever*.

Em is collapsed in Colin's arms – *Colin's!* – and crying. Adam's crying as well, and smiling. Niah's asleep again.

'Mum, wake her up, she'll miss it,' I say. 'Niah!'

Mum doesn't hear, but Jim shakes Niah's shoulder. Out the blurry corner of my eye, I see Michael and his mum, but I don't look properly. Gabriella is a mother. She is a *mother* cow, suddenly. She pushes and licks the calf, swiping her tongue over its body, nagging. The calf moves its legs, like swimming. It's not slimy now, it's just damp, and already tufty.

'So?' says Finbar, reappearing. 'Christ, just tell me, did it live?'

Bryn grabs his hand and pulls him to the sheep hurdles. 'See?'

'Oh, yes,' he says. 'All four legs. One head. That's grand.'

'And she's nearly standing up,' says Eden.

The tiny heifer is blindly trying to get her legs under her. Amy says, *she has a white face!* It's small and dished, like Gabriella's, when she first came. The muzzle is no more than a snout.

'That's altogether too much humanity for me,' says Finbar. 'And the little thing's not even human.'

Her splayed back legs push up, but her front end is still floppy. She falls. She tries again. Every time she falls, Gabriella nags her. It stops feeling like life or death. We even laugh. At last, she's up.

'We've got a calf!' says Harriet, smiling like crazy.

Jim kisses Niah, all over her face.

Then he hugs me.

And the girls.

And then Mum.

'Love,' he says, taking both her hands and kissing them. 'Love.'

The calf falls on her nose again, but then she's up, and looking for food. Gabriella shuffles about, trying to put her udders in the right place for the tiny snout. Adjusting into just the right position.

'It looks like the moon landing,' says Bill.

'Well,' says the Guest Mother, and everyone turns around.

'Goodnight, and thank you. That was . . . amazing.'

'See ya,' says Michael, and smiles at me and Amy. Just like a kid. Just like anyone. Happy.

'See ya,' I say.

'Bye,' says Amy.

They go off together. He's letting his mum keep her arm round him.

We don't see them when they leave the next day, we're with Gabriella. Hours can go by, watching a cow and her calf.

I have a bath on my own, without Josh. Amy and me stopped sharing baths a while ago. When I take off my clothes, they're thick with mud. The water's hot for once, and I duck under. There's mud in my hair. On my neck. It's even fun doing the soap. Did I wash yesterday? The day before? It's half-term mud. Tomorrow will be a very clean Monday. School corridors, with that shine on them. And the smell. I climb out, tired, and pull the plug, and watch the cow poo and mud, and whatever else half-term has left on me, swirl and float and disappear down the drain, leaving grit. And dry myself. And get pyjamas on. I hope nobody mentions homework. I did have some, but I can't remember what it was. I haven't done it. They probably won't ask, they don't usually.

I hear them all downstairs and I go down to look. The girls are ready for bed already, but everyone's standing around the Big Room, including all the parents, and Adam is taping a notice to the Snug door with gaffer tape.

COMPUTER ROOM

'New rule,' says Harriet. 'Computers in here. Only in here.'

The girls start moaning about *child protection* and Bill's yelling about his freedom, but they hardly ever even *use* the computer.

'That means Guests, us, everyone,' says Adam. 'And it includes smartphones. They can leave them here, and use them in here, if they need to.'

Until he said 'smartphones', I wasn't sure, but now I know. I feel my face go hot. I would run out of the room, but then everyone will look at me. Do they all know?

'Won't the Guests mind?' asks Eden.

Adam mimes pointing at a big, lit-up sign.

'Frith Farm is a tech-free environment,' he says. 'It can be our USP.'

'If you need the laptop, ask,' says Mum. She smiles at me, kindly.

I stare at the floor.

'You will talk to us, if you need to?' says Jim. 'You know you can?'

I want him to stop going on about it.

The little kids have lost interest.

'OK, fine, I don't care,' says Eden.

They all start wandering off, going, *boring! Can we go see Angel Rocket?*

Angel Rocket. That's the calf. She's perfect.

'Yeah,' I say, 'let's go.'

'It's nobody's fault,' says Jim. 'Nobody's done anything wrong. We just want to keep you safe.'

Safe. I remember that first Guest Dad, after the kid fell down the hole in the haystack, yelling at Jim – *this place is a deathtrap!* I nearly laugh, but I can't yet. I suppose I might think it's funny later, but I don't think so.

16

Angel Rocket Starry Skies

AMY

We called the calf Angel Rocket Starry Skies, but maybe the name is too big for her, she's very small and weak. She isn't eating, and she's not standing up nearly as much as she was two days ago. Gabriella pushes her, bossily, with her nose, and licks her all over, but she seems sleepy. If we can't make her eat then she won't get stronger, and her legs are really wobbly. She pushes at Gabriella's udders, but not *hungrily*, like Gabriella used to when *she* was new. She was so strong. You'd think she would have made a strong calf.

We ran into school the first day after she was born, because we were so excited to see her afterwards – we felt like if we ran we'd get home quicker. Coming home after school the first day and probably the second, we were happy, but now – I think it's three days – we're just more and more worried. Angel Rocket's poo isn't right, she's got diarrhoea, and it's *stinky*. The grown-ups are scared it's *scours*, and if it is scours, what kind. They're reading everything they can about it, and they even called Bony-Eyes. I hope they understand better than us.

Me and Lan aren't allowed inside the sheep pen, because of salmonella and E. coli, so we sit just outside it on bales. And they took Rose and Lily out, and put them in their own electric, separate from the goats. Everyone's walking around scared of germs. They've put buckets of hot water with bleach, and we have to dip our boots and wash our hands the whole time. She's just a *calf*, she hasn't got a *plague*. I guess the grown-ups don't know what else to do.

I'm sitting with Lan as close as we're allowed, looking at Gabriella and Angel Rocket, and there's a strong smell of disinfectant and poo. Mum and Gail are arguing outside the barn. They think we can't hear them, but the barn is open all down one side and the walls are just gappy planks. I wish they'd talk more quietly, they're scaring Gabriella. They're not screaming or anything, but they're not bothering to whisper either. Mum's calling Gail *ignorant*, because she doesn't want to call the vet.

'Well, Harriet, you can do what you like with your goats,' says Gail. 'Give them all the drugs you want—'

'You *know* I don't,' says Mum, 'that's not fair—'

Martin comes in. He's still in his suit, which he normally isn't around the farm, with the trousers tucked into boots, looking silly. He must be just back from work. Me and Lan didn't go in to school again and I don't know what time it is.

'Kids,' he says, 'how's the patient?'

Mum and Gail come in, and stand with their arms crossed, looking furious, like Lan's sisters when they've had a fight. I want to say, *don't be stupid, make friends*, like I do to Eden and Bryn. I hate when Gail and Mum fight.

They shouldn't fight, they're best and oldest friends, it makes everything feel wobbly.

'I brought the electrolytes back from Evans,' says Martin, and hands Mum a paper bag. He crouches down, takes one look at Angel Rocket, and says, 'We need to call the vet.'

'Martin, you said we don't have the money,' says Gail.

Martin stands up.

'There are more important things than money.'

Martin not minding about the money makes it worse, not better.

'I'll call them now,' says Mum.

'Wait, we haven't all agreed,' says Gail.

Mum stops.

'If she needs antibiotics, then she does,' she says.

'Calcarea works,' says Gail.

'Calcarea was *preventative*,' says Mum, for the *fifty millionth* time. She's being so *patient*. She's not even this patient with me and Josh. 'It's not working now.'

'I've only just started her on the Arsenicum,' Gail says. 'I think we should wait.'

And they start up again. Mum is calm, and Gail is stubborn, but they just say the same things, over and over again. I do an impression of Gail in my head, like Lulu Hodge, a little squeaky voice, like *I think the Calcarea is working, I'm trying the Arsenicum* ... Then Mum loses it.

'Gail! This is all *fine* but this animal is *dying*! And you're only worried about your ego and your *bullshit* therapies.'

Then Dad comes into the barn. He's only heard the last part – Mum yelling at Gail.

'Harriet,' he says, 'there's no need to attack Gail.'

It's not fair of him. Martin knows it isn't, but he's staying out of it.

'It's not *bullshit*, Harriet,' says Gail. 'It's *science*.'

I feel kind of fascinated. She's as calm as a deaf chicken. Maybe she *likes* fighting with Mum.

'It's not *actual* science, is it, though, Gail?' says Mum, sounding all vicious and ugly in front of Dad. She's not being fair either, Gail's homeopathy does work loads, even on the animals, even if I don't like admitting it.

'Gail's potions work a lot of the time,' says Dad, like he's reading my mind.

He takes our mums' hands, one each.

'Girls,' he says. 'Let's be friends.'

I think Mum's head is going to explode. She takes her hand away.

'We're *not* girls. And that was *not* OK,' she says, and walks off.

'I'll call the vet and let you know,' she shouts over her shoulder.

Martin follows her saying something about bottle-feeding. We thought we'd try it, like Mum's done with the goats sometimes. We've still got Gabriella's old bottle.

I think Dad and Gail have forgotten we're there.

'Are you all right, Gail?' says Dad, in a sort of teacher voice, not like he knows her very well. He's not standing anywhere near her.

'Fine, thank you, Adam,' says Gail. 'Remember what we said? Always other people around.'

She walks out really fast. I nearly say *what was that*

about? to Lan, but I decide not to. It's just boring grown-up stuff. Me and Lan don't want to think about it.

The vet can't come until tomorrow. It's night-time now, and the dark feels much *more* dark than usual, because of waiting, and the night seems like the longest thing in the world. We've funnelled Gabriella's milk into a lambing bottle from a bucket. We keep having to milk her, because Gabriella's producing so much, but then we chuck most of it away. Her udders are massive. I think of Mum saying *ouch*. They do look like they hurt.

'Should we milk her again?' I ask.

'Later. The more we milk, the more she'll produce. It's a balance. Don't touch your face. Wash your hands after.'

We don't know anything about breeding cows. We're not proper farmers. We don't know anything about pathogens, or viruses, or parasites. I gently put the bottle teat into the calf's mouth, and count each swallow. She doesn't suck very hard, not like Gabriella used to. Lan is stroking her throat to help it go down, but a lot of the milk runs out and just falls onto the straw.

'Maybe we should tube-feed her,' says Mum.

Rani and Jim have come to look. The grown-ups are keeping the little kids away, taking turns looking after them and coming to check on the cows. I bet it's nice in the Carthouse, watching TV, and being like five years old and not knowing what's going on.

'How's it going?' says Rani.

Fine, me and Lan both say. We're trying to make Angel Rocket feed and Mum is cleaning. I've got my finger on the measuring line on the bottle. The calf gives up. Her throat sort of – fails. The straw is all wet with milk. I try to get the teat back in but it won't go.

'All right, honey, stop now,' says Mum.

'A hundred and sixty mil,' I say. 'Better than last time.' I feel like I'm trying to convince the grown-ups.

Rani kneels on the straw.

'Oh my darlings, I'm so sorry.' She hugs us. 'Whatever happens, you've done your best.'

Jim puts him arms around Lan, and Lan leans back on him, against his jacket and squeezes his eyes shut but tears come out anyway.

'Life and death, eh, little boy,' says Jim, softly. 'Life, death and love.'

I don't know where Dad is. Mum says he's too upset to look at Angel Rocket, but when she's asleep she looks so peaceful and pretty. Gabriella has laid her head right next to hers, I think so that when she breathes her calf will feel it.

The vet came. She said how clean the farm is, and we did feel really proud about that, and less like it must be our fault. She examined the calf and took samples. She said it wasn't a virus, and it wasn't a parasite. Angel Rocket was just weak. It *was* scours, but not the kind of scours she could treat. There wasn't anything we could do to help.

Anyway.

She said a lot of things, but Angel Rocket died on Saturday, exactly a week after she was born. By then, Gabriella had given up trying to make her get up. She still stood over her, protecting her, and then started mooing. Jim took the dead calf away after a while, but she *still* kept mooing, and she hasn't stopped.

We're burying the calf way down at the bottom of the hill, by the woods. Mum says it's against the law, and *nobody must know*. It took Finbar and Jim hours to dig the grave, so deep nobody will find her for years, or ever.

The little dead calf is on the trailer, under a tarp. They said me and Lan could stay if we wanted – it's not like we *want* to, but we feel like we *should*. The grave is big and gaping and scary. Gabriella is still crying, we can hear her, even from here. Mooing and mooing from her field. All the way up the hill, like the sound she made when we left her alone for the first time.

It only takes one person to pick up Angel Rocket, even me or Lan could do it. Mum carries her over, and drops her in. I think it must hurt to be dropped, but then I remember she's dead, she can't feel it, and I start crying. They shovel all the earth in on top of her. It makes a high, black, loose-looking heap. Finbar and Jim hit it with the backs of their spades, and nobody says anything.

Finbar walks away up the hill, but the rest of us stay. All the grown-ups stand in a line, and we do, too. Gail is too upset to do any speeches or chanting. Jim hugs her and she buries her face in his chest.

'We do our best,' he says. 'We all do our very best.'

I wish Gabriella would stop calling. We walk back up the hill in silence, towards the sound of Gabriella's crying.

17

Pigs

LAN

Me and Amy are meant to be herding pigs, but nobody's here yet, so we're building a dam in the stream in the woods. We haven't done that for ages. It feels like we're playing at being young kids again. I like it. It's better being a stupid young kid than lots of things. Angel Rocket being dead, and secondary school. Phones. And all the fighting. Things like that.

I've always hated cold water, so Amy's in it, and I'm handing her sticks and rocks. There's woodsmoke on the air now it's nearly winter, and the smell of leaf mould, and the stone-smell of the stream. Yellow leaves float, slowly before the dam, then swooping off after, into the woods. We can hear the pigs crashing about in the holly and brambles. Frith pigs live as wild as pigs can live, once they're out in the woods. Nobody sees much of them, but we've got used to the sound of them crashing about in the bushes, rustling and rummaging. *It sounds like they're clearing out a road or something,* says Amy, knee-deep in freezing water,

streaked with mud. *Or, like, building houses out of sticks.*
She squashes stones and mud into our dam, and pushes
back her hair. *There could be like a whole pig village in
there. With shops.* I think she knows we're playing at being
young kids, too.

We hear the Lada coming, the trailer bouncing behind. I
can tell Adam's driving because it's coming down the hill
fast. *That's your dad,* I say.

The dam reaches halfway across the stream. It's pretty
impressive. There's no way *actual* little kids could do it.
The water runs faster as it goes round it and debris bumps
up against the barrier. *Good engineering,* I say. We're not
supposed to mess about too much with the stream in case
we change the course. It's fine. Whatever we do, me and
Amy can't make a real difference. There were minnows
and water boatmen and dragonflies in the summer. The
grown-ups used to talk about getting trout in it, but they
don't so much now. We hear the Lada brake and skid and
two doors slam shut.

Amy comes out of the water swearing at how cold it is
and hopping about. The bank is slippery with slimy roots,
and I help pull her out, then she takes her T-shirt off to dry
her legs, and I look into the trees, pretending I see something interesting. That's what we do now, since about the
time we stopped sharing baths. My mum's always wanting
to have *open and honest chats* with me about things like
growing up and *changes,* but me and Amy know what's
private and what isn't, and all about that stuff. I don't need
to talk to my *mum* about it.

Poor little pigs, says Amy. The grown-ups have come

down to chase them out into an enclosure in the Baldy Wild, so they're easy to catch when they take them off to slaughter. She's got her T-shirt back on now, and her muddy trainers, so we go out to meet the Lada.

It's only Adam and my mum. We see them through the trees, walking together. When they see us, they stop, and Adam does a big wave, like he's amazingly happy and relieved to see us. He's such a fake.

'Season of mists and mellow fruitfulness!' he shouts.

Mum holds both her arms up in the air, like she always does when she's about to talk about nature.

'What a day!' she says 'What light!'

'Any sign of the pigs?' said Adam.

'No,' says Amy. 'We can hear them, though.'

'The others are on their way,' says Adam. 'Give us a hand.'

We pull up the white plastic electric poles from along the treeline, and lay them out in the open of the Baldy Wild. The netting between them lies loose, on the bumpy ground.

We can't hear the pigs now, maybe they can sense something's up. There's ten acres of our woods, so they could be anywhere. The idea is to go right to the back and form a line, and drive the pigs ahead. Everyone else is coming down the hill, the grown-ups and kids fanning out. It looks like such a crowd when we're all together. I sometimes forget there's so many of us. I think it's everyone. I squint up the hill. Except Em. Then I spot her – she's at the back with Niah.

It looks like proper reinforcements, says Amy, which is just what I was thinking.

We walk into the woods, and all start out together at the back boundary, by the stone wall with the footpath on the other side. As we walk, we spread out and the trees come between us. Me and Amy are together – I catch sight of Josh's hair as he walks into a patch of sunlight, holding Jim's hand. Everyone else is out of sight, just the sounds of voices and twigs breaking. Sometimes we hear Eden laughing, and Em and Niah, yapping away at each other. Niah's gone from never speaking to never stopping. Her teacher in Reception tried to call Mum in about it, but Mum didn't bother going.

'I heard Niah call Em "Mum",' says Amy. 'And your actual mum was in the room!'

We both laugh, but I don't think it's funny. Mum doesn't even *mind*. She doesn't care. Maybe that's why I do. Mum says, *love isn't ownership*, but if it isn't, what's it for?

There's still lots of midges and my neck is itchy and stinging where I've scratched it.

We've all got sticks, to beat with.

'A deer!' says Amy.

We see the flick of tail, back legs, and it's gone.

Don't make too much noise, says Harriet's voice, sounding miles away. We can't see her, it's like a ghost has spoken.

We can hear Bill stamping and shouting.

We're in a police line! Eden shouts. *Look out for clues!*

Shouts. Hisses. People saying *shush* to scare the pigs out. Woods all around us. And above. And dampness in the air.

We fight our way through brambles. There are clouds of midges in the beams of sunlight. With the dry leaves and brambles, our feet are so loud, you can't hear anything but our crashing, louder than the pigs. I say –

Stop . . .

And we wait. Noticing every spiderweb, every leaf. The rabbit holes at the bottom of trees.

Away to the left, Finbar shouts, *here's two – there are two here!*

There's blundering, and an *oink*. That side of the hunting party sound as if they're moving forward, we hear more shouts.

Jim calls, *anything?*

No!

Nor here!

'Remember Ellis, Wallace and Gary?' says Amy.

Ellis, Wallace and Gary were our first-year pigs. They followed the stream along, broke out through the gappy wall, and got all the way into the village. When one of them walked into the Spar, Leslie Robinson got on the phone to us up at Frith – *small black pig just looked in the door of my shop. Yours, by any chance?* Me, Amy, Finbar, Adam and Jim chased them all round the village, and eventually cornered them against Racist Rick's garage, but not before they wrecked his posh front garden, and shat all round his car.

We're laughing about it.

After Ellis, Wallace and Gary, Josh said, *no sausages, please,* and he's never had one since. He doesn't even eat bacon – or chicken. Amy says, *Josh is an actual vegetarian, except he doesn't go on about it.* He eats a lot of eggs. I don't eat the pigs either – except sausages. And I do eat bacon, because I can't resist it, it's smoked by a friend of

Jack and Joffrey's. But I don't eat chops, usually. Amy says I'm a hypocrite, but Jim says I'm *working things out*. Amy doesn't eat any meat at school, but she does at home, because it doesn't have hooves in, or stress chemicals, and like Martin says, the animals live better than we do.

The pigs aren't dirty at all, they're friendly, and curious, and into everything. Last year, we hung around Long Field with them loads. We watched them wallow in the shallow pond the grown-ups dug for them, and watched how their big, flopping ears shaded their eyes, and flicked the flies away. We saw them scratch the others' backs, and take naps together. Then, in the autumn, the Trailer of Death was put in the field for them to get used to. They were massively big by then. We watched them having fun running up into the trailer, and out again, looking for food. They loved it in there, and we felt so bad. When Martin and Dad closed the ramp on them for the last time, they made surprised sounds inside. Jim drove the Lada into the field, and hitched it up, and I got it in my head the pigs could read our minds and *knew* we were taking them to be killed. I tried to think innocent thoughts, to fool them, but I could only picture them being herded off the ramp the other end, and being stunned with the electric gun. The trailer was rocking as it left, because they were barging and squealing inside. I'm not watching this year.

The sound of the other herders has faded. We feel like we're alone.

We've reached the tall beeches; no undergrowth, just deep dry leaves on the ground, and the sound of a woodpecker, knocking on a tree.

'I don't want to be in the woods any more,' I say. 'I hate it.'

We run past the beeches, and then holly and oak trees, and out into the Baldy Wild, where the earth is cloddy and sprouted with thistles.

Angel Rocket's black heap of a grave is right in front of us, and we stop. It's started to grow grass on it, but it's still mostly earth.

'I didn't realise we were so far along.'

'Nor me,' says Amy.

We stand by it. Not wanting to. I think of how decomposed the calf's body might be. It's so far down. I've only seen rotten birds. We haven't visited Angel Rocket's grave – except once. Neither of us like it here. Without saying anything else, we walk away. We haven't talked about what happened, except just after, when Amy was upset and blamed my mum. I know she still does, but it wasn't Mum's fault. Angel Rocket. It was nature.

When the grave is far enough behind us, we stop and sit on the trunk of a fir that's been felled for wood, kicking logs over to see the beetles scatter, and looking at the blood-beads where the holly pricked us drying on our arms. There isn't any sun now.

'Maybe they've got the third pig already,' I say.

A hummingbird moth wobbles with the weight of itself near some yellow flowers.

'It *should* be a bird,' says Amy. 'I mean, it's *weird*.'

We're staring at it when we hear a clatter.

'Is that the trailer ramp?'

We go towards the sound. The fence netting is still lying

on the ground. Adam and Mum were meant to put it up, and we can't even see them, but Harriet is standing there, doing nothing.

'Mum! We need to get the fence up!' shouts Amy.

Harriet doesn't answer, staring at something we can't see. The woods are sticking out, there are trees in the way. We carry on towards her, round the bend, until we can see what she's staring at – it's Adam and my mum. They're not doing anything, they're just staring back at Harriet. Harriet's body looks braced, like it's a very windy day, but it isn't, there's no wind at all.

Two of the pigs come trotting out of the treeline, and the third one is just behind. Adam, Harriet and Mum don't move.

'MUM!' yells Amy.

The pigs are massive after a whole summer getting fat, they don't look like the same pigs, not cute at all. Frightening, if you get too close. They're big enough to trample a grown-up. We've nearly been knocked over before, when they want food. The three massive pigs jog happily past Harriet and out into the Wild, where the fence is still just lying uselessly on the ground. After all that planning.

'Weren't Dad and Gail meant to be doing it?' says Amy.

She looks at me. And I see her face change. She's heard herself say *Dad and Gail*, and realised how it sounds.

I think, *if neither of us says anything about it, it will be OK*, and say, 'They are doing it now.' Or something. I don't know what.

Harriet is still just standing there, but my mum and Adam are running fast as they can in a panic, up and down, sticking the poles into the ground, and tripping over. It should be funny, watching them fumbling around in case the pigs realise they can just run off, up the hill.

'Give us a hand!' yells Adam. He jabs a pole in, and Mum runs to help, then changes her mind and runs back, slips on the mud and falls flat on her back – whump – in the mud.

Harriet doesn't move. She watches Mum scramble up. The beaters come out of the trees in different places, some excited, some slow and tired. Gradually, they realise there's no fence to shut the pigs into.

'Shut the gap!' shouts Bill. 'Adam! *Shut it!*'

Martin does his weird short-stepped run to go help. He always runs like he's scared of falling over.

'It's fine,' says Amy, in a dead-flat voice, 'the pigs are only interested in eating.'

It's true, the pigs are halfway up the trailer ramp, eating turnips. They haven't even realised they could run to freedom.

Mum looks upset, she's all covered in mud from falling over, and nobody's gone to see if she's OK. Adam is bashing a pole in with a rock, but it's bendy so the rock is slipping off and keeps hitting his hand. Jim goes to Mum and helps brush her off, just like the way he does to me and the girls when we fall over. Mum pushes his hands away.

'I'm fine!' she snaps.

'Let's get these in, shall we?' says Jim. Everyone's watching. He acts like she hasn't been rude. He always does that.

I notice Harriet, quite far away up the hill. I hadn't realised she'd gone.

'Do you want to go up with your mum?' I ask Amy.

'No, it's OK,' says Amy, and pushes up her sleeves. 'Let's finish helping.'

Once the fence is up and switched back on, we all start for home. Adam takes the Lada with Niah and Em, and the rest of us walk back up the hill, together and apart.

Ahead of us up the track, Jim is walking along with Josh. Josh is chatting, and Jim has his head bent towards him in that way he always does with us, like he's hanging on every word Josh is saying. He always made me feel like that, too, even when I was very little.

Mum should be with Jim, but she isn't. Nor are any of the grown-ups. I look at him, walking along with Josh, pretending to be interested, and his kindness doesn't seem strong to me, like it always has. Not bigger, or above the mess of ordinary things. It seems like being weak.

The pigs will be taken off to slaughter while me and Amy are at school, so we don't have to see.

18

Rare and Precious

AMY

The grown-ups don't even *notice* when me and Lan steal the Lada.

If they hear it, they'll think it's the Hodges, says Lan, *and it's dark, they won't see us.*

I can only drive when it's in first gear, but that's OK if I go slowly, and we've already put the stuff in the back, wrapped in a blanket, but first we have to unhitch the flat-bed trailer.

We crouch over the tow bar, whispering. I'm so scared and excited I'm boiling over, but Lan's gone all serious, like Jim. It's not even funny but it's so hard not to laugh my eyes are watering. We can hear the Western galloping music from *Spirit* coming from the Big Room where the other kids are watching TV – it must be so loud in there. The Farmhouse kitchen window, where the grown-ups are fighting, is so close I start giggling again and I nearly pee myself, and have to sit on my heel and shut my eyes while Lan gets the handle loose.

Amy! he hisses. I get a grip and help him, and we crank it, squeaking, till the trailer is clear and then get in the Lada – but we don't slam the doors.

I hold my breath and we both keep our eyes on the houses as I turn the key. It starts first time, with a cough, and sits, grumbling.

Careful! says Lan as I take my foot off the clutch pedal. I don't stall it. The Lada jerks forward, but I'm ready. We lurch towards the corner of the house.

Turn! goes Lan, and makes a grab for the wheel.

Get off!

We inch forwards, feeling every rut and puddle. The Lada creeps round the side of the Farmhouse. We're not near the trough, so that's OK, but it's too dark to see exactly where Mum's flower bed is. If we drive over it, she'll kill us. We can *just* see the track, because light from the houses is shining on it a bit.

Careful! goes Lan again.

I am! Shut up!

My door is swinging open because I can't grab the handle and drive at the same time. Lan's holding his with both hands.

We're halfway across the Yard. The Lada engine is so noisy, and the squeaks it makes on the bumps sound like screaming in the quiet night. With the houses all around, where anyone could look out and see us, it's almost less scary, because there's nothing we can do – just bobbing along in the Lada, me and Lan, eleven o'clock on a school night. I start smiling. I don't care. I hate them. We check out the Carthouse as we roll by. They've got the curtains closed, glowing from the light behind. The won't see us unless they come out for wood or something.

Slowly, we roll past Finbar's, and New Cottage, into the pitch-black. It closes round us like a curtain. The Yard near the houses isn't dark like this is. The moon isn't even up yet, I can't see a thing.

Where's the gate? I whisper. We can't see it, or the wall, or anything. *Shine the torch!*

Black-velvet darkness, woodsmoke and wet grass, and the Lada engine is the only sound. I'm not even sure how far we've come, or where we are, at *all*. It feels lonely. Lan shines his torch and the wall is suddenly right in front of us. I slam on the brake, and the engine cuts out with a kind of hiccup.

We sit, out of breath and cringing, waiting for a door to open and a grown-up shouting. But it's dead quiet. Nothing. Just some foxes yapping. Just peaceful.

Neither of us say anything. It's not funny now. It's very cool, like being on patrol. Lan gets out, and I see his blurry shape, walking along the wall with the torch bobbing. Then he signals – *here . . .*

With my foot pressed down hard on the clutch, I turn the key. The Lada starts up again, like it's keen to get going, it bounces and growls. I glance over my shoulder at the houses behind us, and ease off the clutch.

I roll gently past Lan, turning right along the wall, following his signal, and I see the gatepost. I'm hunching over the wheel, but it's not even that narrow, we're clear. Then left, through it, and it's downhill again. Lan runs next to the car and leaps back in next to me.

Cool, he says, full of confidence, and forgets not to slam his door – it's like an explosion.

Shit!

I slam mine too, and put my foot down.

Lights! Lan! Lights!

We cannon into the dark, with the engine yelling. Lan's hand fumbles and turns the stick, and the hard-white glare hits the manky long grass and thistles, right in front of us. The shadows leap like the ground is wriggling, and the darkness is like driving off a cliff.

We roar down the hill – Lan checking behind as we go. I want to shout or laugh. Or yell. Or cry. I grip the wheel so hard my hands hurt, and I can hardly see over the bonnet. Cold air pours through the open window, super-clean and wild.

'*Fuck them, fuck them, fuck them,*' I think, '*we're free! We're free!*'

At the bottom of the track, in the Rough, we leave the Lada, swinging our blanket of stuff between us. We've planned the perfect place, where there are small hills like sand dunes and not too many thistles. Way, way out of sight.

We light our fire in a hollow with the wood we stole from my house. It takes nearly all the matches. When it's hot, we put the frying pan on, only squabbling a bit. I pull a chunk of butter off the packet with my fingers and put the sausages in before it's even melted.

We can put them straight on the fire, if they don't get brown enough, I say, sucking butter off my hand, but the sausages are already sizzling. We're pretty much experts.

We sit hugging our knees and taking a break. We're looking over our shoulders, but we know we're safe. Dad would never drive all the way down here in the stupid Last Remnants.

The sausages pop and scorch – they smell amazing. We break two eggs each into the pan, and put more butter.

Let's chop them up and make a sausage omelette, says Lan. We get our penknives and do it, burning our fingers, the smoke stabbing our eyes so they stream.

What's that? says Lan, suddenly.

We hold our breath, with thumping hearts. We hear crashing, breaking twigs and then, clearly, small hooves on wet ground. *Deer,* we both say, and carry on.

We cook and eat, turning on the torch some of the time, but mostly just seeing by firelight, huddling near it, scorching hot. After we finish, we push everything off the blanket, and get wrapped up in it, because it's much colder than before, and a mist has come down and is making everything wet. I realise I still haven't peed, and I really need to. I get up, taking the torch.

My bum's wet! I say, going into the dark, flashing the torch about, looking for a place.

Peed yourself?

No, stupid—

Lan laughs. I put the torch on the ground and yank my jeans down. There's rustling all around, and an owl hoots, answered by another.

My finger hurts, calls Lan.

Yeah, so does mine. And I feel sick . . .

Don't puke in your pee!

Gross.

I get my jeans up and run back like I'm being chased by something. I know I'm not, it's just running with the darkness behind always feels like something's about to reach out.

The little fire's still hot, but getting lower, and it won't last forever. I don't want this feeling to be over. I don't ever want to go back up into the stupid boring house.

The moon is rising over Foy's Wood, clear of the treetops, and bright, so the branches are black against the silver. Our toes are wet and getting cold. We pull the blanket around our necks and grip it closed. We could get more firewood, but it rained today, it would be wet. Anyway, it's late.

Back to back, says Lan. We shuffle round, against each other, backs like radiators. I'm facing Foy's Wood and Lan's facing the Baldy Wild.

I hear a sound, like a deer again, but this time there's something different. It's not crashing, and there are no hooves. I nudge Lan. We turn our heads together, and listen. It's coming closer. I feel Lan's heart inside his bony back, beating just as fast as mine.

What is it?

We strain our eyes.

The weak firelight doesn't do anything except make it harder to see. Lan's twisting round, close to me, trapping the blanket. *Get off*, I say and shove him. Then we see – just barely – like an old photograph, the grey, black and white nose of a badger. Its nose. Eyes, glinting. We look at it, and I think it's looking at us. It feels as if everything all around has been frozen still in time. Then it moves. It turns slowly in the gloom, broadside, like a ghost ship, and disappears. We let out our breath. Things are normal again.

It looked like a bear, I say.
It was a badger.
Yeah, Lan, thanks, I'm not thick . . .
After a second, he says, *rare and precious.*
And I nod.

We leave the Lada by the gate and carry the blanket between us, not risking driving back over the Yard.
They'll think one of them left the Lada there.
Yeah, let them find it.
The houses are dark, except the Farmhouse kitchen. We creep into my house, and hide the blanket, rolled up behind the boots.
Night, whispers Lan as he goes off across the Big Room.
Night.
I go upstairs. There's a light under Mum and Dad's door, and I can hear them talking again. I don't care what about.
My eyes in the bathroom mirror are red with woodsmoke. I'm smeared with ash, and streaks through the soot where my eyes were streaming, and my hair's got a big sausage crumb in it. I eat it before I remember not to, then smile at myself, because we got away with it. We stole the Lada. It felt like it was ours.
I wash my face as quietly as I can, turning the cold tap as far as it goes before the weird sound starts. And eat a bit of toothpaste and swoosh it round, and spit. I love the smell of the bathroom – soap and wet matting. The clean laundry-liquid smell on the scratchy towel.

WINTER
2010

19

Snow

LAN

It's a new decade, and it's January, and it's snowing. The whole farm is covered, and it snows more nearly every day. In the mornings, the snow has a hard layer of ice on top that breaks when you step in it or poke it. Deep, deep snow. Weeks and weeks.

The first day it fell so thick we couldn't see the Cart-house from the Farmhouse. It was fun. Then everything disappeared under it – wheelbarrows, vegetable beds, walls, ditches. We keep tripping over things we've forgot-ten are there. And it's cold, like it's snowing inside a freezer and we're all trapped inside. The troughs are iced over and the plastic goat buckets frozen solid. We tipped them up, and bucket-shaped blocks of ice fell out and didn't even melt. Then they got snowed on, and now they look like giant white pom-poms.

It feels like it might never stop. We've had so many snow days off school, we've stopped counting. Sometimes even the Lada can't get to the village. We've made paths, some with shovelling, others just from walking, criss-crossing the Yard like a wobbly spider's web. The wind off Colin's hill has blown snow so deep against the front of the Farm-house, it's higher than our heads. We couldn't get to the front door. We had to dig a path to it. The sun doesn't come up until way after breakfast but at night it's never properly dark because the snow glows, all the time. When there's a moon, it's like blue, weird-looking daylight.

I'm meant to be collecting snow to make more bricks for the igloo, but I'm looking at the tracks in the snow through the Rough. It's very quiet, no birds singing or anything. It's afternoon and the sky is grey except where the sun must be, where it looks like an old bruise. Some-times I hear the shuffle of snow dropping off a branch, and I can hear Amy and the others working on the igloo. I'm being a Canadian tracker in a fur-lined hat. I can see the tiny, three-toed prints of a robin, maybe – and bigger ones that could be a pheasant, or a crow, and round holes, prob-ably made by a fox, and a shallow trench like something has been dragged, which must have been a badger, or—

LAN!

Coming . . .

I wish my fur-lined hat was real. I'm freezing. I scoop snow into my plastic bag and head back to camp. I can see Amy, Josh and Niah, working hard. The igloo isn't any-thing at all like an igloo. We wanted to make big, sharp-edged ice-bricks. We tried, but you can't tell. We pictured it perfect, but it's not even good.

'What?' says Amy.

'Nothing.'

Bryn and Eden stamp up, panting, carrying a tarp full of snow, and dump it on the building heap.

'We're on the second layer,' says Josh. He wants me to say well done, so I do.

Niah, sitting down, is patting the igloo flat with both hands.

'We'll need tools,' says Amy. Her face looks small and sharp. 'D'you think we should make the corridor to the second room now, or hollow it out later?'

Corridor? Second room? The igloo looks like a sandcastle after the waves have hit it but Amy's waiting for an answer.

'Maybe later?' I say.

It takes ages to walk home up the hill. We made the track into our toboggan run and it's hard ice, so we have to walk in the deep snow up the sides, getting our legs soaked. It's almost dark. The snow creaks and squeaks. The farm looks like a circle of gingerbread houses, lit up and welcoming, but I don't want to go in.

I'm hungry! yells Bryn, leaping off like a rabbit. *Me too,* says Niah, shoving her hand in mine. Her gloves are drenched. Em's curtains are drawn, glowing red. Finbar has his shutters closed, showing splinters of light. Every chimney has smoke coming out in a solid line, against the sky.

In my kitchen, Em is knitting in the armchair by the Rayburn, with Poacher on her lap. He's too big for anybody's lap, let alone Em's, his bony black Lab legs are everywhere. Neither of them can be comfortable. She's resting her weird knitting on him so he looks like he's wearing it. He rolls his eyes at us guiltily.

'All right, Em?'

'Shut the door, it's freezing.'

Eden and Bryn grab bread off the table and run upstairs, screaming, *put the kettle on, put the kettle on!* and Josh goes off through the Big Room, yelling, *MUM!*

'Gail's with the chickens,' says Em.

If Mum was with the chickens every time someone says she's with the chickens, she would be a chicken, and live with them. I don't know where she is.

Niah holds up her hands and I peel off her gloves and hang them on the stove rail. *Shepherd's pie,* she says. There's a pie dish with leftovers on the warming plate. I scrape some off onto a plate for her. She climbs up on the bench.

'After this, it's bath time,' she says. She's an organised kid. 'Then bedtime.'

'Yup.'

Me and Amy sit opposite to keep her company.

'And don't forget teeth,' says Niah.

We hear Jim's footsteps and stamping as he knocks the snow off, then he comes in.

'Daddy!' says Niah.

He has snow on the shoulders of his big tan jacket, and snow in his hair. He takes off his work boots and hangs his jacket on the peg.

'Hello, my darling. Hello, my little beauty.' He kisses and hugs her.

'I'm eating,' she says. 'Then it's bath time.'

'Then bedtime,' I say.

She nods.

'You're not wrong.' Jim grinds the kettle down on the hotplate.

'Look.' Em holds up her knitting.

'Wow,' says Jim. 'Enormous.'

There's someone shouting out in the Yard. Rani's voice first, then Martin's.

'What now?' says Em.

Jim tries to peer out through the window over the sink.

What's going on? What's going on? scream the girls, above us, in their rooms. We can hear them trying to open the stuck window, and scraping. *Don't smash it!* shrieks Eden.

'Who's shouting?' shouts Harriet, from across the Big Room.

'Rani! Wait!' yells Martin, in the Yard.

Em tips Poacher off her lap, and we all go to the back door, and open it.

Rani is storming through the snow from the Carthouse, yowling and waving her arms, and Martin is trying to catch up, looking frantic.

'D'you know what, Martin? I don't fucking care!'

We all crowd to look – except Niah, who carries on eating with her hand around her glass like someone's going to take it away from her.

Rani is in her long quilted coat; she looks like an upright caterpillar, marching away from Martin, who is slipping around behind her. We can just see Bill and Lulu, in the Carthouse doorway. It looks like Lulu's crying.

'*God,*' says Amy. 'Grown-ups.'

'Don't tell me to calm down!' screams Rani at Martin. 'You tight-arse! You bastard accountant!'

Rani and Martin are always nice to each other. Rani doesn't scream.

'What did he do?' I ask.

'I think she's just had enough of this snow,' says Jim. 'We all have.'

He leans out.

'Cup of tea, Rani?'

Rani skids.

'Fuck off, Jim,' she says. 'I'm getting the hell out. I haven't left the house in over two weeks.'

'She's got the keys!' Martin calls to him, desperately. 'She's taking the Mondeo.'

Not the Mondeo, I say, and Amy dashes her hand on her forehead – *call 999.*

Rani disappears past the house to the front. Martin tries to run, and slips. He falls really hard onto his side in the snow.

'Ow, Jesus, God, ow, God! Why is this path not gritted?'

'Daddy!' cries Lulu from the door of the Carthouse. 'Mummy! Don't go!'

She's loving it, says Amy. *Stupid.*

We all go to the front door to see what Rani's going to do.

Pulling car keys from her pocket, she staggers to the Mondeo and leans over the bonnet, sweeping the snow off it with her arm.

'Rani . . .' says Martin, catching up.

She's scraping the windscreen with her bare hands, ignoring him. Jim puts on his boots.

'Where you gonna go, Rani?' I ask.

'Out,' says Rani, looking mad. 'For a cappuccino.'

Martin limps towards her through the swirling snow.

'Rani, be sensible . . .'

Harriet and Josh lean out of the Cowhouse door to watch too.

'Seriously,' calls Harriet, over the wind, 'the drift by the gate at the top is about ten feet deep.'

'Well, fuck it,' says Rani, and pops the car unlocked.

'You'll be killed!' shouts Martin.

'Then I'm *killed*,' screams Rani, tugging at the driver's door.

Lan, says Amy, *they've completely lost it.*

Then, out of a curtain of snow, come Adam and Mum, running from the direction of the Orchard and Tumbledown.

'What's going on?' says Adam.

They look pink and happy. They look completely different to everybody else. Different to the whole day. The snow. Everything. They look like it's both their birthdays, and we're all on a summer picnic. Everyone stares at them as they stop, and they stare back. It's like they're trying to look worried and miserable, and cold, like every single other person at Frith, but they just can't.

'I was with the hens,' says Mum.

Martin walks towards Rani.

'Stay back!' she shouts, and waves the car key at him, like a gun.

'What the hell is going on?' says Adam.

'Rani, please—' says Martin.

Rani gets in the car.

'I may be some time,' she says, and laughs. She slams the door, and turns the engine on.

'No!' shouts Martin. 'Rani! It's dangerous!'

It's very dangerous, says Amy. *It's unbelievably dangerous*, I say back.

'Shut up, kids,' says Harriet, 'it actually is. She'll get stuck and tractors won't see her.'

We imagine Colin speeding in his tractor, the Mondeo in pieces on the road. Amy laughs.

Rani puts on the headlights, wipers skidding. Plumes of exhaust billow as the car backs towards us. Jim bends down to make a hole in the snow on the car window and looks in at her. She gestures violently at him. The tyres skid as she lurches towards the gate. Martin bangs on the boot, stumbling into a run behind the car.

'Stop!' he shouts. 'I'm begging you to stop!'

Jim suddenly makes a great, weird barking sound. Me and Amy look at him. For a second I think he's choking on something. But it's a laugh. He does it again. Like a crow. Like *KAH!* Me and Amy exchange looks. Then Harriet does it, too. They're both laughing. Barking and choking with laughter. The two of them staggering about, completely out of control, covering their faces, whimpering and stamping the ground. All us kids are just watching. It's not funny. It's horrible. It's an attack. I might have missed something. Maybe there was something I didn't see. I check on Mum and Adam. But they aren't laughing. Not at all. They look – like they're far away. Like they're watching it all happen from somewhere else, from a boat or something. A really nice boat, maybe a yacht, the sun shining just on them.

The snow falls thicker and thicker as Rani drives out onto the lane. Jim and Harriet are still pissing themselves, saying – *God, stop, oh God, stop, help.*

Martin is chasing the Mondeo, waving. Rani's driving so slowly he doesn't even need to run.

Then Jim says, 'Oh, no. Oh, Harriet,' in his normal voice – sadly.

There are giant snowflakes in Harriet's hair, like a big fur hat. She's gone pale, like someone frozen, and her laughing has turned into crying. Her mouth is twisted up, but she's hardly making a sound, just her chest heaving, and tears coming down her cheeks.

'Darling . . .' says Adam, as he starts to towards her, the snow groaning under his boots. 'Sweetheart—'

'No,' says Harriet, in tears. 'No, Adam.'

'I am so, so sorry, Harriet,' says Mum. 'We just can't keep fighting it.'

'Inside,' says Jim. He holds his arms out, to herd us. I can't see past his big, solid arm in the tan jacket. 'Kids? Inside.'

We all obey him.

Niah is still at the kitchen table.

'It's bath time now,' she says. 'Don't forget.'

Eden and Bryn have first bath with Niah. Me, Amy and Josh go into Josh's room, peeling off wet jeans and socks and wrapping up in quilts, then we kneel in the corner by Josh's incubator, and pick up one egg each.

'Don't scare them,' whispers Josh. 'Remember they can hear you.'

Adam's and Harriet's voices come up through the floor, and we listen to the chicks as hard as we can, to see if they've started cheeping inside their shells. We hear tiny, tiny, distant cheeps. Then we put them back.

'They'll hatch soon,' he says, 'it's Day Twelve.' He's got a wallchart, and he's ticking off the days. Recently, he and Harriet painted his walls in rainbow colours. He's stuck pictures of animals up: sloths, pandas, all kinds of bears. We all look at the grizzly bear with the salmon in its mouth, and sprays of water flying up. Harriet's and Adam's voices come up quietly through the floor, talking and talking and talking.

'My tummy hurts,' says Josh.

'Mine does that,' I say. 'It goes away.'

'Do you want a hot-water bottle?' says Amy.

'It's downstairs.'

None of us want to go down there.

'There's one in my bed,' I say. It's been there ages. 'We can use the tap. It can be a warm-water bottle.'

We're filling it in the bathroom when we hear voices out front and all crowd to the window to look, Eden and Bryn wrapped in towels for the bath. Rani and Martin are trudging home down the lane.

'No Mondeo,' says Amy. 'They must have had to leave it *abandoned*.'

'Rani has cabin fever,' I say.

'It's lucky she didn't have a gun,' says Eden. 'She could have gone on a rampage.'

We imagine Rani on a rampage in her caterpillar coat.

'We'd all be splatted dead everywhere,' says Eden. 'And there'd be blood all over the snow.'

We can picture it so clearly, we almost check there hasn't been a massacre and the snow is still white, not drenched with blood.

Martin and Rani have their arms around each other. They look like they normally do. Happy.

Me and Amy are sitting out on the Bridge with Josh, dangling our legs through the holes. Josh hugs his warm-water bottle. Eden and Bryn come and sit next to us. Eden has got a quilt round her now, and Bryn's wearing bunny slippers that used to be Amy's.

'How cold is it?' asks Amy.

'Needs a kettle,' Eden answers. 'Maybe two.'

They sit on the Bridge with us.

'We put Niah to bed,' says Bryn.

The five of us sit in a row, which makes the Bridge dip, which makes us want to swing it. We begin to rock, and the Bridge swings, and the fat ropes creak, and the stone floor tilts.

'No, it's only a cradle,' says Bryn, so we slow down.

'Remember when Gabriella lived in the Snug?' says Amy.

'I don't, I was too little,' says Bryn. 'It's not fair.'

'I do,' says Eden. ''Em used to sleep on the sofa.'

'Remember when Perdy had her kittens?' I say.

'And stupid Bill squashed them.'

Squeaker is a girl.

How do you know?

I think she's pregnant.

Remember when you found that Guest Kid we thought was lost?

Toby?

Oh yeah . . .

He nearly died.

I thought he did die?

No, he nearly died.

Remember when the pigs got out, and went into the Spar?

Ellis, Wallace and Gary . . .

We remember, and remember, and rock the Rope Bridge slowly.

SPRING
2010

20

Goats

AMY

It's the first warm week for so, so long. The new grass is
electric-green, and the air is soft. Josh is sowing seeds with
Finbar, and me and Lan are against the wall of his house,
where it's sunny, arguing about who would win a battle
between Spider-Man and Iron Man. Everywhere we look
things are growing, and it's like the chickens and chicks are
in a springtime competition to get into everything, pecking
and preening. I could sit like this my whole life. I want the
sunshine to last forever. *No, if Iron Man is covered in web,
he can't shoot, can he?* says Lan.

Mum comes to the back door and calls, 'Amy! Give me
a hand?'

It should be normal, and innocent, but there's something about the way she says it that makes the day stop
still. I think I must've been waiting, that I knew this
moment was coming. I have the feeling I'm stepping out of
myself, and looking back at me and Lan, still leaning

against the wall, Lan scraping the ground with a stick. I look at Josh's head bent over the seedbed, carefully planting, and Finbar saying, *that's right, Josh, drop them in, just like that.*

'Amy!' Mum shouts.

'Your mum wants you,' says Lan.

Following my ghost-self, I get up from the ground.

'See ya,' I say, so he won't come too.

Mum is waiting by the back door.

'Will you feed the goats with me?' she says.

It's OK, she only wants help feeding the goats.

'Sure.'

We take a bucket each, turn off the current, and open up the fence. We walk through the shoving goats, who are jostling about and lifting their faces. Gabriella is in the middle, pushing me with her nose.

'Do you think Gabriella would like another calf?' I say.

'I need to talk to you,' says Mum.

I want to pretend I haven't heard, but she stops me. We're standing in the sun, near the goats' house Jim and Dad built.

'Do you want to go somewhere else?' she says.

'No, it's OK.'

'Are you ready? I need to tell you something.'

'Yes.'

'I'm so sorry, Amy, we're going to have to leave.'

'Who?'

'Me and you, and Josh. Move out.'

'What?'

I don't know what I expected. I'm crying before I have any time to think, or take it in. It just starts.

'Leave Frith?' I say.

We can be seen from anywhere. She puts her arms around me.

'Come on.'

I'm blind with tears and she guides me, saying how sorry she is, and she never wanted this to happen.

'Amy, we just can't stay. We have to leave.'

'Why can't *Dad* go?' I say, pulling back. '*He's* the one who should go.'

She looks surprised, then not surprised. I've never said anything about Dad and Gail. Not once. Even to myself. Now it's everywhere, and everything is broken.

'He and Gail don't want to,' says Mum tightly. 'It was your father's money, when we moved here. The flat we sold to buy Frith was all his. So he owns our share, not me.'

'Don't make me – please, please, Mum, don't make us leave.'

I'm begging. I know I shouldn't, but I can't stop.

'I can't help it,' she says. 'I'm sorry.'

I cry more. I sit down.

'Mind out for thistles,' says Mum.

We sit together, in the middle of the goats, near a cowpat. Of all the places to sit in the whole of Frith, it's the least comfortable and the least beautiful.

'Is Jim leaving Gail?' I ask. 'Is he going, too?'

She looks at me, steadily.

'Gail and Jim aren't together any more, but he doesn't want to go.'

Gabriella still hates being on her own. She's followed, and she's standing over me. She licks my leg.

'I think Jim's hoping things will change,' says Mum. 'He loves her.'

I think of Gail, and her stupid ideas, and her annoying laugh, and how she never bothered teaching Lan to read, and ignores Niah totally.

'Fuck sake, *why*?' I say.

'I have no fucking idea,' says Mum. 'He just does.'

I feel so sad I can't speak.

'Why does Dad love *her*?' I say. 'He should love you.'

'He tried not to. Really. They both really tried.'

'Why couldn't they try *harder*?'

After a second, like she's come to a conclusion, she says, 'Because they're both fucking arseholes. If you want to know the truth, they are both *fucking arseholes*.'

She looks crazy and ugly. I want to hit her. I want to hit him, because she's right. I'm a child and he's my father. I'm a woman, and he's screwing Gail.

'No, he's *not*,' I say. 'Dad's *not* an arsehole—'

She hugs me. We're sort of laughing. I think we're both slightly mad. I feel so grown up. But then I glimpse, past this, the future, lying ahead of me like black water. We're leaving. I stop crying. After a while, I'm breathing normally.

'I've got a sore throat,' I say.

'I'm so sorry, Amy.'

'Will you get divorced?'

'Maybe.'

'But . . . where are we going?'

'Bristol, London. I'm not sure.'

'*Bristol*?' Bristol is Dad's.

'I haven't decided yet.'

'When?'

'Two weeks.'

Two weeks? It's still very sunny and there's no wind. The other kids are playing somewhere. I can hear them laughing and calling.

'I'm so sorry, Amy. I'm so, so sorry. We messed everything up.'

I wish she'd stop saying sorry. I need her not to be wrong.

'It's been a long time coming,' says Mum.

I'm looking down the hill towards the Rough, where we built the igloo that never really was an igloo, in the winter. Working day after day, making all the others work with us. It wasn't any fun. Did I know then? Did I know before? Maybe I've always known.

'I guess,' I say.

Gabriella is grazing. I want to watch her forever, and never have to go on to the next bit, where my parents are breaking up, and I'm leaving Frith.

We walk back slowly. Mum keeps checking me, to see if I'll faint or die. I don't have anything to say. I've got nothing in my head. She's all business.

'Can you not tell Josh?' she says. 'I don't want him to find out until after his birthday.'

I nod. She takes my shoulders, looking into my face to check I'm listening.

'I don't want him to know yet,' she says. 'But I had to tell you. You're my big, grown-up girl.'

I look at the broken veins in the corner of her nose, and her hay-covered jumper, full of holes. I say what she would say to me, if I asked her.

'Sure. Don't worry, we'll give him a really good birthday, OK?'

'Thank you, Amy.'

We walk back to the house holding hands.

Lan isn't where I left him.

'They're telling Lan now,' says Mum.

'Right now?'

Looking up from the seedbed, Josh sees me, and stands up and waves.

'Hey! Amy! We did all the beans!' he shouts. 'They're in!'

21

Chopping

LAN

Jim tells me that Mum and Adam are in love. He says that soon Mum is going to be living in the Farmhouse with Adam, instead of him, and that Amy, Josh and Harriet are leaving. We're in his workshop. Mum's walking up and down behind him, crying, while he talks in a calm voice. The sawdust floats and swirls in the air. *We both love you,* Jim keeps saying. And, *I'll still be here for you all.* My heart closes up small and tight. I feel sick. Tears pour out of my eyes while the two adults walk and talk and sweat, telling lies and lies and lies. They make me dizzy.

We want what's best for you
I'll always love you
We're doing our best
I will always love Jim, but I just can't be married to him any more

I don't say anything. Not for ages. They run out of lies and excuses and start to look frightened.

'Lan?' says Mum. 'Lan?'

She can pretend all she likes, but I knew before.

'It's the same as Gray Parks,' I say. 'You think you're in the wrong life.'

That makes her cry even more, and go on about *loving* me and *loving her life at Frith*, and how it's not like that at all. *I left Gray, not you*, she says.

At least Jim has stopped talking. I look out of the window at where my sisters are playing in the Yard. I can't hate Jim. And I can't hate Mum, even if I want to – I'm too scared she won't bother trying to get me back. But she never would have done this if it hadn't been for Adam.

'Lan?' she says. 'Please?'

'You can't make me live with Adam!' I shout, like a little kid. 'I'll leave. I'll go with Amy.'

'I'm sorry,' says Jim. 'It doesn't work like that.'

'I hate that you're hurting, Lan,' says Mum. 'But I can't regret living my right life.'

Afterwards, I'm surprised I can even get up and walk. They've broken me into little pieces. I feel it.

While we're at school, Jim puts a mattress in his workshop, and Adam moves into Tumbledown. It's a bit like that song we used to sing when we were small – *Honeys in the Farmhouse, Connells in the Cowhouse, Hodges in the Carthouse, Finbar, Finbar – no more beds* . . . Except all mixed up.

Now they've told us – now it's happening – we can't pretend we don't notice the fighting, and the way the parents are when they're around each other. Mum says, *aren't you relieved you don't have be in denial any longer?* I'm not relieved. We were fine. Everyone says it's always better to be honest. Of all the grown-up lies, it's the biggest. The truth is bad. I hate it.

The little kids still don't get what's going on. Even when they saw the mattress for Jim being carried out of the house. Even when Adam went off to Tumbledown with a bag of his pants and socks. He was doing his 'sad walk', like it hurt him so much to go. It was the same as his recycling walk. He's such a bad actor, he can't even do that.

Mum told my little sisters it's normal for grown-ups to need a break from each other sometimes. And they *believed* her. It's sort of pathetic.

I'm with Niah, looking for frogs in the trough before school. There's some frogspawn with black dots in that's about to be tadpoles.

'Are they going to be eating ones, like French ones are?' she asks.

'No.' But I tell her if they were, when we cooked them, we'd have to boil the water slowly, so they wouldn't realise it was getting hotter. I don't know if that's true. Someone told me. It's a cool idea.

'And eat them after with butter?' says Niah.

Jim and Martin come across the Yard, carrying a big piece of plasterboard.

'What's that for?'

'We're creating a little bit more privacy for everybody,' says Martin.

I follow them in. Amy is already there, with Harriet. She's with Harriet the whole time now. They're never apart.

Adam honks the horn outside.

'School,' says Harriet, but we're watching Jim and Martin carrying the plasterboard up the Farmhouse stairs. They keep bashing the walls because it's narrow.

'What are they doing?' says Amy. 'What's going on?'

'Just go to school,' says Harriet.

When we get home, the Rope Bridge is sealed. It's cut off at both ends. I run up my stairs and Amy runs up hers. I stare at where we used to look out onto the Bridge, and the whole of the Big Room. I guess Amy's doing the same thing, but I can't see, just a wall. When the little kids argue and complain and cry to the grown-ups, Adam says, *we can't all carry on living in each other's pockets.* In the end, they lose interest. Lulu and Bryn put on a DVD, Josh runs out to see his sheep. I don't know where Bill is. He doesn't even live in the Farmhouse, and he complained the loudest. He cried a lot. They all seem to have forgotten about it now. I think about the boiling frogs. The little kids' lives are changing, like mine and Amy's, but they haven't realised yet. They'll catch on when the water boils.

I just keep going back to look at the new wall from the Farmhouse side. I can't get used to it. They even painted it. It shocks me how easy it is to make the Farmhouse and the Cowhouse stop being special and be just normal, boring houses, with a big room in between. Today, Jim saw me staring up at the Bridge and came and stood next to me. I felt like he was going to say something nice, he started to, but I interrupted.

'You should take the whole Bridge down,' I said. 'It looks dumb.'

22

Sorting

AMY

I find Dad in the Cowhouse bathroom, sitting on the edge of the bath, holding the yellow rubber duck we've had forever, crying on it. It's shocking seeing Dad cry, Mum hasn't cried since she told me.

'What are you doing with Ducky?' I say.

He says he's crying because he can't stand it, because he gave Ducky to Josh when Josh was small.

'No, Dad, Ducky's mine.'

I don't say that I don't remember him playing with us in the bath, because I don't want him to be more upset. I keep trying to hate him, but it doesn't work. *Give me a hug*, he says, *let's cheer up.* So I do. I don't want to be comforting him. He should be comforting me. But I don't want that, either, I just want him to love Mum again, and us not to have to leave. It makes me feel weak how much I don't hate him. I look all through myself for anger, but I can't find any, anywhere.

'Thank you, sweetheart,' he says. 'I love you.'

The stupid thing is, right then, while he's hugging me, I believe him. I feel like he'd do anything in the world for me, if I just ask. I'm very careful not to ask.

Mum's told me to go through my clothes. There are so many. Things I haven't seen for ages. They look sort of sad and crumpled, without anyone wearing them. I put all the ones that are too small for me in a pile for Bryn and Eden. I feel strong, and capable, and for a minute, part of a journey forward. It's almost fun. I find my favourite T-shirt, which has long sleeves and a big star on the front, and hold it up and imagine wearing it in London, where I've never been, even once. And walking into a classroom full of kids, and them all staring at me. The T-shirt isn't white any more and has grass stains on it. It's way too small now, anyway. I think of the Tumbledown kids from London, who always say the country smells. I wonder if they'll say it when I'm there, that *I* smell. I didn't know I even *liked* secondary school in Ross. Turns out, I love it.

I'm so scared, I feel sick, so I go and find Mum, and try not to cry trying to tell her, but she just says, *don't worry, we'll buy new clothes.* She's not even listening. I want to yell – *what with? We don't have any money!* But I don't want to hurt her feelings, I know she's worried about money.

I guess she can be a piano teacher anywhere, only not one with a farm, and three families. Not one who has a herd of beautiful caramel-coloured goats. She won't be able to bring Honey. But Honey's old. She might not live that long anyway. And we can't take any of the dogs. Not even Christabel. Christabel will probably die soon, too. I'm thinking too much. Once I start, it's difficult to stop.

DVDs. Homework. Tidying. DVDs. Homework. Tidying.

And I won't go outside or look at anything. Everything I look at hurts.

I'm in the Spar with Mum, staring at a ham sandwich in a packet while Ruby Wright and Leslie Robinson talk about doctors' appointments. *Be with you in just a moment,* says Leslie. *It's fine,* says Mum. The ham is pink and wet – it doesn't even look like ham. Now Ruby's started talking to Mum as well. I wonder where the pig came from, that's in the sandwich. Maybe it's lots of pigs, ground up. If you folded our ham like that, it would break. I think of Angel Rocket's grave. And Dad and Gail not bothering sticking in the poles for the electric to keep the pigs in, because they were busy being in love.

'Remember when Ellis, Wallace and Gary came in your shop?' I suddenly say to Leslie, in a loud voice. I didn't know I was going to say it. I've interrupted.

'Yes, love,' says Leslie.

We pay, and leave, and go out onto the pavement, and Ruby follows, chasing after Mum, and touching her arm.

'You all right, Harriet?' she says. 'You all right?' Like asking twice will show how much she cares.

Everyone knows what's happened to us all at Frith. Everyone knows me, Josh and Mum are leaving. Mum hates people being nice, it makes her angry.

'I'm fine, Ruby, thank you,' she says and glares at her like a lion.

I'm scared for Ruby's safety.

'How are your Dexters?' I ask, to put her off the scent.

'Tammy's pregnant!' she says. 'We're expecting twins!'

When me and Mum are safe again, on our own back in the Lada, she winds up the window and grips the steering wheel.

'Where now?' she says. 'I'm losing my mind.'

'Jack and Joffrey.'

'Right. Good.'

But she doesn't start the engine.

'Do you miss having Gail be your best friend?' I say.

She looks at me a long time.

'Yes,' she says. 'I miss it a lot.'

'You darlings,' says Joffrey, when we give him our eggs and rhubarb in a crate. 'Come in.'

Jack and Joffrey's house looks like a giant doll's house on the outside and has a massive, shiny kitchen. Josh's birthday cupcakes are in three bright white boxes. Every single one says *Josh* on it, in curly writing.

'Jack brought them down last night,' he says.

'They're gorgeous,' says Mum.

We've always had Rani-made cakes before. But Mum wants Josh's birthday to be special, she keeps saying, *I want it to be extra-special*. Rani cakes *are* special. Josh doesn't know yet, that we're leaving. I think she should have told him.

On the way home, the boxes bounce on the back seat,

and we're scared the icing will fall off. They look out of place on our muddy seats.

'In London we'll have lots of shop-bought things,' says Mum.

I'm so lost and scared, I can't breathe.

When we get back, it's pouring with rain. We shield the boxes from the rain and hide them in the cellar. Rani says we can have the Carthouse for his party, but Mum says we'll use the Big Room. Rani's made chirotis, like always. The sugar-syrup cardamom smell floated out into the Yard today, and made me think of all our birthdays. It's probably a good idea to do something different.

I feel bad for Rani and Martin. It's not their fault our parents are so stupid, and have wrecked everything. Martin leaves for work every morning looking excited and happy, like an animal escaping from the zoo, and gets out of the Mondeo every night miserable, like he's been trapped and brought back to captivity.

I wonder if Lan feels bad for them too. I bet he does. I bet he'd think it was funny, about Martin escaping from a zoo. I'd like to ask him. But we're not talking.

We aren't even looking at each other.

I feel weird about looking into his face. I'm scared if I look at him, I'll see how bad I really feel. I can't do it. Even when I try. I don't think he can either.

We're just ignoring each other.

We don't even speak on the way into school, and it's far to Ross.

No more *Traviata*, no more 'Purple Rain', like when

were kids. Dad plays the radio, and I sit in the front, and nobody says anything, the whole way. And I feel so, so lonely.

It's *Gail and my dad* now.

Gail and Adam.

Adam and Gail.

There isn't anything for me and Lan to say, is there? Gail has taken my dad away. Me and Mum are the only ones who know what this is like. And we haven't even left yet, and I miss Lan. I don't know what it was like, just feeling normal.

23

The Hay

LAN

I'm sitting on the floor of Jim's workshop not doing home-work. Jim's finished Mum's dresser, but now he doesn't know how to give it to her, so he's just sanding the shelves, smoother and smoother and smoother. The dresser is in the corner, and three of the shelves are leaning up against the wall, next to his mattress, which he sleeps on at night and takes up off the ground during the day. He's got a ket-tle in the workshop, but he doesn't keep food in here, because of mice, so I've been bringing him breakfast in the mornings. Not proper breakfast, just bread and butter.

Jim looks very calm and peaceful when he works. He doesn't look like the things that are happening are happening.

'I miss you making breakfast,' I say.

He looks up.

'I miss it too,' he says.

He carries on sanding, and I try not to think about

where Mum and Adam are, or what they're doing. I try
not to, but it's like that game Finbar taught me and Amy.
*Try not to think about white elephants for one whole min-
ute, and you can join my club.* It's impossible. That's why
there isn't a White Elephant Club. Now, because of thinking about Jim's breakfast, I'm trying not to think about
Adam cooking, but I keep picturing how he shows off
when he's making spaghetti, and imagine running at him,
and bashing his skull in with a mallet. I'd have to jump
quite high to reach his head, I'm still way shorter than
Amy. People keep telling me I'll grow, but nobody knows
how tall I'll be. Gray Parks might have been short. Mum's
never said. He might be shorter than Martin. Maybe she
left him because he was too small. Maybe she left Jim
because he took too long to make her dresser. No. I think
it was because he didn't fight for her, and shout, and shake
her, and yell, *don't leave me! Please, please, don't leave me!*
That might have worked. He hasn't even tried. She needs
to be stopped. She could leave Adam next, like she left
Gray Parks, and Jim. She might go on leaving forever.

'Lan?' says Jim, in a voice like he's said it more than
once.

'What?'

He comes and sits on the floor by me. I don't want him
to give me *a talk*. He'll say he loves me and grown-ups'
lives are complicated. I don't want him to. But then he
takes my hand, so I look at him and get ready to nod or
whatever, and agree with him so he'll go away.

'You're a wonderful boy,' he says.

I don't feel that. I don't think I am. But he likes me
enough to say it. He strokes my head.

'Right then. I think we should go in to Josh's party now,' he says.

'Oh. OK.'

Me and Jim run across the Yard in the rain, and come into the Big Room, quietly, dripping on the floor. The party has already started. There's a huge pyramid of cupcakes on the table, next to the chirotis. The cupcakes must be from Joffrey, but he's not here, just Josh's class from school, no non-Frith grown-ups.

Harriet is in the corner, not saying anything, and I can't see my mum – she probably won't come. Amy is pretending to be a grown-up, asking the kids what DVDs they want.

'*Scooby-Doo, Night at the Museum* or *Iron Man?*'

Not that asking them that is pretending to be a grown-up, it's the way she's doing it, acting big, like Adam. It's just annoying. '*Iron Man! Iron Man! Iron Man!*' yell the kids. Josh's favourite is *Night at the Museum.*

'Happy Birthday, Josh,' say me and Jim.

Adam is clapping his hands together.

'*Iron Man*, then! Kids?'

I start backing out.

'Lan?' says Jim.

But I don't stop. I see Amy, from right across the room, looking at me. It's a shock. For days, I've felt like she couldn't see me. I freeze where I am, and look at the floor.

'Stay a few minutes for Josh?' says Jim.

I shake my head.

Adam's big actor voice is booming around the room. I

leave. I'm out. I don't care. I'm outside in the rain. It's better. Jim stays in there. Pretending. Why does he do that? He must have been doing it for years.

I look behind me, through the glass into the brightly lit Big Room, and the rain makes the afternoon more like night. The kids are jumping about now. Adam's waving his arms. Rani and Martin are handing out food and paper napkins, then Martin goes to help Adam with the movie screen. They've rented a proper one. Josh looks worried. He doesn't even like parties. None of the other kids are talking to him, not even my sisters. I walk further into the rain. *Iron Man! Iron Man!* yell the kids inside the house, but their voices get quieter as I walk away.

I hear the door slam and feet splashing.

'Lan!'

Amy, behind me. *All right?* she says. I half turn, and shrug, and say, *all right?* to show I'm not ignoring her. Then I walk on.

She keeps coming after me. I can hear her steps.

'What you doing?'

'Nothing.'

'Where you going?'

'Nowhere.'

Her footsteps stop. Then start again.

'Fucking hell, Lan.'

I nearly stop. She's angry. I should stop. I don't want to ignore her. I don't want to be mean. I just don't want to talk to her. She should go back inside.

'You OK?' she says.

I don't know what to say. She keeps following me.

'Did I do something?' she says.

'No.'

'Did I though?'

'No.'

'Stop it, Lan!'

I shake her off. I'll stop answering her. That's what I need to do. Then she'll go away. We're passing the Orchard. I don't know where I'm headed. Maybe the barn.

The chickens startle and flutter as we pass the barn. And Tumbledown, which is where Adam's living, so I can't get away from her in there.

She's catching me up. She's so annoying – can't she see there's no point talking? She never knows when to shut up. But she doesn't say anything. She *pushes* me. Hard. So I nearly fall over. I spin round –

'Hey!'

'*What?*' I've seen her this angry before, but not with me. I'm not scared. I stare her down.

'Whatever, Lan,' she says. 'I don't fucking care.'

She pushes me again. She's bigger than I am. Both hands. And I stagger back and nearly fall on my bum.

Get off!

Make me.

Get off.

No.

And then I rush her – head down – and knock her back, and we're fighting. I punch her first, then run, because she scares me, but she runs after and trips me, and then I'm down. She punches me back. We're rolling over on the ground, off the track and through the gate of the Hay, into the soft old stubble and the earth, water soaking through our backs. Clawing, smacking – her foot catches my head, and we both fall, shoving each other. My knee lands on her hair, and I feel it tear, and she screams. I pull back and she jerks up, her head smacking the underneath of my chin, so my teeth smash together. I flail, and hit her, and she falls. I hear her go down, more than see her.

I open my eyes, and drop onto my knees, getting my breath back. She isn't moving.

'You OK?'

'Fine,' she says, immediately. '*Stupid*.'

I sit back, and check my wounds. It's the best I've felt for as long as I can remember. Blood is trickling down my chin. I taste it.

'I've got a cut.'

'Do you need to go in?'

'No. It's OK.'

We sit.

We don't say anything, but we stay sitting there, long enough to stop sweating and start shivering. Long enough to feel where the bruises will be, and for it to stop hurting in some places and get worse in others. And to know exactly what's true.

'Your dad's an arsehole,' I say, slow, and careful. 'And I hate him.'

'Your mum's a bitch. And she's a whore.'

'Your dad's a dirty fucking liar.'

She doesn't answer that one for ages.

'They're having sex,' she whispers. 'I hate it.'

'I hate it, too.'

Her head is resting on her arms.

'Lan. What's happened to everything?' she says.

And I don't know. And I can't tell her. It's dark enough now we don't have faces, just ourselves.

'I don't want you to go,' I say. I'm going to cry.

'I'm so scared,' she says, like she'll cry, too.

We hold hands with the ends of our fingers. We haven't done that since we were six or seven. It isn't like those kids at school who say they're dating. It's just being nice. We stay like that until it gets embarrassing.

'Anyway,' Amy says, and rubs her face, and sorts herself out. I do the same, and wipe my nose on my jeans.

'Your cut OK?'

'Yeah, it stopped,' I say.

The night has got very cold. I can smell the stubble and the earth. And grass. And the Orchard.

'Do you think we'll ever cut hay in here again? When we're older?'

'I don't think I will,' says Amy. 'I won't be here.'

'You don't know that.'

We get up, and start walking back.

What did you cut yourself on?

   Your head

         There's blood in the soil now, isn't there?

          Yeah, like a battlefield

          The Battle of the Hay, 2010

      It's not that dramatic

   Yeah, it is, your head is like a rock

Shut up. You shut up. No, you shut up. Whatever . . .

24

Hodges in the Carthouse

AMY

It comes suddenly, the day before we go. One minute we're dreading something far away, the next, we're saying good-bye *tomorrow*.

Mum wants to go round the whole farm to say goodbye. She lets me and Josh drive the Lada. At the bottom of the track, we get out and walk across the Rough, to Foy's Wood, along the boundary to the Baldy Wild and into our woods. We check the hedges, nearly all of them.

In the woods, Bryn, Eden, Lulu and Niah are playing in the stream. They're working on the dam, and act like they don't see us. They don't want to be interrupted.

When Mum and Dad told Josh, about us leaving, he went completely white, and then he screamed, like he was being killed by a fox. Mum hugged him, and Dad was so upset he had to walk out of the room. I think Josh was in shock for days. Maybe we all are. It still doesn't seem real.

The bluebells are out, everywhere. Mum's face is rigid looking at them. She stares at everything like she hates it, hard as ice. I keep trying to think of things to make her laugh. All her goodbyes are regrets.

I wanted to finish off the hedging
We never got the stones out of Big Field
I wanted a dairy herd, I wish we'd had the money
I've told them they should put the weaners in Barrow,
for the soil, I bet they won't
I wish we'd planted trees there
I thought we had time
That's what she says the most: *I thought we had time.*

Later on, me and Lan take some bread and cheese and sit with Gabriella, Lily and Rose. Josh won't come, he's too upset about his sheep to see them now.

'I'm going to ask Mum to get me a phone,' I say. 'So we can call.'

'Cool, and we can Facebook.'

'Yeah.'

We're not going to do those things, and if we do, they won't be the same. They won't be anything. What would we say? *How was your day*, like grown-ups?

'AMY! DARLING!'

I see Lan go still at the sound of Dad's voice, and I jump up quick to see what he wants.

'Amy! Josh!'

Josh walks a little way behind me along the back track to Tumbledown.

'What does he want?' he says.

The door of the cottage is open. Out of everywhere on the farm, Tumbledown has always been the most properly clean and perfect, but now it's got Dad in it.

'What did you do?' I say. It's an unbelievable mess – and Mum says I don't see mess, so it must be bad.

'Come on,' says Dad, 'come in.'

He's been cooking, and it smells of that and grown-up duvets in a really bad way. He's been very sad since Mum said he wasn't allowed to talk to us kids about him and Gail. They kept trying, saying things about Love, and it was horrible. *You're just upsetting them,* said Mum, *you don't get to be the good guy.* But if Dad can't be the good guy, he doesn't know who to be. I try not to notice how unhappy he looks. He's not moving into the Farmhouse for a while; maybe he's feeling left out. I won't feel bad for him.

'I've bought this Wi-Fi booster,' he says, 'but I have no idea how to set it up.' He smiles at me, really sweetly.

'He's just being a suck-up,' I say to Josh.

'I am being a suck-up,' says Dad. 'I miss you.'

'I don't know anything about Wi-Fi,' I say. 'Nor does Josh.'

'Well, never mind,' says Dad. 'Would you like something to eat? Or drink?'

He shuffles about, tidying up, and he's so bad at it, and so slow, that in the end we help him. Josh washes up, and I do the cleaning. He thanks us, and looks so sad I nearly have to shut my eyes.

'When you come, would you like to stay in Tumbledown with me? Or where?' he says.

I don't know. I can't imagine it. I know Mum says she'll

never come. She says she can't ever see Frith again, if she can't live here.

'Dad—' I try to stop him talking, but I don't know how. I feel like he's cornering me.

'I'm going to miss you both, so much,' he says. 'Promise you'll come see me?'

'You're throwing us out!' I suddenly say, surprising myself.

Josh looks shocked, and I shut my mouth. Josh doesn't ever snap at anyone, he just gets tummy aches.

'I understand,' says Dad. 'I know it feels that way. But if you come – *when* you come – I think, maybe . . .' he smiles, '. . . we might be able to get that pony you've always dreamed of.'

I can't believe he's said it. Next to me, Josh startles, beginning to be excited. It's not fair. He doesn't know he's being tricked. Seeing my face, Dad stops, and gets a guilty look, like one of the dogs caught doing something bad.

I think of Mum. I think of all their dreams of Frith. And about all her work. Dad and Gail are planning another holiday cottage; they want Frith to *fulfil its potential*. They'll do it when we've gone. There, there it is, at last, I'm angry.

'I'm not *ever* coming back here to see you,' I say. 'Not *ever.*'

I feel a wave of pride, like a big bright light is shining onto me, and I think, *I'll remember this moment. I'm right. I know I'm right.*

Then I think of Josh.

And that we're leaving.

'Josh can come here, if he wants,' I mumble. 'I'm not.'

I'm going to cry. So I grab Josh's hand, and run. *Are you OK, Amy?* he keeps saying, trying to keep up. *Are you OK?*

Me, Lan and Josh stand in the Big Room, looking out down the valley. Rani and Martin have invited us over to the Carthouse for the Last Supper, but we don't want to go. There's a pink-and-orange sunset at the end of the valley, and all the light is pink, everywhere. Jim and Mum are sitting on the edge of the trough together, looking at it. Jim's arm is round Mum's shoulders.

'I hate Dad,' says Josh.

I want to argue, but I can't. Now I've started being angry with Dad, I don't know when I'll ever stop.

'Jim's nicer,' says Josh.

We go out where Mum and Jim are.

'Come here.' Mum puts her arm round Josh, and me and Lan sit on the ground near their feet. It's slimy, but I feel like it's an important moment, and I can't complain. *Nice sunset,* says one of us, and the rest of us agree.

'We're the best people,' says Josh to Mum. 'Me, you, Amy, Lan and Jim.'

'And your sisters, Lan,' says Mum.

'Yeah, they're OK,' says Lan. 'And Finbar.'

'And Em,' says Josh. 'She's OK, too.'

'And Rani,' says Jim, 'and Martin.'

Remembering, I say, 'Me and Lan used to wish you and Jim were married.'

'I know,' says Mum. 'You were always saying it.'

Really? I don't remember that.

'Thing is, even we wished it,' says Jim. 'Didn't we, Harriet?'

'In a way.'

'Sadly, we both have the misfortune of loving very silly people. And the silly appear to be on the winning team.'

Rani shoves homework and drawings off the table, and Bill lays it. Lulu is upside down on the sofa. 'I don't want you to go,' she says, with her legs in the air.

'Finbar isn't coming to dinner,' says Martin.

We didn't think he would. This dinner is the most *inside* anything could be. Everybody is nice and kind, even Bill and Lulu. I don't know how grown-ups pretend, and eat, and talk, when awful things are happening. I hope I'm never like that. Lan and me are more like Finbar. We feel trapped, and want to escape. Except I don't want to have to go to bed, and it be tomorrow.

Sarah lives in Finsbury Park, Mum is saying. *I don't know north London, but I'm glad I'll be sharing a room with the kids, I think we'll need each other, and we'll have two beds, and a camp bed, so we can take turns* . . . On and on and on.

The future.

The past.

How they *feel*.

It's bad enough living it, without talking about it all the time.

When finally it's time to go, the grown-ups hug.

'It's the eve of Agincourt,' says Rani.

'Except then, there was a chance of winning,' says Mum. Her hair is scraped back and her lips thin and tight.

We're at the door. *Sleep well, sleep well, take care –*

'I still can't believe it,' said Martin. 'I really can't. I never thought they'd really, actually do it.'

'But they did,' says Mum. She feels far away, like I wouldn't be able to touch her if I tried.

We walk back up to the house. We can't see the Frith, there isn't any moon, but I know it's all around me. Invisible. Beautiful. I smell the smoke from a just lit roll-up. *All right?* says Finbar, from the direction of his house. We see the small red glow – then Finbar himself.

'Are you OK?' says Mum.

'I was just, you know,' he says. 'I don't want you to think I was being rude, not coming to your farewell dinner.' *Rude* is not a Finbar word.

All right, kids? he says. *All right, Finbar?* we answer back. Josh is tired and leaning on me, like he did when he was small. He's too heavy to hold up for long.

'Harriet —' says Finbar, but he does not go on. 'Harriet,' he says again.

Mum waits.

'Fuck,' he says. 'Oh, fuck it. You know?'

'I know,' she says. 'Fuck it. I wish I had something, but I don't. Goodbye, Finbar.'

She kisses his cheek. And I do, even though he's so electric I feel like he'll run away any second. Josh hugs him. He doesn't seem to mind. We go quickly, before we get any more upset.

We're halfway to the house.

'You gave me a home,' shouts Finbar, his voice carrying on the still air. 'You saved my life.'

Mum turns round, and we look, too, but we can't see him anywhere.

'What would we have done without you?' she says. 'We were the lucky ones.'

I love her always saying the thing I would never have time to think of.

'Fuck that,' says Finbar. 'It wasn't for the others, it was for you.'

I don't know if he's still there as we go in, or if he's gone back inside.

25

Goodbye

LAN

I wake up in the very early morning. Amy's never up before me, so I go downstairs and across the Big Room to wait for her in the Cowhouse kitchen. They keep the door closed now, and when I open it, she's by the Aga, making tea. The kitchen's dark. She looks weird.

'I was going to feed the goats so Mum won't have to,' she says.

'OK.'

We walk up together with the bucket of scraps.

The goats don't know anything's different, stamping in the muddy patch near the fence, hopping on each other's backs, Gabriella, Rose and Lily joining in like they always do.

'They definitely all think they're goats,' I say.

Amy's being quiet. We tip the bucket out, and nearly get pushed over. The day is beginning to warm up. We stand and watch them eating.

'Amy! Bloody hell! What are you doing?' Harriet is out of the house, and blazing, storming at us.

'What?' says Amy.

'You've fed the goats! I was going to!'

Then the anger drops out of her, and she just looks tired.

'I'm sorry. I'll milk them. I'm sorry, darling.'

'It's OK.'

'Ten o'clock, to leave?' She goes back in, and slams the door.

I'm not going to say anything at all. *Tensions are running high,* as Finbar might say. I put my hands in my pockets and look back at the goats.

'Will you say goodbye with me?' says Amy.

'Sure.'

We walk back to the electric.

Goodbye, Hazel, says Amy. *Goodbye, Satan. Goodbye, Erica, Conny and Olive.* They don't look up. Why would they care?

Goodbye, Gabriella Christmas.

It isn't enough. She goes into the field and kisses her.

I'm sorry about Angel Rocket.

It feels like my goodbye, too, it's so long since we named them those babyish names.

We walk down, past Finbar's house. Normally he'd be out by now – vegetables in the morning, painting in the afternoon – but there's no sign.

Goodbye, Finbar's house.

Rani and Martin are in their front garden, and they wave. The other kids are all getting up. The very early-morning feeling has gone.

'Goodbye, Em's house,' says Amy.

We stand at the top of the track, shut one eye and turn a circle with our arms straight out, pointing. We trace our fingers over the horizon. The top of the barn, the woods, the distant hill shaped like a dolphin's head.

'Ooo-eee' – we hear Harriet's call. 'Amyyy . . .'

'It's only the first one,' I say.

We run to the gate of the Hay, and climb it. We can still see the scars of our fight in the new grass and stubble.

Amy . . . Amyyyy . . . Oooo-eeee.

AMY! Jim's voice.

It's time to go. We're children, there's nothing we can do about it.

'Look—' says Amy.

A bird, its tail twin darts, swoops low over the field.

All eight of us watch Jim add the new date to the wall.

2010 – 14th April

'Well spotted,' he says.

The Lada's all packed up with their stuff. Everyone is waiting while Amy and Josh say goodbye to their dad. They didn't want to. Harriet made them. When they come back, Amy's holding Josh's hand and neither of them say anything. My mum's with the chickens – she actually is this time, I saw her.

We all say goodbye, hugging and saying the same things to each other and feeling awkward. Me and Amy just kind of make a face, there isn't anything to say and I'm not hugging her, it would be weird.

'OK, let's go,' says Harriet. 'This is intolerable.'

Jim starts up the Lada, and Harriet gets in beside him. Amy and Josh go in with bags between them, and two under their feet, and duvets on their laps. She doesn't look out of the window. She doesn't even look up. The last I see of her is the tip of her nose, disappearing as her hair falls forward and hides it.

I can't even see the back of her head, there's too much stuff piled in the boot.

Jim drives out of the gate. And up the hill, and over it.

The rest of us are left standing around, not knowing what to do. It's too small a moment for such a big change.

Bill picks up a piece of flint. He walks over to the Last Remnants, and slowly scrapes it along the shiny red car. Rani and Martin, and Em, and Finbar and me, all watch him scratch a jagged line in the red paint. Nobody says anything.

When he's done it, Bill smiles. I turn to talk to Amy about it, but she isn't there.

AMY

The Lada bumps down the hill. Nobody speaks. It's already boiling under the duvet. I shove it off. *Don't*, says Josh, shoving it back. I shove it off again, stamping it into the floor of the car.

'Kids,' says Mum.

At the end of Colin's lane, Jim pulls up and honks. I roll my eyes. They open the windows and wait, and in a few minutes he looms over the hill, at a slow run. I don't want to feel impatient with Boring Colin, but I need to be gone, not watching him look for the right words, when there aren't any. I clench my fists and try to look friendly. But

Colin doesn't say anything. He shakes Mum's hand, and nods at us in the back, then gives a sort of salute. Jim drives on. I twist round to see him through the tiny square of clear glass, waving. I try to wave back, but he can't see me.

Jim drives very slowly, as if the Lada is made of glass, or Mum is. She doesn't look it, she looks stony, staring straight ahead. I hear a noise beside me. Josh is crying.

'My chicks,' he says – all tears and spit. 'I don't want to leave my chicks.'

'Painkillers,' says Mum. 'Can you stop at the Spar?'

Jim turns off the engine, staring into space. Josh looks like he's been travelling for ten hours, and we're only in the village.

'Want a Twister?' I say. We haven't said goodbye to Kyle and Lily.

'Hey—' says Jim, but we're gone.

We stop dead in the door of the shop. Leslie Robinson is hugging our mother. And Mum's crying in her arms. I've never seen her cry like that before, like a little girl. Her whole body shudders, her face rests on Leslie's shoulder. Leslie is patting her on the back.

'There, my love, it's all right,' Leslie's saying, like a different person, pillowy and kind. They separate. Leslie puts both hands on the sides of Mum's face.

'The land will always be there,' she says. 'It will *always* be there. Everything else passes. The land endures.'

Mum nods. 'Thank you,' she says.

Leslie turns to us, the same as always.

'What can I do for you?'

'Are Kyle and Lily here?'

'Out with Chris. Next time.'

I open my mouth to say there won't be a next time, but then I realise Leslie knows.

'Will you tell them, *all right?*' I ask.

'Surely,' says Leslie.

'Come on,' says Mum. She takes my hand and Josh's. We all get back into the Lada.

And Jim drives on, and away.

We leave the village, past fields, and trees, the Robinson land, and the sign to their old house, onto the B-road, and then a wide, big road, where we join the other cars. The Lada is the slowest, piled high.

I look out at the white lines, the verges, the trees, and the fields beyond them, up to the green horizon, like a wave, gliding by. I think of the future. Not the Future the grown-ups said we should be *prepared for*, which is scary and cold. Not secondary in London with strangers. The real future. My life. When I can be in charge of it. I'm a practical person. I'm very strong. I know I am, Mum says so, and I feel it. When I was born, she looked into my eyes and she felt confident. I feel confident, too. Frith is home and I will come back to it. It won't last forever, being away. And maybe it won't be so bad. I'll have adventures. And then I'll come home. I don't know how yet. But I know it. Whatever happens, like Leslie said to Mum, Frith will still be there. And I'm lucky, because I've lived there, I know what it feels like to belong. I take Josh's hand.

'OK?'

He nods, and smiles a bit.

'Mum,' I say. 'OK?'

Mum turns round to look at me, and smiles. She doesn't need to say she loves me, I know she does.

LAN

There's nothing for me to do. The grown-ups have gone off to work around the place, and Rani's taken the girls with her kids, to do cooking or something. I said I didn't want to. I just stand there, until the last smell of diesel has gone from the air, and the only sound is the birds singing.

I think I'll just go inside, but I look up at the houses and I realise I don't know which one to go into. The Farmhouse doesn't feel right. And the Cowhouse should be Amy's family, and Amy's. Jim will be living in it, soon. He'll have the whole thing to himself. Maybe I can sleep in Josh's room, or Amy's, and be near him. I think I might. But I don't really want to think about it. Or anything.

'Lan?' It's Mum.

She walks towards me from the Orchard.

'Are you OK?' she says. I shrug. I don't know what to say.

She gives me a hug, and while she's hugging me she says, 'I'm sorry I wasn't here, for you, to say goodbye to them. It's difficult.'

I don't move or say anything. I don't want to sulk or make her angry, I just don't know what to say or feel, and I don't want to cry. Then I feel her sort of startle, and she straightens up. I look where she's looking, and see the long scrape on the Last Remnants, that Bill did. She frowns.

'It wasn't me,' I say, feeling like a coward. She looks down at me, her face like she's doing a sum in her head, like she does. Then she smiles, and I feel warm, like the sun has come out.

'I believe you,' she says. 'But it's all right if you're angry with Adam. And with me. And I know you'll miss Amy. But *we're* here, Lan. You, me, your sisters – we're *here*, and I would *never* leave you.'

I feel choked and my voice comes out weird. 'I know,' I say. I didn't know. But I'm very glad she said it.

'See you in a bit,' she says.

And she walks off. I know she's going to see Adam. I guess that's what will happen now.

I'm on my own again, standing in front of the houses, alone. The stone walls, and the gate, the tufts of grass and daisies growing between the stones. I lift my foot, and watch some blades of grass spring up. And a daisy springs back up, too, the stalk slowly recovering, until it's just like normal again, like my foot was never even there.

Then I remember Josh's chicks, in the incubator in his room. When Amy was saying *goodbye*, she didn't say it to the chicks, maybe everyone's forgotten them. I'm still feeling bad, and I resist. But they'll need someone to take care of them.

There's nobody in the Cowhouse. And it feels completely different. I go up the stairs, and stop on the landing.

The horizon drawing Amy and me did on the wall is still there. We got in so much trouble. Now it's covered in other pictures us kids have done over the years – animals and rainbows and stick people. I go into Josh's room. The bed is there, and his empty plastic wash basket and bedside table, but nearly everything else has gone. It looks really old and dirty – it didn't when he was in it. Now it looks a mess. The incubator is on the floor, plugged in and lit up. I kneel down to look. The chicks are bobbing and bumping and cheeping. They've got water. They look OK. Most of them of them are fluffy now, and getting fat. A couple still look damp and stringy. I open the top, carefully, take one out and hold it to my chest with my hand over it, so it won't feel scared. It cheeps and pecks softly against me. I go back out onto the landing. My sisters are playing together down in the Yard. I can't see Bill and Lulu, but my sisters are playing down in the yard, all three of them, laughing about something.

I sit on the window ledge, with the chick tucked under my neck. It feels like the most alive and breakable thing in the world.

Amy is probably still in the car, not at the station yet. I am going to call her and Facebook and stuff. I thought I wouldn't, but I probably will. *Obviously*, I practically hear her say.

The chick feels so alive it's almost humming, quivering on my chest. Soft and precious. And somewhere inside it, a tiny, tiny little heart, beating.

I look out at the hills going off down the valley, dipping up and down, into the distance, and the morning sun and shadows moving over them, changing them from green to blue. The furthest distance is under a dark cloud. I watch it until it turns bright, golden-green, a patch of sun so far away it's like looking through time. I wonder how long it would take to walk to it, and what it would be like, if I did.

I get up, and put Josh's chick back with the others, and go to wait by the gate for Jim to come back. He'll want to know they're all right.

Acknowledgements

This book would not exist without the candour and patience of my exceptional editor and publisher at Chatto & Windus, Clara Farmer, to whom I will always be grateful.

Thank you to my tremendously gifted US editor, Terry Karten, for her unerring guidance and love for Frith.

British thanks to Priya Roy, Isobel Turton, Amanda Waters, Mollie Stewart, Victoria Murray-Browne, and Beth Coates.

American thanks to the excellent Tracy Locke and Katie O'Callaghan.

I thought I wanted an idyllic pastoral cover for this book. I could not have been more wrong. Thanks to Stephen Parker for the wonderful Chatto/Vintage cover design, to Milan Bozic at HarperCollins for his super-cool American counterpart – and to both for their perseverance.

Many thanks to Emma Lopes for her fabulous map of Frith.

A huge thank you to the brilliant Cathryn Summerhayes at Curtis Brown, and to Jennifer Joel at ICM.

I am grateful and honoured to have the support of Hannah Telfer and Jonathan Burnham.

The books, websites, places and people who helped me imagine Frith were:

The New Complete Book of Self-Sufficiency, by John Seymour; *The Smallholder's Handbook*, by Suzie Baldwin; www.accidentalsmallholder.net; the very special Linhay in Devon at www.smilingsheep.co.uk, where I wrote the scything chapter; the uniquely beautiful Drovers Bough, www.droversbough.com, where I hope to write, but haven't yet; Jane Howorth at the British Hen Welfare Trust, and the RSPB.

This book more than any other so far had the help of early readers. It's a particular skill and kindness. Thank you, Tabitha Boyd, Tim Boyd, Benita Garvin, Rebecca Harris, Anna Parker, and Angel Parker.

The songs in the book, referenced or in fragments were:

'Do You Want To', by Franz Ferdinand. Alexander Paul Kapranos Huntley, Nicholas John McCarthy, Paul Robert Thompson, and Robert Hardy.

'Take Me Home, Country Roads', by John Denver. Bill Danoff, John Denver, Taffy Nivert-Danoff.

'Purple Rain', by Prince. Prince Rogers Nelson.

'The One I Love', by David Gray. Craig McClune, David Gray.

'Top of the World', by The Carpenters. John Bettis and Richard Carpenter.

This book is dedicated to Mark and Tarn, whose inspiring lives I plundered to make it. For the rope bridge, for the goats and Harriet's goat-call, for the perilous haystack, for so many little pieces of Frith – and our friendship – thank you.